Breaking Free

Tori Minard

Breaking Free

Gage and Nova Trilogy Book 3
An Avery's Crossing Novel

Tori Minard

Copyright 2015 Tori Minard
Cover art by Tori Minard from photos by : © Bjørn Hovdal (smoke)
and © Daniel Sroga (handsome man)

Enchanted Lyre Books

Chapter 1

Gone

Gage:

The master bedroom smelled like sex and vanilla, both musky and sweet, knowing and innocent. The hard light from the glittering chandelier sent bewildering patterns of light and shadow across the black and white bed, the zebra-patterned bench, the gleaming wooden floor. Once pristine white bedding spilled over the edge of the mattress, still tumbled from a long and vigorous session of lovemaking.

The cold, hard floorboards pressed ruthlessly against my knees. I bent my head against the side of the mattress, my hands tangled up in white sheets. My joints hurt. My fingers looked almost as white as the bedding.

My heart slammed against my ribs as my stomach wrenched itself into a whole new shape.

More light spilled out of the bathroom and across the bedroom floor. So much light. It showed me everything in the room and nothing at all. Outside of the light, the black night stared in through the windows, through the slats in the white plantation shutters, mocking me.

The scent of my girlfriend's body still clung to my skin and the beloved taste of her coated my tongue with salty musk. I licked my lips, tasting her again. Inside my chest, my heart shredded itself.

The silence mocked me. There should be sound here, laughter, a soft feminine voice. Instead there was nothing except the harsh in-and-out of my breath.

An animal groan ripped its way out of me. Then another. I tilted my head back and screamed, roar after roar tearing at the tissues of my throat. I filled the room with all the wretched noise of my anguish.

All the furniture was present—fancy-ass bed, girly lamps, zebra-patterned bench—but Nova was no longer there. She was gone, taken by Lucifer, the devil himself. She was gone. Gone.

I'd asked him to take me instead, since it was my puny soul that had been promised him. But that motherfucker would rather punish me by stealing Nova than take me.

I'd failed. All I'd wanted to do was protect her, and I'd failed.

A drawing lay face-down on the floor next to the bed. I reached for it. A self-portrait Nova had drawn for me in pencil. Her beautiful face smiled up at me from the paper. What if this was all I'd ever have of her? I folded the drawing carefully and put it in my jeans pocket.

Light footsteps clacked along the wood floor behind me. I turned my head. My mom stood in the doorway, staring at me, her eyes wild as light from the hallway lamp flooded into the bedroom. She wore pale blue satin pajamas and slip-on high heeled white slippers with bows on the toes. Her toenails were painted Easter-egg blue to match the pj's.

"What happened?" she said in a frightened whisper, the reek of whiskey drifting in on her breath. She'd been drinking again and I didn't even give a shit.

"He took her," I said, forcing the words past the pain in my throat. "He took Nova."

She put her hand over her mouth. "Oh, my God."

Not exactly.

"Why did you let him in?" I rose to my feet and confronted her. "You knew who he was. You let him in the house."

"What was I supposed to do?" She put her hands on her skinny hips. "He's the devil. I couldn't exactly shut the door in his face."

"Sure you could." I advanced on her, suddenly furious, my feet oddly quiet on the throw rug.

She took a step back into the hallway. "Gage, he's not like a vampire, where he has to be invited in before he can enter. He could have come in any time he wanted."

"Then why didn't he?" I growled. "How come he didn't get in here until you let him in?"

"I don't know." She shook her head, her eyes glistening.

Crocodile tears? She hated Nova, so I didn't know what she was so upset about.

"Were you hoping he'd take her?"

"What?" She gaped up at me. "No. Of course not!"

"You sure? I know you thought Nova wasn't right for me."

"That doesn't mean I wanted *him* to take her." She drew herself upright, glaring at me. "I warned you, didn't I? I told you this would happen but you didn't listen. This is your fault."

Damn right it was.

I covered my own eyes with a groan as sour bile rose up in my throat to choke me. Right before he'd shown up, I'd finally confessed to Nova that I loved her. I'd said the words, even though I knew it would bring the devil down upon us.

My mother had made a pact with him when I was ten—my soul in return for fame and fortune in my budding career as an actor. She hadn't consulted me on this, and because she didn't have my consent, the devil knew he couldn't really take my soul. But he'd allowed her to think he could, because it amused him to watch us turn ourselves into emotional and social pretzels trying to hide what we'd done and protect the people around us from her piss-poor decision.

All my life, I'd avoided close emotional ties because of The Deal. Especially with women. I'd never had a girlfriend before Nova, just one-night stands and short flings. This was easy considering my career. An A-list star can get all the sex partners he wants without any promise of commitment.

But Nova was different from the beginning. She'd saved my life, pulled me from a freezing river when I'd fallen in because I was a drunken, drugged-up idiot. And she hadn't judged me. She was the best person I knew, and this was how I thanked her for her love. By allowing the devil to take her down to hell.

I hadn't really believed the devil would take the people I cared about until my best friend, Jeremy Lindstrom, had died of a drug overdose. There had been something in his apartment when I'd found his body, something potent and invisible. Something dark. After that experience, I'd known in my bones that I had to stay away from others.

I'd fought my love for Nova, trying to keep some distance in order to protect her. But I was weak and selfish and I couldn't stay away from her. I'd been dumb enough to think if I could just keep from saying it out loud, keep from saying those three little words, she'd still be safe enough. And then I'd gone and blurted it out anyway, like the selfish prick I was.

Now she was gone, in a terrible place, and I couldn't even bear to imagine what she must be going through at the moment.

"Wait a minute," Mom said, pursing her glossy lips. Who wears lip gloss and pj's at the same time? "How do you know he took her? Maybe she went for a walk."

I stared at her, appalled. "In the middle of the night? When I left her, she was asleep."

"Maybe she woke up. You should wait a while and see if she comes back."

"Mom, she's not coming back. He told me he was going to do this. He said he'd take someone else instead of me, and now he has." I groaned again at the thought of what she might even now be enduring.

My guitar stood propped up beside the door, reminding me of the songs I'd written for her that she hadn't heard. I had the weirdest thought that it was mocking me for thinking I could ever really have Nova. I should have known he wouldn't let me keep her, love her.

No. I wasn't going down that road. She was mine and I was going to get her back, no matter what it took. Starting now.

***

Nova:

I had the cutest two-bedroom apartment in Avery's Crossing, much better than the one I'd shared with Skylar. The building didn't look like much from the outside, just a big dark box, but my unit had clean white walls I'd decorated with posters that picked up the red and gold tones in the throw rug I'd bought for the small living room. It had a pretty kitchen with a big window that looked out on some trees I thought might be maples. I would know for sure when they leafed out in the spring.

I'd bought café curtains for the window and hung them on tension rods. They were red and white toile. I didn't have a boyfriend, so I could put as much girly stuff in as I liked.

The building was quiet, too. Extremely quiet. Most of the time, I couldn't hear anything but the noise I made myself.

The second bedroom was kind of overkill, since I didn't have a roommate, but on the other hand I could use it for studying. As a pre-med student, I did a lot of studying. I had a sweet little desk in there and toile curtains that matched the ones in the kitchen.

It was the nicest place I'd ever lived besides my parents' house. Nobody ever complained about the loud metal I played, no matter how loud I played it. I could dance around in the living room and the neighbors never came up to bang on my door and tell me to knock it off.

Lately, though, I'd had the oddest feeling something was wrong. I couldn't put my finger on what it was. I had a great apartment a lot of students would kill for, with a sunny little balcony off the dining nook where I could grow flowers in the summer and flowering kale in the winter. It had a big kitchen too, for an apartment, and I spent a lot of time in there cooking, at least when I could fit it in between study sessions.

My pre-med studies were going better than ever. Subjects I'd found difficult or boring at one time seemed to come easily to me now. I could actually envision my future as a doctor, with a private practice a lot like those of my parents. But something was missing and I didn't know what it was.

On a Saturday morning in February, I stood at my kitchen counter rolling out sugar cookie dough and pondering the elusive missing piece as I stared at the drizzly weather outside. Typical Willamette Valley winter, gray and wet. The kitchen smelled like the lemon zest I'd used to flavor the cookie dough. I planned to use a heart-shaped cutter in honor of Valentine's Day, although I didn't have a sweetheart and now that I thought of it I wasn't sure why I was bothering.

The thought of a lover or boyfriend made something in my chest ache with a vague, nagging pain. Someone ought to be with me. I wasn't supposed to be alone in this apartment; I was supposed to be with a man.

Which was ridiculous. I didn't have time for romance. I had to stay focused on my studies so I could get into the medical school of my choice. Someday, when I'd established myself as a doctor, I'd find a partner for myself. Until then, I was all about the career.

So what was the point of all this romantic baking? Why did I feel like I ought to be sharing this with someone?

Maybe I'd bring the cookies along when I met my study group in the afternoon. That would be sharing, even if it wasn't the least bit romantic.

Someone knocked on my door. I wiped my hands on an already-floury kitchen towel and went to answer it. Had one of my study buddies shown up for an early session? They were as obsessed with success as I was.

I opened the door. A man stood there in the outdoor hallway of my building, looking at me with a slight smile on his lips. I didn't recognize him.

He was tall, with blond hair that curled around his ears, and unusual green eyes. Although he wore a wool winter jacket, I could see the athletic build of his body beneath the lines of his clothes. He was hot, so hot that the idea of using him to fill in that missing piece flitted through my head.

He's a stranger, Nova, and he wants something from you.

"Um, can I help you?" I said, hoping he wasn't here to sell me religion or ask me to vote for his candidate.

"Hi. My name's Declan. I just moved into the neighborhood, so I thought I'd come over and introduce myself."

"Oh." I blinked up at him. "Um, hi. I'm Nova."

"Hi, Nova." He stuck out his hand, so I shook with him.

His skin felt warm and dry. He was good-looking enough to render me slightly tongue-tied, as I'd never been confident with attractive men. I cast around for something appropriate to say, but found nothing.

He glanced at my flour-covered apron and grimaced. "I'm sorry. You're busy. I'll let you get back to your cooking."

There was something lonely in his voice, although it was so low-key I almost thought I'd imagined it. He probably didn't know anyone, since he'd just moved in. I knew what that felt like; the only friends I had were my study partners, and those were more like work relationships than real friends.

"Do you like to make cookies?" I said.

His eyes crinkled at the corners. "I have no idea."

"You've never made cookies?"

He shrugged, giving me a self-deprecating smile. "No. I haven't."

"You wanna come in and help me? I'm doing heart-shaped ones for Valentine's Day." Oops. I probably shouldn't have said that. He might think I was some kind of creeper putting romantic pressure on him, a guy I'd just met.

But he only smiled wider. "Sure. Sounds like fun."

"My study group is coming over in a while, but I'm free until then. Come in." I stood back to let him enter.

He walked into my apartment and gave a quick glance around. "Nice place."

"Thanks." It wasn't much, nothing fancy or chic, but I'd tried to make it look like home with a couch and chairs, a cheap throw rug in red and sage green, some colorful floral and landscape posters on the walls.

"So what are you studying?" he said as he followed me to the kitchen.

"Micro-biology. I'm a pre-med student."

"Wow. Gonna be a doctor, huh? I'm just a bank manager."

"Hey, somebody's got to handle the money," I said, throwing him a smile.

Wow, he was cute. He had dimples in his cheeks. Long, lean fingers, too.

"Mind if I take off my coat?" he said.

"Nope. Just throw it on a kitchen stool." I pointed at the cookie dough. "You got here just in time for the fun part."

I glanced at him with a teasing smile and caught him staring at me, a searching expression in his eyes. It was an odd look for someone who didn't know me. Almost like he was trying to figure me out, or wondering exactly what thoughts were going through my head.

It suddenly occurred to me that I'd invited a stranger, a male stranger, into my apartment while I was home alone. I knew better than that. What had I been thinking?

Now I had him inside, however, I wasn't sure how to politely get rid of him. And he wasn't threatening me, although that watchful expression he had made me a little nervous. He noticed me looking and the intent focus on his face disappeared.

"So, Valentine's Day, huh?" he said in a jocular tone.

"Yeah. Hearts. Too cheesy for you?" I picked up my heart-shaped cutter for emphasis.

"Not at all. I don't have a girlfriend to get jealous." He grinned flirtatiously at me, putting his dimples on full display.

I merely smiled. I shouldn't have invited him in after all. Normally I'd never ask a stranger to enter my apartment, not when I was alone. Again, what had I been thinking?

But he made no ominous gestures. He just watched as I pressed the cutter into the dough and removed a heart-shaped piece to carefully set on my baking sheet.

"Can I try one?" he said.

"Wash your hands first." I pointed at the sink.

"Okay, doc." He winked at me.

Doc. Something about that nickname made my insides twinge. A memory. No, not a memory, more like a mental ghost. Someone else had called me Doc once, someone I cared for deeply. But who? I couldn't picture his face.

Declan washed up and returned to me. He stood close, so close I could feel his body heat. It stirred the loneliness inside me, making me feel just how long I'd been without a man. I pushed the feelings down and handed him the cutter.

"Just press it straight down," I said.

"Like this?" He pushed it into the dough.

"Perfect. Now separate the cookie from the cutter and put it on the baking sheet."

I watched him follow my instructions, a little frown of concentration on his handsome face. "I'll bet you didn't think you'd get roped into making cookies when you decided to come over here."

He set the dough on the sheet and smiled at me. "Nope. But this is fun. Do you bake often?"

"Yeah, I guess." I did a lot of cooking, especially considering I lived alone. That was another oddity I hadn't thought of until now.

"Boyfriend?" he said.

"Huh?"

His smile broadened. "Do you have a boyfriend?"

"No." I backed up an inch or two. "I've been too busy to meet anyone."

"So there's no-one to take a swing at me for spending time with you?" He bent over the cookie dough again, cutting out a second heart.

"No, I guess not," I said, wondering where he was going with this. Wishing my study group was going to get here about three hours earlier than scheduled. Like, within the next five minutes.

He glanced at me and frowned, his green eyes full of genuine-looking concern. "I've made you uncomfortable. I'm sorry."

"No, it's all right. I'm not used to flirting." I widened my eyes. "Not that I think you're flirting with me. Just, you know, hanging out with a

7

guy who isn't part of my study group and someone I only just met, and oh, God, I'm totally babbling, aren't I?"

"Yes, and it's adorable. I was flirting, by the way. Because I find you very attractive."

"Oh." My cheeks began to burn. "So are you."

"No pressure, though," he said lightly. "Since we just met a few minutes ago."

Right. No pressure.

"So what bank do you work for?" I said as he cut out another cookie.

"Central Willamette."

"Really? That's where I go."

"Huh. It's a small world. I hope you're satisfied with our service." He extended the cutter to me. "You want to do some more?"

Our fingers brushed when I took the cutter from his hand. A little tingle of sexual awareness shot through me, making me even more awkward than usual. I nearly dropped the cutter on the floor.

This is what's missing.

My earlier thought repeated itself—I was supposed to be with a man. I gave Declan a surreptitious glance out of the corner of my eye. Could he be the one? Maybe Fate had sent him here just for me.

Chapter 2
Help

Gage:

The kitchen looked wrong with Nova missing. She loved it in here, loved to cook for me even though I never told her I wanted her to do that. There were still dirty dishes in the sink from when we'd had dinner together.

My mom had done nothing but pace back and forth across the kitchen since Nova had disappeared. She hadn't even had a drink, which had to be an all-time record for her. Instead, she'd guzzled down all the crappy coffee I could give her and droned non-stop about how I had to think of myself and my career and how I was endangering myself by telling people that my girlfriend had disappeared.

The smell of coffee, something I ordinarily enjoyed, filled the room and made me feel like hurling. I could still taste the bile in the back of my throat.

"Mom." I interrupted her in the middle of yet another tirade. "I have to call the police. Someone is going to come looking for Nova, and what am I going to tell them? If I don't report this, it'll make me look even more guilty."

She wrung her hands. "I knew you never should have gotten involved with her. I knew it."

"You didn't even know she existed until a week ago."

"That's not the point. And I told you not to get emotionally involved. Didn't I tell you? He took her because you cared about her, although why I have no idea."

Yeah, that was my mom, to slip an insult to my girl right in the middle of telling me how much she cared about me.

I pulled my smart phone out of my pocket. "I'm doing it."

She put her hand over her eyes. "Oh, God," she moaned. "This is going to be the end of everything."

I ignored her as I searched for the number for a missing persons report. There it was.

"Gage, don't do this." She wrapped her fingers around my wrist, pleading with her eyes. "It's not too late."

"Her parents are staying at the Holiday Inn. They'll probably be here later today."

Her skinny shoulders slumped. "We're doomed."

I almost said it—we wouldn't be having this problem if she hadn't let the devil in the door. If she hadn't made The Deal in the first place. What kind of mom sells her son's soul to the devil? Who does that?

She'd wanted me to be a famous actor, never mind what I wanted. I'd only been ten years old at the time, and my career hadn't advanced at the speed my mother wanted for me. Or more accurately, for herself. So she'd struck a deal to speed things up. And now the woman I loved more than anything else in the entire world had been caught in the crossfire.

"They won't even look for her. You know that, don't you?" my mom said as the phone started ringing.

"Things have changed," I said.

"Yeah, but she's an adult. She doesn't have dementia, does she? So why would they look for her? Give it a few days and see if she comes back."

I cut the connection on my phone. "Comes back? How's she going to do that? She's in hell, Mom." I covered my eyes as a surge of pain threatened to make me start bawling like a little kid. "He might be hurting her. Anything could be happening to her."

"And what are the police going to do about it?"

"Nothing. I'm more concerned about her parents."

"So tell them you had a fight and she left and you haven't seen her since." She stopped pacing to stand in front of me and put her hands on my shoulders. "You could go to jail over this, Gage, and you haven't done anything wrong."

"Yeah, I have. I fell for her. I should have stayed away from her."

"It's too late for that now."

I knew that. It was too late for Nova to stay safe by staying the hell away from me. But that didn't absolve me of my responsibilities. I had to save her. Somehow. Some way. I had to get her out of hell.

"Marie," I said.

"What?" Mom sent me a look of bafflement.

"A friend. Marie. She might be able to help." I stuck my phone in my back pocket and went to find Nova's purse.

My mother tagged along behind me. "I don't think anyone can help us with this. Don't you think I've tried that? I've tried everything, but there's nothing we can do."

I took a breath and grabbed onto what little patience I had left. "I doubt you've tried anything at all."

"Ever since you met Nova, you've been disrespectful to me," she snapped as I started down the stairs.

She could think that if she liked. The truth was I'd been holding in a lifetime of rage and resentment toward my mom and she simply hadn't noticed it. She rarely noticed anything she didn't want to see, and I hadn't wanted her to see it. Until now. I figured it was time for her to face up to the forces she'd unleashed fifteen years ago.

I stalked into the foyer, where Nova's purse hung in the entry closet. Fishing it out, I dumped its contents onto the foyer table and sorted through them until I found a piece of folded-up scratch paper with Marie's name and a phone number.

"It's two o'clock in the morning," Mom said as she came up behind me.

"Don't care." I dialed Marie's number.

It seemed to ring forever before someone picked up. "'Lo?" said a fuzzy female voice.

"Marie?" I said.

"Yeah? Who's this?"

"It's Gage. Gage Dalton. He took Nova."

"What?" Her voice turned sharp and wakeful in an instant. "When?"

"Tonight. Uh—about half an hour ago."

"Are you saying she's gone?"

"Yes. She disappeared. I left her in the bedroom. He got into the house. We talked. He vanished. I ran upstairs and Nova was gone."

"How do you know she didn't leave on her own?" Marie said.

"He said he was going to take someone else instead of me. Plus, where would she go in the middle of the night?"

I heard a muffled male voice from the other end.

"It's Gage," Marie said. "Nova's disappeared."

"We have to get her back," I said. "I have to get her back."

"Oh, dear." Something on Marie's end rustled. "I'm not sure that's possible."

"It has to be. There must be something I can do."

"Can you come over here? I'm going to do some research and you can help."

"I'll be there as soon as I can." I got her and Brad's address and cut the connection.

"Where are you going?" my mom said.

"To Marie's house. She might be able to help."

"I'll get some clothes on."

"No." I stopped her with a hand on her arm. "I need to do this by myself."

"But—"

"Mom, you don't even like Nova. I don't want you at Marie's."

She looked so hurt I almost winced and gave in. But she'd caused this problem and I didn't want her making any more trouble. Maybe justice demanded she play some role in making this thing right again, but helping me and Marie research wasn't it. I didn't trust her.

"I feel like you don't trust me," she said.

I just looked at her.

"Okay, fine. Be like that. I'll stay here and wait." She sighed heavily.

Whatever. She could play the martyr if she wanted, but nobody was buying it, least of all me.

I stuck my feet in my shoes without bothering to tie them. "I'm going. I don't know when I'll be back. Cindy and the guys will take care of you if you need anything. She should be here by nine o'clock."

"Be careful, Gage." She clasped her hands together, her blue eyes wide and innocent-looking. What an actress. She should have pursued the Hollywood career instead of me.

"Yeah. See ya." I abandoned her for the garage and my car.

Chapter 3
Frater Umbrarum's Library

Gage:

I took my gray sedan, as the most nondescript car I owned. The one least likely to be marked as belonging to a celebrity.

As I left the circular drive that fronted the house, I also left all light behind. The long, narrow, unpaved lane that led from the house to the nearest road was so dark I couldn't see anything at all except the arc illuminated by my headlights. The car crunched over the gravel and bumped along the ruts of the drive—I really needed to get my assistant, Cindy, on the paving project—in what felt like a tunnel of darkness, tangled bushes rising up like walls on both sides of the car.

The ruts and potholes kept me from driving as fast as I wanted. If I had my way, I'd floor it all the way to Brad and Marie's farm, but getting myself stuck in a ditch wouldn't help anyone. So I crept along, leaning forward as if that would help me see better.

My headlights lit up a deer by the left side of the road, all slender legs and spreading antlers. I figured the antlers meant it was a male. Its big eyes seemed to glow red in the light from the car.

Normally, seeing a deer would have pleased me. I hadn't had a lot of nature growing up in L.A. Right now, though, I couldn't care less about some wild animal that had nothing to do with my current problem. I pulled my attention back to the road, to what lay ahead.

My peripheral vision caught movement. I turned my head, just in case that deer had decided to jump out in front of me. But it wasn't a deer. It was a man.

He strode from the left side of the road, the deer's side, seeming to emerge right out of the bushes, and walked directly in front of my car. I frowned as my heart slammed up against my ribs and my hands bore down on the steering wheel. What the fuck was this dude doing out here in the middle of the night?

He turned his head and stared right at me and I jumped. Jeremy. Holy fuck, it was Jeremy. I could clearly see his facial features beneath the curtain of messy blond hair that hung on either side of his face.

The look he gave me was strangely detached, as if he didn't recognize me. He passed before me and disappeared into the bushes on the right side of the road.

I put the car into park and jumped out, engine still running. "Jeremy! Hey! Jer!"

13

He didn't answer. There was no sound at all, not even the frogs we'd been listening to every evening. Nothing but a soft sigh of wind through a nearby tree and the low rumble of the car's engine.

"Jeremy," I said loudly. "Are you here? Talk to me."

Still, nothing. *Of course there's nothing. He's a ghost.* Either that, or I was hallucinating.

Feeling strangely energized, I got back into the car. I didn't know what it meant, but seeing Jeremy's ghost on the same night Nova disappeared had to be significant.

Fifteen minutes later, I pulled up in a dark farmyard. A small, cottage style house painted dark blue sat under a giant tree with no leaves. With its steeply pitched gable roof and dormers in the attic, it looked like it belonged in a fairy tale. An evil fairy tale, the kind with blood and monsters in it.

The huge, gray hulk of a barn reared up to the right of the house. I could just make out its silhouette in the darkness. Here and there, some metal fencing glimmered in the beams of my headlights.

I parked the sedan beneath the spreading branches of the tree. As I shut the car door, the house door opened, silhouetting a dark-haired woman in the light spilling from inside. She raised her hand in greeting. Marie.

I dashed toward her. She looked exhausted, with dark circles under her eyes, her long dark hair tangled. She wore an ankle-length blue-plaid flannel robe clutched together in the front by one hand.

"I'm sorry to wake you up," I said, suddenly embarrassed at what I was asking of her. Nova and I barely knew her and I'd gotten her up in the middle of the night.

"Don't be. Come in. Would you like some coffee?"

"Yeah, sure."

I followed her into the little house. A small kitchen to our right had a red and white checkerboard linoleum floor that looked like it might be completely original to the house. The cabinets, too, looked really old, along with the red Formica countertops with silvery metal banding. The appliances seemed to date from the seventies, judging by the dark brown and harvest gold all over them.

The rich, dark smell of coffee filled the small room. Marie pulled a huge mug from a cupboard and filled it from the coffee pot on the tile counter.

"We were combing our library for ideas." She handed the mug to me.

"Find anything?"

"Not yet. It's through here."

She led me through an archway into the living room. Bookcases crammed with books lined every wall in the room. Her lanky, brown-haired husband, Brad, sat on a sagging gold couch surrounded by stacks of books. He wore black sweatpants and a baggy, gray T-shirt with a tear along the hem. He glanced up at me, his face somber.

"Gage," he said.

"Hey, Brad. Sorry to wake you and Marie."

He waved that off. "Don't mention it. We're glad you could call. Glad we can try to help."

These people were too good to be true. I'd never met a couple more willing to give their time and energy to other people, and I wasn't about to complain. I needed all the help I could get.

"Is Max around?" I said.

"He's got his own place. When the sun comes up, I'll call him. He and Caro can help too." Marie patted a chair. "Come sit. I'll give you some books to flip through."

"I don't even know what to look for." I sat down.

"Any mention of the devil, to start," Brad said. "Or hell. The only story I know of someone physically raised from the dead is when Orpheus tried to resurrect Eurydice, and that didn't go very well."

"I don't know that one," I said, picking up a book at random.

"Eurydice was his wife. She died of a snake bite. He was so grieved that his sad music moved Hades and Persephone, the Greek deities of the underworld, to allow him to rescue her from their realm. But he was supposed to lead her out without looking back at her or he would lose her forever."

"And?"

"He looked." Brad set aside the book he'd been reading and picked up another one.

"Wait. So he lost her?" I said.

"Yep," Brad said.

"Holy crap."

"That was Hades, though, not the devil," Marie said. "Completely different mythology."

I peered at her in bafflement. "Are you saying one story is true and the other isn't? Like the devil is real and Hades is just a myth?"

"I'm not sure. All I know is the rules for dealing with Hades and Persephone are different from the rules for dealing with the devil."

I scratched my head. "Okay. I'm not sure I understand what you just said."

"Neither is she." Brad gave me a wry smile.

All righty. They were doing an excellent job of shaking my confidence in them.

15

"There are so many different mythological systems," Brad continued. "Are they all true? Are none of them true? Nobody really knows, even those of us who work with the spirit world."

"Let's just concentrate on the task at hand," Marie said. "Find out if there's any kind of mention of rescuing someone from hell in any of these books. Gage, there are snacks in the kitchen and I'll cook something later for us to eat."

"I'm not hungry anyway." I bent to the book in my hand.

By sunrise, I'd gone through uncounted mugs of coffee, a plate of scrambled eggs and toast, and a whole pile of books with titles like *An ABC of Witchcraft, Abramelin the Mage*—a book I'd already encountered once in L.A.—and *Three Books Of Occult Philosophy.* But I hadn't found any mention of rescuing people from hell.

The three of us were surrounded by piles and stacks of books. The shelves were now almost empty. Nobody had found anything of use.

The front door opened and shut. A moment later, Max showed up in the living room archway, a petite curly-haired blonde on his arm. I thought I recognized her from a picture he'd once showed me and Nova. Max's black hair and her blonde contrasted in a dramatic way I thought Nova would like. God, I couldn't stop thinking of her.

"Are we too late?" he said.

"Nope. We haven't found a thing." Brad waved the two into the room.

"Have you eaten breakfast?" Marie said.

"We got something on the way," the blonde told her.

"Sorry this happened," Max told me. He nodded to the girl. "This is my girlfriend, Caroline. Caro, this is Gage Dalton."

She gave me a shy smile. "I recognize you. I've seen all your movies."

"Yeah. Uh, nice to meet you."

"I'm so sorry about your girlfriend." She glanced at Marie. "What can I do to help?"

"You can go through some of these books, see if you can find something we missed," Marie said. "I'm going to make some calls. Maybe some of my friends know something."

She got up and left the room, while Max and Caroline settled on the floor in the midst of all the books.

"This is going to be a bitch to put away," Max remarked as he picked up one of the volumes.

I turned and grabbed another book from the shelf. It had the weird and unpromising title *The Black Sow,* with a line drawing of a large, presumably female pig on the faded, brown hardback cover.

Thumbing through it, I scanned the text for any mention of the devil or hell. The style of the thing seemed to be even more archaic than most of the other books I'd scanned, making it slow going. Around me, Brad, Max and Caroline talked in low tones. Marie's voice came from some other downstairs room, but I couldn't make out what she was saying.

The book I'd chosen seemed to be about magically enchanting a black sow to make her capable of finding treasure. It was such a ridiculous idea, so obviously a hoax, that I was tempted to toss the book to the side as useless. But then the phrase "resurrected from hell" caught my eye.

Examining the passage in detail, I found it referred to another book called *The Secret Rites Of Necromancy*, which supposedly contained a method of contacting human spirits in hell and even of extracting them.

"Guys, I think I found something." I handed the book to Brad, pointing at the right paragraph.

He scanned the book. "Holy shit. I was beginning to think we should give up. Good work, Dalton."

"I'll call it good work when Nova is back." I rubbed my eyes, which were starting to hurt. "You think we can find this Secrets book?"

"I've heard of it but I've never seen a copy," he said. "I'll get on it."

"I'll look it up on F.U.L.," Caroline said.

"What's that?" I said.

"Frater Umbrarum's Library. It's a database of obscure occult books. A lot of them are available as PDF's, so we might not even have to order anything." She stood up and left the room.

Max watched her go, an affectionate expression on his face that made me want to deck him. I couldn't stand that he could look at Caroline—and touch and kiss her, talk to her—and I didn't even know if I would ever see Nova again. Selfish of me, I know. But Nova's fate was tearing me up inside and seeing a happy couple just made it a hundred times worse.

Chapter 4
Gloom

Nova:

Everything in the world was gray. Thick white fog clung to everything in the neighborhood, draining it of color, and filled in the spaces between so I couldn't make out any of the shapes around me with any certainty. What little sunlight made it through the gloom of the mist was diffused and weak.

There had been a lot of fog lately. It muffled sound and made me feel closed in. Alone.

You can't bake all the time, or even during all your time off. So I'd decided to take a break from the cooking and go for a walk. With my peacoat, a scarf wrapped around my throat, and a knit beanie on my head, I felt pretty cozy. Except for the fog.

It made no sense to think the fog could see me, that it was watching me, but that's what it felt like. As if there were eyes hidden in it somewhere. Intelligence. I shivered in spite of my warm coat and pulled my scarf a little closer to my chin.

Dark green and gray shapes emerged out of the white as I made my way down my street. Bushes. Trees. Clumps of ornamental grass like enormous heads of hair. No birds sang. There didn't seem to be any animals around at all.

Didn't anyone in this neighborhood have pets?

Come to think of it, I hadn't really met any of my neighbors except for Declan. And he didn't have any critters, not even a goldfish. He claimed he was too busy working to take care of a pet.

One advantage of the walk was it got my blood moving and made my body feel more alive. That was good because I'd been way too sedentary lately. Except for all the baking, I'd spent most of my time sitting with my books and notes.

I rounded a corner onto another suburban street, this one with all single-family houses. At two o'clock on a Saturday afternoon, you'd think there would be people on the street. Cars going by. Something. But the place was as empty as a ghost town. Where was everyone?

Lately, I'd had that nagging feeling of something missing more and more often. It came to me now, sharp and aching. My world was off-kilter in a way I couldn't see or explain or even understand.

I sighed. It was just loneliness. Lots of busy people, people like me who worked and studied hard, were lonely. It was part of the price you paid for success in the world.

From somewhere ahead of me came the sound of footsteps. I tensed, wondering who it could be. This might be an opportunity to meet someone else in the neighborhood, but it could also be an opportunity to be mugged. Should I hide? Run away?

God, I was being silly. Why would I need to hide? It might be a foggy, gloomy day but it was still broad daylight. People must be around here somewhere, so there was nothing to fear.

My heart pounded frantically in spite of my reassurances to myself.

A figure approached me from out of the fog, tall and dark. I swallowed. It came closer, seeming to grow larger as it neared. Closer. Now I could see it was male, a man wearing a dark knit hat.

The man's features resolved out of the mist into someone I recognized. His blond hair peeked out from under the edges of his hat.

Declan.

I smiled in relief. "Hey, you."

"Hi, Nova. What are you doing out here?" He paused in front of me on the sidewalk, smiling in return. He seemed paler in the pale, gray light.

"I thought I'd take a walk. I'm tired of being cooped up in my apartment."

"You're not baking cookies today?"

"No." I shook my head. "A girl can only bake so many cookies."

He laughed. "I guess so. Would you like to walk with me? I'm getting some exercise too."

"Sure. But aren't you heading back?"

"It doesn't matter. I've got plenty of energy." He turned so he faced the same direction as me. "Have you seen the park down this way?"

"No."

"I'll show you." He took my hand and tucked it in the crook of his arm, like an old-fashioned gentleman, and I let him, although it seemed like an odd gesture.

"It's so dead around here today," I said.

Declan laughed at that. "It sure is."

"Where is everyone? I mean, it's Saturday." I peered up at the darkened house we were passing. "Doesn't anyone have shopping to do? Where are the kids?"

"They're probably inside, out of this cold fog. Where you should be." He gave me a significant glance.

"You don't think I should have gone for a walk?"

"I understand why you felt the need to get out, but it isn't all that safe around here. With this fog, you could get hit."

"Yeah, if there were any cars around. But there aren't."

"You never know when one will come along," he said, tucking my arm through his a little more tightly.

"Are you worried about me, Declan?" I said teasingly.

He smiled and shrugged. "Yeah, kind of. You should be more careful, Nova. You let me into your apartment and I could have been anyone. I could have been some kind of evil freak who wanted to hurt you."

That sent a chill through me, something much icier than the fog. "You're not a freak, are you?"

His green eyes turned serious. "No. But that's not true for everyone around here."

"I thought you just moved into the neighborhood. How do you know all this?" He was starting to scare me.

"I did a little research."

"Ookay. I'm not sure what you're really trying to tell me."

He patted my hand where it rested on his arm. "I'm not trying to tell you anything bad about myself. I just don't want you wandering off alone. You never know who you'll run into."

"But there's nobody around except us."

"I saw a man." Declan sent me a sidelong glance. "He was lurking in the bushes of one of these houses, watching me. Didn't seem like friendly behavior."

"Wow. Okay. I'll be careful. I promise."

"Good." He pointed ahead. "See there? That's the park."

Mostly what I saw was a curtain of white, but there were some column-like shapes rising out of it that I took for the trunks of some huge trees. "Are you sure this place is safe?"

"You're with me."

I shot him a glance out of the corner of my eye. "And you're safe?"

"I would never hurt you."

I wasn't sure if I believed that. But I also wasn't sure I wanted to bolt and run for home. Stupid me, I didn't want to insult him or hurt his feelings by acting like he was threatening me.

"You know, guys don't usually warn me the way you just did," I said.

He drew me closer to the park. "That's probably because either they didn't care about you or they didn't know enough to warn you."

"Are you saying you care about me?"

He paused to gaze down at me, completely serious now. "Yes. I do."

"Why? We just met the other day." The only thing I'd given him was a few Valentine's Day cookies.

"I like you. I wouldn't want to see you get hurt."

I shook my head. "You're very odd, do you know that?"

20

"Sorry. I guess I'm in an overly serious mood today."

"I guess so." I gazed around the park as we left the sidewalk for closely cropped grass. Ahead, there was a small sort of outbuilding, that really looked like a tiny house. It had a Victorian style to it, with tall narrow windows, shiplap siding, and carved corbels supporting the hip roof. For some reason, it gave me the creeps.

The tiny place couldn't have been big enough to live in, unless there were only one or two people in residence. Yet it felt occupied. That really made no sense. It didn't look any more occupied than any of the other structures in the neighborhood. Its windows were dark. There was no-one gazing out, no vehicle nearby, not even a bike. It didn't look occupied, yet I could feel a presence there and it made the hair on the back of my neck stand up.

"What is that place?" I whispered to Declan.

"I'm not sure. Want to go inside?"

"Hell, no. It gives me a major case of the creeps."

"Okay. We won't," he said.

"Besides, doesn't it belong to someone? Wouldn't we be trespassing?"

"I don't think so. It's in a public park."

I supposed that made sense. I still didn't want to get close to the thing. I glanced around, looking for something park-like. Benches, playground equipment, stuff like that. But there wasn't any. Nothing. Just a single path curving around the trunks of those enormous trees. And the house.

Then I saw the headstones. Rows and rows of headstones, gray and pink marble, black granite, some kind of white stone, some of the plain slabs with only a couple of lines of text on them and others elaborately carved. The stones disappeared into the clinging fog, but I could sense there were a lot of them just out of sight.

My hand tightened on Declan's arm. "This isn't a park. It's a cemetery."

"What?"

I pointed. "Graves. We're in a cemetery."

"Huh. I was sure this was a park."

"I want to go home now," I said.

"Don't you want to have a look around? Cemeteries are interesting."

Walk around in all that fog, with creepy graves just waiting for us to stumble on them? "No, thank you. Let's go back."

"Okay." He shrugged. "I'll bet there are some good ones in here, though."

We turned and headed back toward the sidewalk.

"Good ones?" I said.

"Yeah. Cool stories. Cool names. You know, the history and stuff. Don't you ever wonder about the people buried in cemeteries? Where they came from, what they were like, how they died?"

"Not really," I said, shivering. "Graveyards are places I've always avoided." And I planned to continue avoiding them in the future.

"I love them. They're so peaceful," he said with a dreamy expression.

This whole episode was giving me the willies. I had no idea Declan was so...odd. He'd seemed totally normal the other time. There didn't seem to be anything peaceful in that place, just a lot of death. The fog only underscored the themes of death and forgetfulness and isolation.

"Would you think less of me if I told you I'm scared?" I said. "I don't like the idea of ghosts."

"Ghosts won't hurt you," he said firmly. As if he knew some of them personally. "Most of them are totally harmless."

"Uh...okay. If you say so."

He laughed. "Come on, Nova. Don't worry. They're dead. They can't hurt you."

"Well, after you went to all that trouble to tell me how dangerous it is around here, you can't blame me for getting spooked in a foggy graveyard."

He grinned at me. "I guess you're right. Let's go back to your place and warm up."

I left the cemetery with enthusiasm. If I'd known it was there, I'd never have rented my apartment. It was only a block from my place, for crying out loud. Ick. I shivered again at the thought of all those dead people lying so close to the place where I slept.

Great. Now I'd never have a decent night's sleep again.

Even re-entering the more normal, everyday world of a modern suburb couldn't completely shut off that sense of hopelessness and loss I felt in the graveyard. The houses looked even emptier, their windows even more blank, than before.

"I think you need a hot toddy," Declan said.

"A what?"

"A hot toddy. It's tea with whiskey in it." He winked at me. "You got any whiskey? I'll make you one."

"I don't have hard liquor."

"Well, I'll duck into my place and get mine. If that's okay."

"Sure."

The fright of the graveyard loomed behind us in the fog. My apartment would be warm and dry and brightly lit, and a hot toddy sounded wonderful.

Chapter 5
Rare Books

Gage:

Caroline curled up in one of the armchairs in Marie and Brad's living room, wildly tangled gold hair spilling over her face, and pulled a tablet from her purse. She fired up the thing and started searching, looking for Frater Umbrarum's Library. I rubbed my forehead again, suddenly exhausted. I'd been up all night and I was running on fumes.

Sleep probably wouldn't come, though. I wasn't sure I'd ever sleep again, unless I found and rescued Nova.

"You need some rest," Marie said from her position next to me on the couch.

"Do you read minds?"

She smiled and patted me on the arm. "Only sometimes. You look wrecked, that's all. Want to lie down in the spare bedroom?"

"I don't think I could sleep unless you shot me with a tranquilizer dart."

Max glanced up from his position next to Caroline. "We could do that."

"Screw you, Kincaid."

"Hey, it was your idea." He grinned at me.

I couldn't smile back, although my lips twitched. Having Max harass me and Marie try to take care of me made the empty, jagged places inside of me a little warmer though. I had allies. Nova had allies. Somehow we'd get her back and make everything all right again.

"I can give you an herbal medicine to help you sleep," Marie told me. "If you want it. If you don't, I understand. You need to take care of yourself, though, or you'll be no good to Nova."

I heaved a sigh. "I want to do something."

"I know, hon. But Caroline and Max are looking for your book. There's nothing you can do at the moment besides get some sleep." She gave me a sympathetic smile. "Honestly, you look like you haven't slept in a week."

Nova and I had been doing a lot of other activities at night.

The loss of her suddenly hit me all over again like a fifty-pound dumbbell thrust directly into my gut. I almost doubled over at the heavy, hard pain of it. I grabbed for the back of the nearest chair as my eyes closed on the agony.

"I don't know what he's doing to her," I whispered roughly. "It could be anything. Anything. I can't stand that she might be hurting because of me." Or at all.

23

"You love her," Marie said.

"Yeah. Yeah, I do." And that was the problem. "That's why he took her. So it's my fault she's gone. It's my fucking fault. I did this. And it's up to me to fix it."

"I don't see how loving her is your fault, or how loving her could endanger her," Marie said.

I glared at her. "Because he promised he'd take people I cared about if he couldn't get me. If I hadn't loved her, or maybe if I did but I'd kept my mouth shut about it, then he wouldn't have taken her."

"Gage, you told me he wasn't able to take you because your mom had no authority to offer your soul. Don't you think it's kind of bullshit that he's trying to make you responsible for kidnapping Nova? That he's trying to fix the blame for Jeremy's death on you? He's the one who did those things, not you. He's the one responsible. Don't blame yourself."

I pressed the heels of my hands into my eyes. "I don't know. I can't think straight."

"Exactly. That's why you need sleep. Come on, I'll get you some valerian."

I had no idea what valerian was, but I followed her anyway. She led me up a steep, narrow wooden staircase to a second floor. A cramped landing led to several bedrooms and a bathroom so old-fashioned with its black and white hex tiles it reminded me of a movie set. Hell, everything had been reminding me of movie sets, when they weren't reminding me of Nova.

Instead of going to the medicine cabinet, Marie opened a small cupboard fixed to the wall of the landing and pulled out a plastic bottle. "Take these with water," she said, dumping four green capsules into my open palm.

"They smell weird." Like smelly cheese or sweaty socks.

"That's how you know the valerian is good. If they don't stink, they've lost their power. They'll help you relax. I gave you kind of a strong dose because you're a big guy and you're so tense right now. You should sleep for a few hours anyway."

"Okay. Thanks, Marie."

She patted me again. "You're welcome. The room's right through there."

I staggered into the bedroom and closed the door. The ceiling slanted down to short walls. Thin winter light came through the cotton curtains on the dormer window. The room felt chilly, too, as if they never turned on the heat up here. There was a single twin bed with a little-girl quilt on top. It had blue ribbons printed on it in a diamond pattern, and a different girl in each diamond. Every girl had an enormous pioneer-type bonnet on her head and some kind of loose smock.

Clearly, I'd been transported back to the seventies. I should have known the instant I saw the harvest gold fridge downstairs. I kicked off my shoes, peeled back the quilt, and stretched out on the mattress.

No way could I sleep with Nova missing. But maybe I'd lay here and rest for a while before going back downstairs to help with the search.

***

Nova:

The whiskey Declan brought over was in a crystal decanter rather than in an ordinary bottle. I made some tea—nothing special, just English breakfast—and he poured generous amounts of the whiskey into each mug. I added milk and sugar to mine, because that's the way I always take my tea.

Damn, toddies are good. Don't let anyone tell you different.

We sat on the couch, me with my red throw blanket wrapped around my shoulders for extra coziness. The toddy helped take the edge off that nasty feeling I'd gotten in the fog. I glanced over to find Declan watching me with a soft expression on his face.

He liked me. I could tell.

Normally, I didn't think that way about guys. I was kind of dense when it came to flirting, because I never thought guys were interested in me. Especially not hot ones like him. But for some reason I could easily see that he really liked me.

"I'm sorry our walk scared you," he said, reaching for my hand.

I let him take it, let him lace his fingers through mine. It felt good. Reassuring. The lamplight in my living room made a circle of apparent safety, a refuge from the darkness and fog outside.

"It's okay," I said. "You didn't know how it would affect me."

"Yeah, but you're right. After all those grim warnings, I shouldn't have taken you to a cemetery."

"I thought you didn't realize it was a cemetery."

"I didn't, but you pointed out the headstones. I should have gotten you out of there."

All I wanted to do was forget about it, not be reminded all over. I shrugged. "It's over now. I'll be fine."

"Okay."

"Why did you give me all those warnings?"

He paused, studying our clasped hands. "Yesterday I saw some things that worried me. Some of the people around here aren't exactly upstanding citizens."

"Oh, yeah? I don't think I've seen any of the people around here. You're the only one I've met." Which seemed almost weirder than the haunted fog, now that I thought about it.

"You're lucky then." He smiled at me.

"Don't you think it's odd that we're the only ones around here, though?"

"Nova, you're just going to scare yourself again. Let's turn on some music and forget about the frightening and uncanny for a while." He pulled an mp3 player out of his pocket and turned it on. There were no speakers attached to it, yet music immediately filled the room.

The piece was something classical that I'd heard before. I couldn't remember the name.

I took another sip of the toddy, letting the heat of the tea relax me while the booze gave me a pleasant little buzz. "How did you learn about this drink? I never even heard of it before."

"Oh, they're popular where I'm from," he said.

"Where's that?"

He frowned. "Around. Uh, east of here."

"East?" I raised my brows. "That's kind of vague."

"It doesn't matter. I'm here now, and that's all that counts." He scooted closer to me on the couch and stretched his arm along the back, behind me. "Is this okay?"

"Yeah." I smiled up at him with the feeling he was going to try to kiss me soon.

My heart began fluttering. I hadn't kissed a man in such a long time, I could hardly remember what I was supposed to do. And Declan was so freaking hot, much better looking than my ex-fiancé Barry.

My mind gave a little hiccup at the thought of Barry. Hadn't I done something because of him? Besides break up, that is. Hadn't I gone away? And something big had happened when I did, something crucial that I was supposed to remember. But what?

Then Declan's hand came up to cup the side of my face and his warm lips brushed gently over mine. It felt nice. So nice that I raised my own hand to his shoulder, enjoying the strength I felt there.

He toyed with my mouth, skillfully using his lips to caress mine. I moved more deeply into his embrace, while a tiny voice at the back of my mind whispered that this was wrong. We weren't supposed to be together.

Declan's tongue slid across my lips and I opened for him. When he entered my mouth, I found he tasted faintly of whiskey. His arms tightened around me and his mouth delved more insistently into mine, making me warm and tingly deep inside.

Still, the notion we were doing something wrong wouldn't leave me alone. I tensed, my hand pushing at his shoulder, my back stiffening, pulling away from him.

He released me, his blond brows drawing slightly together. "What's wrong?"

"I'm just—I'm not ready yet."

Declan backed off, scooting away from me down the couch. "I'm sorry. I didn't mean to rush you."

"No, it's okay. It's just that I broke up with my fiancé, Barry, not too long ago and I guess I need to take it slow."

"Okay. I can do that." He smiled at me as he took my hand and raised it to his lips. "I like you a lot, though. I hope we can keep seeing each other."

"Of course we can. I like you too."

After Declan left and the hot toddy had worn off, the creepy feeling returned to me. In the graveyard, I'd felt as if the fog had a consciousness, maybe even eyes through which it could watch me. A bizarre idea, but that was the image that kept recurring to me.

By now, it was dark outside and the heavy fog hid all outside detail. I shut the curtains in every room, yet the creepiness persisted, as if it had followed me home from the cemetery. As if something from the graveyard had invaded my home.

Yuck. Now why had I thought about that? I needed to police my thoughts.

I brushed my teeth and got into some pink flannel pj's, then climbed into bed. Even though I couldn't see anything outside with my curtains drawn, I kept imagining the fog creeping into my room, curling its way beneath my curtains and over to my bed. I hadn't been this spooked since I was a kid and had scared the crap out of myself with *The Sixth Sense.*

I'd leave my bedside lamp on all night. Maybe that would hold the boogie man at bay.

***

I wake up sometime later. There is white outside, but it isn't fog. It's falling snow—giant flakes swirling down and down and down, hitting the glass of the window with a barely audible hushing sound. Yet the room feels warm and safe.

I look around, noticing this isn't my apartment bedroom. It's the master bedroom of my parents' cabin. I haven't seen this place in years, and yet it feels like home to me. The walls are made of logs. The curtains on the window are blue and white gingham, and a blue and white quilt covers the big bed.

The door to the room opens. A man comes inside. Not Declan. This man has dark hair and huge blue eyes. His face looks as sculpted and beautiful as if he were a statue. Maybe a statue of a Greek god. He has the body to match, his muscled form on display through the snugly fitting black sweatpants and T-shirt he wears.

My belly flutters and aches at the same time as he comes deeper into the room and stands next to the bed. I want him with a desperation I've never felt before.

I push the quilt off me, an invitation for him to join me. He kneels on the bed. I reach up and stroke his angular jaw, feeling the dark stubble beneath my palm. My thumb brushes his full lower lip.

"I love you," he says.

I slip my hand behind his neck and urge him downward, until his mouth claims mine. He tastes like pure sex and I moan, suddenly on fire to have him inside me. Our hands pull and tear at each other's clothes as we kiss with voracious need.

Everywhere he touches me, I come alive with the most intense desire I've ever felt, until the need for him is almost unbearable. I pant, my hands trembling as I touch his smooth skin, feeling the hard muscle underneath.

"I need you inside me," I whisper.

"Yes. Baby, yes." He sinks into the space between my thighs, his hard cock prodding eagerly at my body.

***

Sweating, trembling, still aching with need, I awoke. I sat up in bed and pushed my hair from my face. My bedside lamp still burned, and judging by the overall darkness of the room, the sun wasn't up yet.

I wanted him back, wanted to complete the encounter. I wanted more from him, even more than sex. The need in me wasn't merely sexual, it was emotional. A heart need.

He hadn't even entered me before I'd been dragged back to waking consciousness. I needed him so much, wanted him so much, and I couldn't even have him in a dream.

But who was he?

God, Nova, it was just a dream. Get over it.

Sensible advice. But it had felt real somehow, as if I should know who he was. As if he ought to be more real to me than my own home, than my flesh-and-blood next door neighbor Declan.

Chapter 6
Secret Rites Of Necromancy

Gage:

The middle of an *old cemetery is the perfect spot for the house. I've never built a house before, yet somehow I know exactly what to do although I have no blueprints or plans of any kind. I wield my tools expertly, putting together the stone foundation, the walls and high ceilings and hip roof like I've built hundreds of them before. It's small, almost like a playhouse, and in a simple Victorian style that I know Nova will love. I lavish bright colors on it to charm her, because I know she loves bright colors—Christmas red and pale green and white and a touch of dark, almost-black green for some of the details on the roof corbels. I know she'll fall in love with this place the instant she sees it, especially since it's in the cemetery.*

She'll know I made it just for her.

Suddenly, I'm with her again. We're in the master bedroom up at her parents' cabin, where I first met her. She's sprawled beneath me in the bed, and I'm loving every inch of her body with my mouth and hands. All I can think of is how good she feels and smells and tastes, and how bad I want to get inside her. She's moaning, touching me, her hands moving everywhere, and it's like her touch fills me up, like it's a kind of food and I'm starving.

I groan, pressing myself close to her hot, wet body. God, she feels so good. Perfect. She'll feel even better when I get inside her; I can hardly wait for the hot, tight clasp of her sheath on my cock.

"Nova," I moan into her hair.

She disappears. Vanishes right from under me.

***

I blinked. A dream. That's what it was. Just a dream.

God damn it. I almost groaned again at the loss of her, my whole body still throbbing with need and my soul dark and empty without her.

I needed her back. I needed to know she was safe and happy, which obviously couldn't be true given her current location.

Gradually, the sound of someone softly playing a guitar penetrated my consciousness. The song was something I used to play with Jeremy, when we were learning ballads to impress girls. I'd never really used my skill that way, but he had. Love songs almost always work to soften up a reluctant girl when she's not impressed with all your other stellar qualities, at least according to him.

My eyes opened. The light seemed even dimmer and chillier than it had when I'd fallen asleep. A man sat on the end of the borrowed bed, his blond head bent over a guitar as he played a whispery tune. I blinked again, narrowing my eyes. He was familiar. Too familiar.

Jeremy. My heart zoomed from a lazy, post-sleep rhythm to a frantic race. I broke out in a sweat. Seeing him in front of my car had been weird enough, but this was in a whole new category of bizarre.

Was he real? Maybe I was still dreaming.

I lay still under the quilt, almost holding my breath, waiting to see what he'd do next. Would he look at me? Would he talk to me?

I could feel his weight pressing down on the mattress, making it dip. I could see his long fingers, bony from all the drugs and not-eating he did before he died. I could even hear the soft, occasional scritch of his fingers against the strings as he picked out the tune.

This didn't feel like a dream at all. It felt real.

"Jeremy," I said.

He vanished. He didn't fade or grow insubstantial; he simply was there one instant and gone the next.

I jackknifed up to a sitting position, my heart still galloping. Why was he visiting me? And if he had something to tell me, why not just come out and say it? Why the guitar playing?

I scrubbed my face. I hadn't expected to fall asleep, but now I felt that I'd been deep under for a while. A couple of hours at least.

"Okay, Jer," I said out loud. "If you can hear me, know that I want to hear whatever message you have for me. Don't worry about scaring me."

Yeah, I felt like a dumbass talking to an empty room, but there was a chance he could hear what I said. And I wanted him to come back. I wanted to have a face-to-face conversation with him, the sooner the better.

Maybe Jeremy knew a way to get Nova back. Or maybe he knew someone who could help us. And even if he didn't, I wanted to see my friend again, to apologize for not being there to help him. For failing to save him.

I padded back down the stairs in my stocking feet, making only the occasional creaking noise on the old steps. Nobody else was making any sound. The old house smelled of moisture and age and loneliness.

At the bottom of the stairs, I glanced into the living room. It was empty. The books still lay over end tables, couch cushions, and the floor, although more of them were back on the shelves.

I noticed a nondescript black guitar case sitting against the far arm of the couch. I hadn't noticed it before, yet it seemed obvious now. Maybe because I'd also seen Jeremy's ghost playing a few minutes earlier. Was he trying to tell me I needed to play?

I didn't really get that. What difference would my playing guitar make? I should be working, looking for a method of rescuing Nova. But it's not every day you see your dead best friend, and the connection between my vision and this guitar nagged at me.

A burst of laughter escaped the kitchen, drawing my attention. The others were probably all gathered there and it sounded like they were having a good time. They wouldn't notice or care if I took a bit longer joining them.

"Okay, Jer," I said. "This is for you."

I went to the case and unfastened it, pulled out the instrument. It was a standard cheap guitar, the kind parents buy their rock-star addled kids for Christmas. But it would do.

Sitting down on the couch with it, I tuned it up, quickly because it was already almost there. Not as convenient as the one I'd gotten on the streets in L.A., which was always magically in tune, but good enough. Someone had obviously played it not too long ago.

The first song I did was a ballad I'd done for Nova months ago, when we'd been stuck in the cabin together. I'd played it in an attempt to make her feel better as she was sick with stomach flu at the time.

Ever since I'd left Oregon without her, I'd played this song to remind myself of her and it still felt like the most solid connection I had with her. She was gone, in a place I couldn't reach, but I could still play this song. And someday, I'd find her and get her back where she belonged.

I finished that piece and segued into one I'd written for her. She'd only heard it once, right before she'd been taken. I would play it for her, I told myself. Soon. It wouldn't be long before she would be here with me.

I didn't fully believe it, but I repeated that thought to myself anyway.

You think I've forgotten you
Your sweet face
The way you kissed me and said you loved me
You think I've forgotten you
But I will never forget

I know I'm not good enough for you
November Daye, you deserve better than me

You think I've gone away
Left your beautiful soul behind
You think I've gone away

I'll never leave unless you make me

I know I'm not good enough for you
November Daye, you deserve better than me

You think I'm moving on
But I'm only moving up
I will make myself over
I will fight my way back to you

Someday, I'll be good enough for you
November Daye, you deserve better than me

You think I don't care
You think I'd rather be with someone else
You think I don't care
But baby, I love you

Someday I'll be strong enough for you
November Daye, I love you
I love you, November Daye

The song felt even sadder than usual. I'd written it when we were apart, and it seemed even more relevant now. My throat tightened, making my voice husky and rough as I sang in a voice low enough to avoid bothering the others.

Nova had loved listening to me. I didn't think I was all that good, yet she kept insisting how great I was at it. She thought I was as good a musician and songwriter as I was an actor, a comparison that made me laugh since I didn't see myself as a great actor either. But Nova did. She believed in me, even though I'd never believed in myself.

Lucifer said I'd built my career on my own, that he'd never honored his end of The Deal. And if that was true, then maybe Nova was right about the music thing. Maybe I did have some real skill. But it wouldn't bring her back, would it?

I finished her love song, the notes of the last chord dying away into silence. When I looked up, I found the others all crowded around the archway listening. Marie, in front, began to clap.

My face flushed with heat as I stuck the guitar back in its case. "Cut it out. I was just fooling around."

"You're really good," Max said.

"You are." Brad grinned at me. "Wanna join my band?"

"Ha ha." I stood up. "Thanks for letting me borrow it. Did anybody find anything while I was asleep?"

Marie stared at me with narrowed eyes. "Don't you know how good you sounded?"

"I want to find Nova." I got up and joined them.

"We'll get to that in a minute," Marie told me. "Seriously. You don't know how good a song that was, do you?"

Max gave me a sympathetic look. "You can't stop her when she gets like this."

"Nova thinks I'm good," I said. "But she's biased." Because she loved me. My chest felt like it was going to collapse.

"Well, she's right. You're really good," Marie said.

Brad clapped me on the shoulder. "I wouldn't ask just anyone to join the band. Only the best get invitations."

I laughed, but it sounded forced. "I'm honored then. So about Nova."

Then I noticed another man standing next to Max. The two of them looked so alike they could have been brothers, or maybe cousins, same black hair and dark blue eyes, same bone structure. The new guy looked watchful as he gazed at me, as if he were assessing me, trying to make up his mind whether I was a friend or an enemy.

He sported one of those handlebar mustaches that a few trendy dudes were wearing these days. That was when I noticed how old-fashioned his clothes were. He wore a loose, dark jacket with an oddly narrow lapel and loose trousers out of the same material.

"Did you get some sleep?" Max said.

"Yeah." I rubbed my face again.

"This is my—uh—ancestor, Fred Marchand." He indicated the guy next to him with a motion of his head.

Ancestor? That was a fucking weird way of saying they were related. But whatever. Max was an odd-ball.

"A pleasure." I stuck out my hand.

Fred glanced at it, then at Max. Then he gave me an apologetic shrug and a smile.

"I'd be glad to shake hands with you, sir, if I could."

I looked at Max with a puzzled lift of my brows.

"Fred is a ghost," he said.

"Huh?" I stared from him to Fred and back again. "A ghost?"

"I'm afraid so," Fred said.

"But you look real."

"I am real. Just not physical."

"Christ. Am I still dreaming?"

"You're awake," Marie said. "Do you feel all right?"

33

"Yeah. But a few minutes ago, I saw another ghost. My friend Jeremy. He was sitting on the end of my bed playing the guitar."

Max and Fred looked at each other.

"I didn't feel him," Fred remarked. "But I did have my attention on this room, so perhaps that's the reason."

"Are you really a ghost?" I said, coming closer. "I mean, you're not pulling my leg, are you?"

"No." Fred stood and extended his hand to me. "Try to shake."

I grasped his hand. At least, that's what I meant to do, but my flesh seemed to pass right through his. The only sensation I received was a kind of electric tingling.

"Holy shit," I said.

Fred laughed. "Indeed."

"I asked Fred to come in case he had some idea how to help you get your girl back," Max said.

"Do you?" I fixed Fred with an eager stare.

"Not really. I'm sorry I can't be more helpful. But there may be others who know more than I."

A sigh escaped me. "Fuck. I have to *do* something. I can't sit around on my hands while she suffers. Did anybody find that book?"

"There's one copy," Caroline said. "But it's not on-line."

"Where then?"

"It's in the private collection of this ceremonial magician in Seattle," Max said.

"Okay. Great. I'll call the guy and ask him what he'll take for it."

"I already did that. It's not for sale."

I shook my head, hard enough to give myself a headache. "Everything's for sale if the price is high enough."

"That's not what he said."

"Give me his number. I'll call him and see if I can talk him around," I said, holding my hand out toward Max.

"Go on," Marie said. "It can't hurt to let him try."

I took the number he gave me, scribbled on a scrap of lined paper. The others were standing there, watching me like they expected to be my audience. I might be an actor, but I didn't want an audience for this.

"I'll be outside," I said, and walked out the front door.

The fields around the house were hidden in mist; even the giant tree overhanging the house was shrouded in gray. My skin instantly felt damp. The air smelled strongly of some kind of herb or bush, although I had no idea what it was.

The little house didn't have a real porch, just an overhang sheltering the front stoop. I leaned against the door and pulled out my smart phone and dialed the book owner's number.

"Yeah?" said a careless voice on the other end.

"Is this Adam Freiberg?" I said.

"The same."

"I hear you have a book, *Secrets Rites Of Necromancy,* that I'd very much like to buy."

Freiberg sighed loudly. "Look, those other people called earlier and I told them I wasn't selling. You're wasting your time."

"Are you sure? I'm willing to pay a lot of money for it."

"Yeah, I'm sure. Why's it so important to you, anyway?"

Probably for the same reason he was refusing to sell. "It has some obscure information in it I haven't been able to trace to any other source."

Rule number one of negotiation: never reveal how much you want the doo-dad or how much you're willing to give for it. I was revealing way too much for a smart negotiation, but I didn't give a shit about the price. I'd do, or pay, whatever I had to in order to get the book.

"Sorry. I'm not interested in selling."

"Not for any price?" I said, wondering how much it was going to take to make him change his mind.

"Dude, you can't possibly have enough money to make it worth my while."

He sounded awfully confident about that.

I smiled. "Name your price and I'll meet it."

"No. I don't want money. I don't want anything."

"Would it be possible for me to drive up and look at it?" I said. "I won't take it or pester you to sell it to me. I just want to read it."

"No. Not a good idea."

"What? Why not?" I started to pace back and forth across the little stoop. He was being damned unreasonable.

"You must not know much about magical artifacts," he said, his voice sticky with condescension.

"Maybe I don't. So enlighten me."

"Secret Rites is a grimoire." He announced this as if it explained everything.

"Yeah? So? It's just a book."

Freiberg snorted. "It's not just a book. It's a magical book that has a lot of power attached to it. Its magical charge will be weakened if I allow anyone else to touch it."

"Can't you re-charge it?"

"Maybe. But it would take a long time and a lot of effort and I'd rather not have to go to all that trouble."

I gritted my teeth in frustration. "A woman's life is on the line here. Isn't that more important than your magical toy?"

"*Secrets* is not a toy, and the fact you'd call it that just confirms my decision not to let you near it. You don't have the proper respect."

I ground my teeth together, as gritting them wasn't doing the job anymore. "It's not that I don't respect the book. It's that I have more important things on my mind, like rescuing my girlfriend."

"Dude, if you're talking about storming the gates of hell, that has never worked."

Dude? He'd called me that twice now. It seemed so California, and really out of place in the context. Like a surfer who worked dark magic on the side. Not very believable.

"How do you know it's never worked?" I said.

"There's never been a recorded instance of it working, while there have been several accounts of people trying it with disastrous results."

I stared at the misty tree, tapping my fingers against my denim-clad leg. "I'm willing to take that risk."

"No way. I'm not going to be a part of that."

"Oh, for fuck's sake. It's my neck. What do you care if I break it?"

"I don't. Except there'll be a karmic backlash on me, because the book belongs to me. So no. You can't look at it."

I ground my teeth again. This guy was impossible. If he couldn't see reason, I'd have to find out where he lived and break in, because there was no way I was leaving that book behind. I needed the information in it.

"And don't think you can sneak up here and break into my place," he added. "I've got wards here that would grind you into mush if you tried to breach them. Do yourself a favor and give up on Secrets now."

That wasn't going to happen.

"Fine," I bit out. "Is there anything you can tell me, any other technique that can get someone released from hell?"

He laughed. "You don't ask for much, do you?"

"No, then."

He sighed again. I could picture him on the other end shaking his head at my obstinacy. "People in hell are there for a reason. No disrespect to your girlfriend, but I don't think you really want her back."

"She's not there because she's a bad person," I said, taking a step down onto the front walk. "The devil took her to punish me. She's not even dead. At least, she wasn't when he took her."

Freiberg said nothing. The line went so dead and silent I began to think he'd hung up on me. Rain dripped miserably from the house eaves and the broad branches of the tree. A drop splashed right in my eye. I jumped back beneath the overhang.

"Freiberg? You there?"

"Yeah. Uh...fuck." He paused. "You are seriously fucked, dude. And your girlfriend...Jesus H. Christ."

"That's not helpful."

"I've heard of this kind of shit, but only as part of old stories. Not as something that happens in real life. Truth is, I didn't think it was even possible."

"I wouldn't either if I hadn't seen it happen."

"Fuck." He sighed. "Okay, I'm in."

"What?"

"I'm in. I'll help you. But I can't sell you the book."

My back straightened. "But you'll let me look at it."

"Yeah, I'll do that. And I'll do some research for you, see what else I can turn up. But it won't be free."

"That's not a problem. I can pay."

"If you could come up to Seattle, it would be easier. That way we'll have access to all my shit."

"That's cool. You mind if I bring some friends?" I was willing to go up alone, but I'd rather have Max by my side. Maybe Brad and Marie too.

"As long as they can keep their hands off my tools, they're welcome."

"They seem pretty experienced, so I'm sure they'll be cool."

"What's your name again?" he said.

"Gage Dalton."

He barked a laugh. "No fucking way. *The* Gage Dalton?"

"Uh huh. We need to keep this quiet, though, okay? No media attention or I won't pay a dime."

"No, that's fine. I won't say anything. Gage Dalton. Holy crap."

He sounded way more impressed than I'd expected, given his overall attitude toward me and my dilemma. I wondered if he was the kind of guy who'd come on to me. I'd gotten plenty of that kind of proposition, besides my more usual offers from females.

But Freiberg just laughed again. "Some psychic I am. I never would have guessed your identity."

"Yeah. I don't want anyone to know I'm not in L.A. Paparazzi are not people we want hanging around."

"Yeah, I got you. Okay, so here's the address."

I wondered who would be willing to go with me. Marie, probably. She'd said the farm was her job, so she might be able to swing a few days in Seattle. Max and Caroline, on the other hand, I had no idea. Caro was a student, so she probably had classes. Not that it mattered; If I had to go alone and naked, I'd do it.

"Listen, I've gotta go," Freiberg said. "I have an operation coming due and I can't be late."

"You're a surgeon?" I said, confused.

"No." He gave one of those short laughs. "A magical operation. Alchemical, actually. I'll see you on Sunday, right?"

"Right. Sunday." Tomorrow afternoon, in fact.

Chapter 7
Tombstone

Nova:

We were having a rare sunny day and I'd decided to take a walk. Yeah, Declan had given me all those dire warnings, but it was the middle of the day and it felt safe. The visibility was fine without that heavy fog to hide things.

The only problem with the greater visibility was I could now see how odd the neighborhood really was. Empty, for example. The pretty winter sunlight fell on empty houses, empty driveways, empty streets.

I left the apartment building without seeing a single other person. Maybe everyone in my building worked nights except for me and Declan. That in itself seemed like an awfully odd coincidence, though.

Don't think about that right now.

Damn it, I wanted to just enjoy my walk, without having strange fears and premonitions spoil it for me. I had my walking shoes on, a bottle of water, and my sketchpad and pencil in case I saw something I wanted to draw. I was all set to have a good time. I put my weird imaginings away.

The houses in the neighborhood, a mix of seventies suburbia and twenties charm, still looked as dark and shuttered as they had on all my other walks. Most people were likely to be at work right now...unless they were those graveyard shift people I'd imagined earlier.

A small, seventies ranch painted a faded blue had curtains visible through the living room window. The grass was neatly cut, the boxwood shrubs near the door growing in tidy round shapes. But there were no cars in the driveway, no toys in the yard. I walked a few yards up the driveway, staring at that living room window.

The room had no furniture. It was nothing but an empty rectangle with brown wall-to-wall carpet. Did no-one live here?

Maybe nobody lived in the neighborhood at all, except for me and Declan.

Nope. Don't go there.

Sunny day. Cheerful. I pulled my attention away from the sad little ranch house and looked up at the blue, cloud-dotted sky. A crow cawed at me from its perch in a nearby oak.

If I could get a good look at the bird, maybe I could sketch it. I glanced around for a place to draw and noticed the cemetery. That stopped me in my tracks.

I hadn't meant to end up here. The pillar-like trunks of the trees I'd seen through the fog just looked like big trees today, a mixture of oaks and spruce mostly, but there were still the gravestones. Rows and clusters of them, sticking out of the ground like stone hands raised to get my attention.

I gave another glance around. Still alone. No traffic on the street at all. In fact, I couldn't hear any traffic noise from adjacent streets, either. But in spite of the eerie stillness of the day, the place looked a lot less threatening with the sun shining.

It's just a graveyard. It's not going to hurt you.

Declan was right. Dead people couldn't do anything to me. They were dead.

I crossed the street and entered through an opening in a long, wrought-iron fence I hadn't noticed the other time I'd been here. It must have been hidden in the fog. It had sharp, spear-like points sticking up as if to skewer the unwary.

Inside the cemetery, the first row of stones looked almost new, their surfaces shiny and polished. The death dates on them seemed to be mostly from the nineteen-eighties and nineties. Some were made of shiny, black granite and others of pink marble. Most of them were flat in the ground. I supposed it cost more to buy one of the upright kind.

There was so much silence in this place. No birds sang, except for the crow that still cawed in the oak tree. Sunlight filtered down through the bare branches and cast intricate patterns across the grass.

I wandered farther into the cemetery as a sense of peace came over me. At least here I didn't have the blank windows of all those houses, like dark staring eyes.

The ground sloped upward under my feet. As I penetrated more deeply into the place, the stones became less shiny, more weathered. Some of them bore thick coverings of grayish lichen and bright green sphagnum moss. The dates moved further into the past. The nineteen fifties, thirties, teens. The eighteen hundreds.

I passed a sad little row of small, gray stones laid flat into the ground. All of them belonged to children. The surnames were different—Smith, Grant, McIntosh, Breier—but the dates were all in the same year. What local epidemic had wiped out all of these poor kids?

There were a lot of graves, and the path meandered in a more or less random way between them, wandering around clumps of vine maple and the trunks of enormous oak trees. I rounded a particularly large tree and came on an odd structure. It wasn't a gravestone, but it was clearly meant as a grave marker.

It looked a lot like a miniature temple, the stone carved into pillars in the front, the openings in between them shaped like Gothic arches. In the center was an open space, like a tiny room. It wasn't big enough to enter, though, since the whole thing only came up to my knees. It was like a temple for garden gnomes or something.

I bent closer to it, admiring the Goth beauty of it. Why had I thought this place was so scary? It only felt intriguing and pleasantly evocative now.

The name on the memorial caught my eye. Declan Stanhope, 1840-1869. He'd died so young. I wondered what had killed him. And his name...Declan. What an odd coincidence, especially considering it wasn't a common name in North America.

Fallen oak leaves, acorns, and thick moss clung to the deep places in the memorial. Obviously, no-one had cared for it in a long time and that seemed sad to me. Declan Stanhope had been forgotten.

"Who were you?" I murmured. "How did you die?"

The only answer I received was another caw from a crow sitting in the spruce tree next to the memorial. I glanced up, but couldn't make out the bird. Was it the same one, following me, or one of its friends?

What if the grave belonged to my Declan?

God, that was so crazy I felt embarrassed for thinking it. Normally I'd never consider something like that. It was the strangeness of the neighborhood that put the idea in my head.

No, my Declan was just an ordinary guy. No relation to this Declan Stanhope, just an odd coincidence.

Maybe I'd sketch Mr. Stanhope's memorial. But there was no place to sit except another grave marker, and that didn't seem right. Reluctantly, I turned to follow the path that had brought me here.

After a few dozen yards, it dawned on me that I'd chosen a different route. The row of flat headstones marking the children's graves never materialized. Instead, I walked past a row of elaborate memorials similar to the one for Declan Stanhope, as the overhanging trees grew more and more oppressive and the shrubs larger, encroaching on the path and blocking out much of the cheerful sunshine. The path did move downward along the gentle slope of the hillside, though, so I figured I ought to be going in the right direction.

A huge thicket of shrubs and small trees grew next to the path on my left side, and the way curved around the miniature forest. Whatever was on the other side hid behind the screen of tangled branches, bramble, and dead leaves. I couldn't quite make it out, yet I could see what looked like the peak of a roof.

Something rustled loudly in the bushes and I jumped back, my heart pounding so hard I imagined I could almost hear it. Something was in there, caught among the dead oak leaves and wickedly sharp blackberry thorns. The rustle came again.

A glossy black head peeked out from behind an oak leaf, shiny black eyes peering up at me as the crow cocked its head to the side. I snorted a laugh of relief. Just a bird.

What had I thought it was? A monster? Of course it was a bird.

The crow made a soft clucking noise, as if to confirm my silliness.

Shaking my head at myself, I continued down the path. I rounded the thicket and there was the tiny Victorian-style house. Great. I'd just recovered from the Great Crow Scare and now I had to walk past that haunted-feeling creepfest of a house.

It should have been cute. Tiny, perfectly proportioned, with the tall narrow windows and steeply pitched roof typical of a Victorian, it had been painted in varying shades of gray to pick out the detail in the trim. And the paint job looked new. This small structure was the best-kept item in the cemetery so far.

Yet as I approached it, the air around it seemed to hum at the same time as some invisible weight pressed in on my skull. The sense of being watched, something that had dogged me a lot lately, intensified the closer I got. The hair on the back of my neck prickled and stood up, and I had an almost irresistible urge to look around to see who was there.

No-one is there. It's just you and the crows.

The path promised to take me within a yard of the building, and I couldn't give it a wider berth because of the heavy underbrush that had overtaken this area. It was either get within touching distance of the house or turn around and try to find the other route. I stared at the building, my heart rate now well into the cardio zone.

It's just an old building, Nova. For crying out loud, get hold of yourself.

Okay. Just an old building. I could totally do this.

I straightened my shoulders and started around the house. I could almost smell it, the scent of mildew and dry rot emanating from the clean-looking shiplap siding. When I glanced at a window, I noticed thickly enmeshed strands of cobweb clinging to the inside of the glass and the sill. The smell of rot seemed to intensify.

My steps quickened. Almost all the way around. The tiny front stoop with its thick slab of stone forming the only step appeared. The corbels and the trim around the front door had no cobwebs, so apparently people were cleaning the outside but not the interior.

It wasn't really a house anyway. Nobody could live in a place that small. I had no idea what the structure was really meant for, and at the moment I didn't want to find out. I just wanted to pass it and get back into the sunshine.

A flash of white caught my eye. I turned my head. A shape pressed up against the glass. A shape from the interior of the building.

A face. I could make out the features—they looked female, with long flowing hair and dark staring eyes. Her hand pressed up against the glass and I gave another start.

I ran. Just turned tail and ran down the path, tumbling over rocks and tree roots in my hurry to get away.

What was that thing? A ghost? She couldn't have been a live human, not with such a colorless face and that blank stare. She'd looked as if no-one was home inside her head. No-one at all.

***

Gage:

It's a fair drive from Avery's Crossing to Seattle and we had to swing by Portland on the way. The landscape looked much like what I'd already seen around Avery's—green and misty, with lots of fields full of sheep and cows interspersed with rank upon rank of dark evergreens. I couldn't decide if the gloom made my head hurt or if it was restful. One thing was for sure, though—it was a whole different world from SoCal.

I glanced over at Max, who sat in the passenger seat with his long legs stretched out in front of him as far as they would go. "You ever been to Seattle before?"

"Oh, yeah," he said. "That's where I met Brad and Marie."

"Really. I assumed you'd grown up in Avery's Crossing."

"Nah. We all moved down there about a year ago. Before that, we were in Seattle."

"So how did you meet them?"

He shot me a sidelong glance. "Bookstore. I was living on the streets, but I used to go into this one occult bookstore to warm up and look at the books. Couldn't afford anything, and I wouldn't have had anyplace to keep a book anyway, but I love to read."

"Funny. That's where Nova met Marie, in a bookstore in Avery's."

He smiled as he stared out the windshield at the passing scenery. "Yeah, she probably sensed there was someone in there who needed her. She's really talented that way."

"Until I met you guys, I'd never known anyone into the occult," I said.

He turned his head toward me. "So being caught in a deal with the devil didn't pique your interest?"

"It wasn't like that. There was this whole secrecy thing, like it was something shameful we had to hide from everyone."

"Doesn't that sound familiar." Max tilted back his head for a swallow of coffee from the paper cup he'd gotten at a local drive-thru coffee place.

"You grew up under a deal with the devil too?" I asked, only half in jest.

"No. My dad beat on me." He took another swallow of coffee. "It was the dirty family secret."

"Shit. That's rough."

"That's why I was on the streets in Seattle instead of back home in Montana."

I spared him a glance before refocusing on the road. He looked lost in thought, his dark-blue eyes distant.

"So you were already into the occult?" I said.

"Yeah. I started having weird shit happen to me as a kid. When you're like that, you look for ways to deal with it. Explanations."

"Makes sense. Maybe if I'd looked for information on my own, I would have gotten out from under The Deal a long time ago."

Max looked right at me. "Why didn't you?"

He didn't pull any punches, that was for sure. I shifted uncomfortably, Nova's self-portrait crackling in the pocket of my jacket where I'd put it for safe-keeping. But Max seemed to expect an answer, so I cast around inside my head for some kind of insight. Why hadn't I investigated?

I shrugged. "I dunno. My mom put the fear of the devil into me. She always hinted that bad things would happen to anybody I told, so I kept it to myself. And there was this whole 'there's nothing we can do' vibe going on, like it was Fate or something."

"She did a number on your head," Max remarked.

"No shit."

"You're gonna have to deprogram yourself. Or get help, if you're willing to talk about it with someone else."

I had a shrink back in L.A., but of course I'd never brought up the devil business with him. There weren't many people I'd even consider telling my problem to. Max was one of them. Brad and Marie, too.

"I'm working on it," I said without taking my eyes off the road. "I never gave it much thought until Nova. Guess I was just fatalistic about it all. But Nova changed everything."

"Women will do that."

I'd only known Max a few weeks and we'd already had more meaningful conversations than I'd ever had with Jeremy, except those times we'd been drunk or stoned and he'd chosen to unload on me. He'd told me all kinds of horrible shit about his childhood in the business, things that had been done to him by people in power. Those were the memories that had continued to drive him back to the heroin, the booze. Just to forget for a while.

But there had been only a few of those conversations in all the years I'd known him. Max and I had already gotten about as deep as I'd ever been with Jer. This was a new thing for me and I wasn't sure how I felt about it.

"You hungry?" Max said as he stuck his coffee cup into the cup holder in the door.

"Yeah." Now that he mentioned it.

"There's a roadhouse up at the next exit. Food's not too bad."

I glanced idly at the right shoulder of the road. A man stood there, knee deep in dead weeds, a hundred yards or so ahead of us. He wore a perfectly fitted black suit and he was smoking a cigarette that veiled him in a cloud of smoke.

It was him. The smoking man Nova and I had both spotted watching us at various times and places over the last few weeks. He'd even appeared to invade our house at one time. I'd thought he was the devil, but when Lucifer did appear and steal Nova, he looked nothing like the Suit Guy.

"What is it?" Max said.

"That guy over there." I nodded toward the shoulder. "See him? The suit with the ciggy."

"Yeah. Weird. What's he doing on the side of the road dressed like that?"

"I've seen him before. He was watching me in L.A. Nova saw him spying on her in Avery's Crossing more than once. And one evening he was in our back yard, watching her through the window."

We passed him. He stared openly at my car as we sped by. Max made no bones about watching him from the passenger window, either.

"Not human," he said.

"I figured he was a demon or some shit."

"I don't think so. I don't think he's infernal at all."

I glanced at him. He still had his head cranked around, although the smoking man was long gone, way behind us at that point.

"What do you think he is then?" I said.

"I dunno. There's a lot of power in him, though. We should do a reading or three. He's definitely watching you."

"He scared the hell out of Nova."

"Yeah, I'll bet." Max turned toward the front again, tapping his fingers on his denim covered thigh. "We should have stopped the car and asked him."

I shot him an incredulous glare. "Are you shitting me? No way am I gonna talk to that dude."

"He might be helpful." Max grinned at me. "You have me here to protect you."

"No offense, Kincaid, but that doesn't make me feel any better."

Chapter 8
Master Of The Dark Arts

Gage:

Adam Freiberg lived in a massively oversized Victorian mansion in one of Seattle's older neighborhoods. The house perched on a hill that would have done San Francisco proud. It had a lot almost small enough for a San Francisco house, too, but it was no painted lady. The color seemed drab even for a gloomy afternoon like this one, with a dull, medium brown body and a slightly darker brown shade on the trim. Some of the details were picked out in red, though, giving it more character.

The tiny yard held little but an evergreen shrub of some kind, growing in a perfect cone shape, some leafy mounded bushes near the front windows, and a patch of tired grass.

The windows all looked blank and dark, as if the house were empty. It had an Addams Family quality to it, even though it lacked the Mansard roof. There was something about all the gables and the tall, narrow windows all staring down at us. In the darkness of nightfall, it seemed ominous.

Even the air around it felt heavy, giving off a sense of foreboding that grew thicker and darker the closer we got to the building. In fact, it would have made the perfect haunted house for a movie.

"He's got a flair for the dramatic," Max said.

"You think?"

"I'm surprised there aren't any skulls on posts out in front." He grinned at me. "Or maybe a body hanging in a gibbet."

"So you think the grim look is for show?"

"I'm not sure. But it probably keeps the local kids away."

We moved up the short walk to the front steps. The door looked original to the house and had been painted a glossy black. Or it would have been glossy if it weren't for the cobwebs and dust festooning it. I rang the bell, which gave a mournful sound.

Picturing an arthritic geezer carefully picking his way down the stairs, I took my time looking around the front while we waited. The porch had a hanging lamp that also looked like it could have been original and converted from a gaslight. It was pretty goddamn ugly. I'd always hated Victorian shit—way too fussy and ornate for me.

Other than the lamp and a pot with some dead flowers hanging limply over its sides, there was nothing on the porch. Nothing except a pervasive smell of dry rot and mildew. Gag. It must be ten times worse inside. I didn't know how Freiberg could tolerate that stench, but maybe he was too old to notice it.

The door opened with a horror-movie squeal of un-oiled hinges. A young blond dude stood there, looking at us expectantly. He wore low-slung jeans and a long-sleeve black T-shirt, and his feet were bare.

"Uh, we're looking for Adam Freiberg," I said. "Is he here?"

"Who wants to know?" The dude's voice sounded familiar, so maybe he was Adam's son.

"I'm Gage Dalton and this is Max Kincaid," I said. "We called. Mr. Freiberg knows we're coming."

The blond kid grinned. "Come in. I'm Adam, by the way."

Max and I exchanged a glance. The look on his face suggested he was as surprised as I was. Freiberg looked way too young to be a Master of The Dark Arts, as he'd hinted over the phone. Maybe he was just a Master of the Art of Bullshit.

He stood back to allow us into the foyer. And wow. Holy shit. The place inside looked like a completely different house from the view outside.

You could see the Victorian bones in the high ceilings and fancy woodwork, but other than that it was completely modern. All the woodwork had been painted white, and the walls were some kind of pale grayish blue. Nova would have had a special name for it, I thought, wishing she were here. Of course, if she were with me I wouldn't have to visit Freiberg and beg to see his Arcane Tome Of Ancient Magic.

"Have you got the book?" I said without preamble. Best to get down to business. I wanted the information so I could take it back to Avery's Crossing and make use of it, and any socializing along the way just interfered with my goal.

"Sure, I've got it. You want a drink first?"

He motioned us to follow him through an archway into a starkly modern living room furnished with an angular gray sofa, a pair of black leather Barcelona chairs, and a gray and red abstract rug on the floor. How did the guy afford all this? A fancy Victorian mansion, especially one that had been completely updated like this, must cost a fortune in Seattle. He must have inherited.

Not that I gave a shit. I just wanted the book.

"I'll take a beer," Max said. "If you have it in the bottle."

"Yeah. Me too."

"Bottle only, huh?" Freiberg said with a wry smile.

"You can't be too careful," Max said.

Did he think Freiberg would try to slip something in our drinks? The ominous vibe of the place had disappeared the instant we'd entered, at least for me, but maybe Max was picking up something I couldn't sense. He was better at this shit and had been doing it a lot longer, after all.

"I would never harm a guest in my home," Adam said. "But I don't blame you for being careful."

He disappeared through another archway, leaving Max and me to look around the living room.

The view out the front window seemed to show all of Seattle spread out, the lights of evening just starting to glow like the eyes of millions of demons. I wondered if the Space Needle was visible from here. I hadn't thought to check when we were still outside, and now it was too dark to tell.

Max came up beside me to gaze out. "Some view."

"Yeah."

"What do you make of him?" he said in a low voice.

"I have no idea." I glanced at him. "You?"

"Too early to tell."

"But you don't trust him."

"Nope." He stuck his hands in his pockets and rocked back on his heels. "Not at all."

"Why is that, if you don't mind telling me?"

He shrugged. "Not sure. Just a feeling."

"It seems like a weird set-up for such a young dude. I expected an old guy."

"Me too. Maybe that's part of the glamour he's got on the place. Make himself seem old and weird, with a weird house."

I glanced at him, wondering. "He didn't sound old on the phone. But I still expected a geezer."

"That's probably the glamour." He looked around the living room, as if assessing the value of all the furniture. "Wonder if he's a trust fund baby."

"Could be. Or maybe it's his command of the Dark Arts that got him this place." I waggled my brows when I said Dark Arts.

Max grinned. "I might have to master a couple of those Arts myself, if it gets you a house like this."

"Or you could just become a movie star like me. Then it's easy."

"Sure. Easy. I'll get right on that."

"You've got the looks for it."

Max stared at me like I'd lost my last wit. "Get outta here."

"Seriously. You could be a model or a leading man type, easily."

He snorted. "I didn't know you felt that way about me."

"Fuck off. You know what I mean."

"I have zero desire to be an actor. I'd take some more success with my graphic design biz, though."

"Great view, huh?" Freiberg's voice came from directly behind us, and we both jumped a little.

"Yeah." Max recovered first. "Spectacular."

"We were just speculating on how you scored a place like this," I said, accepting the beer he offered with a smile. I noted the cap was still tightly attached.

"I know, right?" Freiberg said, handing the second one off to Max.

"Isn't Seattle real estate kinda pricey?" I said, hauling out my key chain with its bottle opener. I popped the cap off the beer.

He shrugged. "Yeah, I guess. I inherited the place. All I know is property taxes are a bitch."

"I like what you've done inside," Max said. "Coming up the steps, I thought this would be like a museum or something."

"The haunted house look comes in handy." Freiberg smirked. "Keeps out people I don't want getting close, know what I mean?"

"Uh huh." I nodded, thinking of the paparazzi. Of course, the gossip rags would love a place like this if I owned it. I could see their headlines—*Is Gage Taking His Latest Role Too Seriously? Gage Dalton Believes He's A Vampire.* And so on. They'd probably have me sleeping in a coffin in the basement.

But I wasn't here to gossip about a house or spin daydreams about an alternative life.

"Have you got the book?" I said.

Freiberg lifted his blond brows. "In a hurry?"

"I told you I was."

"We'll get to that. Let's have a drink first." He had a third beer, which he lifted to his own lips.

Max and I exchanged glances, mine exasperated as hell. Why was Freiberg stalling? It's not like he could reasonably expect us all to become buddies over a beer and I couldn't figure out why he'd care in the first place. I was here to do a job, not to socialize.

My regular business was all about socializing, schmoozing, and I'd always hated that part of it.

"So you practice ceremonial magic," Max said.

"Yeah. Not in here, though." Freiberg grinned as if he'd made a joke.

"You have a secret wizard's tower?" Max said.

"I wish. No, but I do have a dedicated temple. It's one of the great things about a house this size."

"No shit." Max looked around. "You could have one on every floor and still have plenty of room for other stuff."

"Are you a magician?" Freiberg said.

"You could say that."

"Got a specialty?"

"Necromancy." Max tossed off the morbid word with casual unconcern, then took a long swallow of beer.

I gave him a sideways glance. Necromancy? So what did he do? Raise corpses or some shit?

"That's heavy," Freiberg said, raising his brows again. "What made you go into necromancy?"

"They came to me first."

Maybe he was talking about Fred. The whole idea of dead people seemed a lot less creepy when I thought of Fred, who looked just like a regular guy. He didn't go around looking half rotted or showing off his death wounds or any of that nasty shit you saw in the movies.

"You?" Max said. "Any specialty?"

"I'm a generalist. Goetia, mainly."

"I'd love to see your set-up." Max raised his brows expectantly, but Freiberg just looked at him.

Chapter 9
Wizard's Tower

Nova:

Declan claimed his favorite food was potted beef, whatever that was. It sounded kind of disgusting, and I hoped the pot roast I'd made was close enough. I had mashed potatoes, too, plus salad and a chocolate cake for dessert. I'd spent the whole day in the kitchen.

My cheap little dinette table was already covered with dishes—a big mixing bowl for the salad, a smaller one for the potatoes. The chocolate cake sat on my counter and the pot roast was waiting on top of the stove.

"It smells delicious," he said, handing me a bottle of merlot.

"Ooh, you brought wine." I set the bottle on the counter.

"Do you have a corkscrew?"

"Uh..." I thought for a minute and couldn't remember whether I did or not. "Let me look."

When I opened my tool drawer, there was a corkscrew sitting right in front. I pulled it out.

"I guess I do." Weird that I had no memory of buying it, putting it away, or ever using it.

That was one more weird thing in an ever-lengthening list of oddities. Like Declan Stanhope's memorial. What were the odds I'd know someone named Declan and there would just happen to be a grave in the nearby cemetery with that name on it? It's not as if he were named something common, like John or Peter.

"Great. Let me open this." He took the corkscrew from me and stuck the sharply pointed end in the cork.

"Hey, Declan, I was just wondering..." I said in an offhand tone. "What's your last name?"

"Why do you ask?" He glanced at me.

"Just wondering." I shrugged and put on some oven mitts before handling the hot roast pan. "Mine's Pennyman."

"I've never met anyone named Pennyman before."

I smiled at him as I picked up the roast. "Well, I've never met anyone named Declan before."

"Stanhope," he said.

I paused, the roast heavy in my hands. Icy worms seemed to crawl through my stomach. "Stanhope. That's unusual too."

"Is it? I guess it's more common where I come from."

"Which is east of here."

He gave me a sunny smile. "That's right."

52

I brought the roast to the table, my gut churning. Until I'd asked him that question, I'd had quite an appetite. Now, I wasn't sure I could eat.

"Are you all right?" he said, peering into my face. "You look kind of sick."

"I'm fine." I straightened and pasted on another smile. "It's just been a strange week."

He set the bottle of wine on the table. "I know what you mean. Can I carry something for you?"

Should I tell him what I'd found? Maybe it was really only a coincidence, although that was some crazy coincidence. A grave with the same name on it as that of my cute neighbor? How often did that happen? It's not like Declan Stanhope was a common name. If he'd been John Smith or Dave Brown, I might be able to blow it off.

"Let's try to forget the weirdness," he said, carrying in the potatoes, "and just enjoy our time together."

"Okay. I can do that." I hoped.

"How is your schoolwork coming?" he said as we took our seats.

"It's great. I'm doing a lot better this term than I ever have before." I scanned some oddly hazy memories of recent class sessions as that uneasy feeling moved through my innards again. Why did everything having to do with school and work feel so vague? It was like my only vivid memories were of this apartment and Declan.

"How's your job?" I asked to distract myself.

"It's good. I might be in line for a promotion."

"Oh, congratulations. I hope you get it."

He went on to tell me some funny stories about his customers. Nice, pleasant dinnertime conversation, yet I couldn't shake the feeling something was wrong. I had the most bizarre image in my head, that this empty neighborhood was a kind of island, floating in a sea of nothingness. Where had that idea come from?

"I went to the cemetery today," I blurted.

Declan looked up from cutting another bite of pot roast. "Why? You hated it the first time."

"I know, but it was sunny and it didn't seem spooky at all when I went in."

"But?"

"What makes you think there's a but?"

He sent me a freighted look. "I can hear it in your voice."

I stalled by scooping up a bite of mashed potato and sticking it in my mouth. Should I tell him about the grave?

"You know, it's a cemetery," I said. "The deeper I got into it, the spookier it felt. And I walked past that little house thing again, and I swear I saw someone inside."

His eyes widened. "No kidding."

"Yeah. It looked just like a ghost. Scared the crap out of me. I think I ran all the way home."

He shook his head. "Nova, you really should stay away from there. I never should have taken you and I'm sorry about that."

"Don't be sorry. It was interesting until the ghost showed up."

"Well, I hope you'll stay away from now on."

Maybe he didn't know about the grave. He seemed completely unconcerned as he put the bite of roast in his mouth and chewed.

"This is excellent," he said, cutting another piece.

"I'm glad you like it." I took a sip of wine, bolstering my courage. "Declan, I found the strangest memorial up there."

"Oh?" He glanced at me, pleasant and entirely innocent-looking.

"Yeah. It had your name on it."

He frowned. "My name?"

"Uh huh. Declan Stanhope. 1840-1869."

He paused with his fork in mid-air and stared at me. "There's a grave with my name on it?"

"Yes, there is. You're telling me you didn't know?"

"Of course I didn't know." His frown deepened until it looked painful. "That's quite chilling, isn't it?"

"I thought so too. Sad, though. He was so young when he died, only twenty-nine."

"A lot of people died young back then. Maybe he was a soldier in the Civil War?"

"But the war ended in 1864. And if he was a soldier, then why was he buried in Oregon?"

He shook his head slowly. "I don't know."

So far, his reaction told me very little. I was pretty sure his confusion was genuine, but maybe he was just a skillful actor. Could my hot neighbor be a ghost? But I'd kissed him, and he'd felt completely physical.

"Maybe he was an ancestor of yours," I said. "Maybe you were named after him."

"Maybe." He shot me a troubled glance. "I'm not sure I'll be able to sleep tonight."

"Dang, I'm sorry. I didn't mean to upset you."

"No, it's all right. That's not something you'd want to keep to yourself." The glance he gave me this time was uncomfortably perceptive. "No wonder you've been skittish tonight. You have had quite a strange day."

"Yes, I have. But there's wine with dinner and chocolate cake for dessert, so things are looking up."

He laughed and we turned the conversation to more pleasant subjects. I could still feel the weirdness, though, waiting to bubble up again, and God only knew what it would bring with it when it did.

***

Gage:

There's nothing like the quiet of a ceremonial magician's living room when he's giving you and your friend the hairy eyeball. The only sound was faint traffic noise from Greater Seattle just outside the windows. Inside, the atmosphere of the ultra-modern room had gone from guarded-but-friendly to unpleasantly searching.

It could have been ugly, except I actually trusted Adam, even though we'd only met him a few minutes before.

Aside from the crazy magic stuff, what interested me most about the exchange between Max and me on the one hand and Freiberg on the other was that Freiberg showed very little interest in the fact that I was a famous movie star. It was like I was just a normal person, an experience I didn't have very often, and I found it refreshing. Maybe even reassuring.

He didn't fawn all over me, like I'd expected him to do. That, I thought, spoke well of him.

At the moment, Freiberg had stopped talking to study Max intently. Almost like he was reading him on some level, although he didn't have the abstracted look Marie seemed to get when she did a reading. He glanced at me and subjected me to the same intense scrutiny.

Finally, he grinned. "Okay. Sure. It's downstairs."

"Is that where you've got the book?" I said.

"Yep. How'd you guess?"

"Just luck."

He laughed. "Didn't you play a wizard in one of your movies?"

"Yeah. I was just the apprentice, though."

"And now you're getting involved with the real thing?" he said, leading us through an archway into a formal dining room and from there into a very modern-style kitchen.

"I told you. My girl's in trouble."

Adam came to a heavy wooden door, painted white like the woodwork. He stuffed his feet into a pair of Birkenstocks waiting by the door and paused with his hand on the knob. "I hope you can save her. I really do. But you've gotta remember, this stuff is unpredictable and the operation you're talking about has a nasty reputation for going wrong." He glanced over his shoulder at Max. "I'm surprised you don't know it, being a necromancer and all."

"I just talk to the dead. I've never tried to resurrect anyone."

"Ah. Gotcha." He opened the door, revealing a plain wooden staircase descending into a dark, old-style basement.

We clumped down the unlit stairs, with only the light from the kitchen to keep us from falling on our faces. My skin and hair started to prickle as we went lower and lower, deeper into what I couldn't help thinking of as Freiberg's lair. The expected smell of mildew and stagnant air never materialized, though. Instead, I caught a note of something resinous and fragrant, like incense.

At the bottom, Freiberg reached up and pulled a string, turning on a single bare bulb and revealing a standard-looking basement room. Low-ish ceiling with exposed beams, pipes, and ductwork, concrete floor, stacks of boxes here and there.

"Window dressing," he said. "In case I have to allow a service person in. Plus the utilities are in here. The temple is this way."

We wended our way between a couple stacks of cardboard boxes and past a big water heater and furnace standing up against a concrete-block wall. A plain brown exterior-type door stood between the heater and furnace, the cheap slab kind like you see on so many apartments. Freiberg pulled a key out of his jeans pocket and unlocked the door.

Inside was what looked a lot like an English gentlemen's club library, if those gentlemen had been members of an occult lodge. Books crammed floor to ceiling bookcases made of some kind of dark wood. A thick Persian carpet, black background with gold and cream designs, covered the concrete floor. He had a leather wingback chair with reading lamp, and more shelves displaying all kinds of freaky shit. Animal skulls, uncut crystals, plain old rocks, weird drawings with notations in a language I'd never even seen before, flasks full of odd-colored liquids. Objects floated in those flasks.

I peered into one. The object inside looked like some kind of animal fetus.

"Nice," Max said, surveying the place.

What can I say? He was batshit crazy, but he was still my friend.

All in all, this room didn't look much like a temple, although I guessed rituals could be performed in the open space in the center of the room. Then I noticed the door on the opposite wall.

Freiberg went right to it. Some kind of geometric drawing decorated the door, with more of that obscure script at various locations around the drawing. I had no idea what I was looking at, but it definitely seemed mystical.

He opened the door and flicked on an electric light, another single bare bulb. It was the plainest thing in the temple room.

The walls were painted four different colors—blue, yellow, red, and black. The concrete floor had been painted black, with an elaborate geometric circular design painted in white. Each wall had its own small table—altar?—along with a larger one in the center of the circle. There were sconces on all the walls as well, which held old-fashioned candles.

"You have good ventilation in here, I hope," Max said, gesturing at the candles.

"Yeah. I've got an air exchange system." He glanced at me. "It's not safe to burn anything in an enclosed space. Uses up all the oxygen eventually."

Hmm. The things you need to know when you're a ceremonial magician.

"I'll keep that in mind," I said.

"Great temple, though," Max continued. "I'm jealous."

"Yeah? Where do you work?"

"Wherever. I don't have a permanent work space."

I was starting to get antsy. "So, where's this book?"

Freiberg pointed back toward the library. "After you."

We filed back into the library. It was obviously furnished for only one person, since there was just the one chair. But I didn't care about getting comfy. I just wanted to see the damn book.

Freiberg went to the shelves and pulled out a volume bound in ordinary-looking brown leather. I looked for some mystical symbols, runes or something, but the binding looked completely plain. He turned with it held in two hands. I reached for it. He kept it close to his chest.

"You can't touch it," he said. "Remember what I told you on the phone?"

"Oh, yeah. You don't want my energy on it or something."

"Can we take it upstairs?" Max said. "You can lay it on the table and turn the pages for us."

"Good idea." Freiberg pointed to the door.

I was really getting sick of all his stalling. Why had he invited us here if he wasn't going to let us see the thing? What would be the point? It's not as if I'd paid him ahead of time. If he wanted to get his money, he needed to show me the goods.

Maybe he'd accepted a bribe to call the paparazzi, tell them I was here. But that might expose his unusual lifestyle, so I didn't think so.

We trooped back up the stairs and into the kitchen, where we sat at the sleek, glass-topped table. Freiberg sat opposite me and Max and laid the book in the middle, facing us.

"I don't normally allow anyone to view items from my collection," he said. "Except for a handful of close friends and colleagues. I hope you understand how much of an exception I'm making here."

"I understand," Max said.

"Yeah, sure." I nodded, even though I was ready to snatch the book from Freiberg and make off with it.

"I also don't normally show strangers my temple."

"What's your point?" Max said.

"I wanted to get a feel for you before I let you look at this." He opened the book.

The title page read *Secret Rites Of Necromancy,* in such an old-fashioned typeface that I had to study it for a second to make out the words. I reached for it, wanting to draw it closer.

Freiberg grabbed it and hauled it back across the table. "No touching."

"Sorry, dude. I just forgot for a sec."

He fixed me with a stern glare. "I'll forgive you this once. But don't try again."

"Okay. All right. I'll sit on my hands. Will that make you happy?"

"It's better than nothing, but I'd rather handcuff you to the chair."

I shifted uneasily. "Not funny."

"Neither is what will happen to this book if you manhandle it. Look but don't touch."

"You sound like my stepmother," Max said.

"This is an important tool for me. It's got a lot of stored energy and I don't want you fucking it up. Can I trust you two or not?"

Max sighed. "Of course you can. Gage just isn't used to this kind of thing. He'll be fine now that you've made yourself clear."

"Yeah. I swear I won't even put my hands on the table top," I said.

"Okay. See that you don't." He began flipping pages.

The paper looked like that thick, ancient kind made out of linen. There were notes in the margin in spidery handwriting, as if made with a dip pen. It sure wasn't ballpoint ink. I wondered if the notes were Freiberg's work or someone else's.

"This is it," he said, stopping at a page titled The Rite Of Retrieval Of A Soul From Hell.

"A soul," I said. "Will this apply to someone who's still in her body?"

"I don't know. You asked to see the book and here it is."

I frowned at the testiness in his voice. "All right."

Leaning over the table, I studied the text while keeping my hands under the top. The ritual required all kinds of exotic supplies, like dirt from a recent grave, human blood, asafoetida, and something called galbanum. I blinked at the human blood. I was fine with cutting myself a bit and collecting what came out, but there was no way I was going to murder someone. Not even for Nova.

"This blood," I said. "How much does it require?"

"Not much. Maybe an ounce," he said.

I relaxed my shoulders. "Okay. Not so bad."

Freiberg grinned. "Did you think you'd have to kill someone?"

"I didn't know. I've never done anything like this before."

"I told you," Freiberg said. "This is some intense shit. You sure you want to go through with it?"

"Yes," I said. I reached into the pocket of my denim jacket and pulled out the self-portrait Nova had made and given to me. "This is her."

Adam took the picture and studied it without comment.

"You talked about things going wrong." Max spoke without looking up from the text. "You mind explaining that a little?"

"I've read some stories, that's all. This rite is supposed to open a gateway, and theoretically creatures can rise up through the gateway. Not just the soul you're trying to rescue, but demons and condemned souls. And there were a couple of stories of people attempting the rite and simply disappearing."

"Like they'd been dragged down to hell themselves?" Max said.

"That's what I would assume," Freiberg said.

"I'd rather be in hell with Nova than up here by myself."

They both turned to me, Freiberg looking incredulous, his brows raised so high they disappeared behind his bangs.

"You're crazy," he said.

"He's in love." Max tilted his head. "I'd probably do the same for Caro."

"I do not like the karmic blowback I'm likely to get if you do this thing and fuck it up." Freiberg shook his head.

"I'm not going to fuck it up." I stared him down. "I'll do it exactly as written. I swear. This has to work, and I'm not taking any chances."

"Jesus." The blond rubbed his eyes before turning to Max. "Does this Caro of yours know what you're planning to do? You are going to help the lunatic here, right?"

"Yeah, she knows," Max said. "And yes, I am. If I could borrow a pen and some paper, I'd like to copy this out."

"Sure, whatever." Freiberg got up, shaking his head again. "And don't even think about touching it while I'm out of the room."

"No touching," Max said. "Got it."

Chapter 10
Where's My Daughter?

Gage:

I dropped Adam off at a local hotel. Max and I continued on to my house, where I planned to pick up some things before we headed to a local cemetery to look for the graveyard dirt the ritual required. Adam planned to take a cab out to Marie and Brad's farm to meet with me, Max, and the others later to discuss the ritual.

Max stayed remarkably quiet all the way over there. He just gazed out the window, like he was trying to memorize Avery's Crossing or something. Since he'd lived here longer than I had, I wasn't too sure what the point would be, but I was too lost in worry over Nova to care much for conversation anyway, so it was all good.

I turned into the circular drive that fronted my country-style house, only to find a familiar-looking gray SUV parked there. "Oh, shit."

"What's up?" Max said.

"Nova's parents are here."

"Do they know?"

"Hell, no. How do you tell your girlfriend's parents that she's been whisked off to hell?"

"You've got a point."

I opened the car door and got out into the mist. What was I going to tell them now? What had my mom already said? I walked up to the covered front porch with my stomach dropping relentlessly toward my toes.

Like an idiot, I'd hoped they wouldn't come looking for her until I'd found a solution to our problem. Until I'd gotten her back. Yet here they were, and I didn't know what to say to them.

The front door opened just as I reached it, her dad glaring at me from inside the foyer. "Dalton, where's my daughter?"

"I don't know," I said baldly.

His glower deepened. "What do you mean, you don't know? Where did she go?"

"She didn't say." That was the truth.

"Your mom's been giving us the runaround for the last half hour," he growled.

"I'm sorry to hear that." I kept my voice as neutral as possible. At last, a practical use for all those acting skills I'd developed.

"I'll bet you are. Where have you been, anyway? Your mom wouldn't tell us where you went either."

"I was up in Seattle visiting an associate. I just got into town."

"Is that so?" He fixed me with a suspicious stare, then turned his gaze on Max. "Who's this?"

"Max Kincaid." Max offered a hand.

Dr. Pennyman stared at Max's hand for what felt like a full minute before grudgingly taking it. "You know anything about what happened to my daughter?"

"No," Max said. "As far as I know, she just went out for a while and didn't come back."

Pennyman snorted.

"Sir, I'm very worried about her myself," I said.

He leaned toward me, his jaw jutting out belligerently. "Then why'd you run up to Seattle? Huh? None of this adds up, Dalton. I don't trust you."

I could see that.

"I wish I could help you," I said. "If you see Nova, tell her I've been looking for her. Say I love her and I want her to come home."

God, I hated spouting this crap. It wasn't lying, exactly, but it was a deliberate attempt to mislead, which amounted to the same thing.

He snorted again. "Sure you do."

Jesus, did this guy ever let up?

He turned back into the foyer. "Louise, let's go!" he bellowed before swiveling back to glare at me again.

I stood there and took it. Arguing would do no good and there was nothing useful I could tell him.

Louise Pennyman emerged onto the porch with obvious strain around her brown eyes. God, her eyes looked just like Nova's, giving me a sickening sense of longing and dread. I wanted my girl back more than anything in the world, yet I couldn't tell these people what was going on.

She laid a hand on my arm. "We came over to see if you and Nova wanted to go out for lunch."

"I'm so sorry," I said, putting my hand over hers. "I wish I knew where Nova is. I'm worried sick about her."

Ray Pennyman snorted again.

Louise patted my arm. "You'll let us know if you find out anything, right?"

"Of course."

"Let's go, Ray," she said.

I didn't watch them leave. It seemed like something a guilty man would do and I didn't want to look any guiltier than I already did.

"That man is not your friend," Max said as we went inside.

"No shit."

"Why does he hate you so much?"

I skinned out of my jacket. "I don't know. Maybe just because I'm with Nova."

"Damn." He shook his head. "You're gonna have fun at Thanksgiving with in-laws like that."

I hadn't said anything to Max about wanting to marry Nova, but he'd guessed correctly so I let it pass. "I'm more concerned with making sure we have Thanksgivings."

"You ready to go out for those supplies, then?" he said, looking pointedly at my jacket.

"Yeah. I'm gonna talk to my mom for a sec."

I walked back to the kitchen. All the lights blazed. Dirty dishes littered the golden granite counter.

"Mom?"

She tottered out of the breakfast area, alcohol fumes wafting ahead of her like heralds announcing her approach. Great. She was still sneaking booze, and to make things even better, she'd talked to Nova's parents in that state. Way to make a good impression.

"Where have you been?" she said in a drunken shriek.

"Ma, I told you no drinking in the house."

She waved that off. "You've been gone two days. You didn't even call."

"Yeah. Sorry about that. I had to make a run up to Seattle yesterday."

"You worried me. And then those awful people came by. You have no idea how stressful that was. The things they said to me."

"Oh? Like what?"

She used a hand to prop herself against the wall. "They accused you of hurting her. Can you believe it? They threatened me. Said they were going to call the police."

"Really. They didn't say anything about that to me."

"Are you saying I'm lying?" Her voice rose in pitch by at least half an octave.

"No, Mom. I'm saying they didn't mention the police to me." I took her by the elbow. "Come on, let's sit down for a minute. I have to go again, though. There are a few things I have to get before tonight."

"Oh?" She looked up at me. "What's tonight?"

"Just a get-together." Couldn't really call it a party.

"Can I come?"

"No. It's not that kind of thing." I tried to urge her into a kitchen chair.

"What kind of thing is it?" she said, swaying as she sat down.

"We're looking for Nova."

"Then I want to help."

I shook my head, resisting the urge to glance over my shoulder and see if Max was listening. "No. I have to do this on my own."

She peered up at me. "You didn't hurt her, did you?"

"Jesus, Mom, of course not." Did she really believe I was capable of something like that? "I love her. I'd never do anything to hurt her."

"I was just asking."

Cindy bustled into the room, looking concerned, lines showing around her mouth. "Gage, thank God you're back. What's going on with Nova?"

"I don't know. I'm looking for her."

"Did you know her parents were here?" she said with an agitated glance at my mom.

"Yeah. I ran into them in the doorway."

Cindy ran her fingers through hair that was usually perfectly styled, making it stick out in random clumps. "They were unbelievable, especially her dad. They acted like you'd killed her and buried the body out back."

"I know. Ray hates my guts."

"I think he's dangerous." She glanced at my mom again. "He said some things—"

"I'm doing everything I can to find her. I have to go back out now, so look after my mom, okay?"

"Yeah, sure. Of course. Should I get Ted for you?"

"No. The security guys can't help. Just have them keep watch over the house."

She frowned, the lines at the corners of her mouth deepening. "But what about the pap? What about fans? You'll be mobbed if you go out alone."

"Not where I'm going. There won't be many people around, so it'll be fine."

"Where is that, anyway?"

I shook my head. "Not sure of the location yet. I'll call if I need you."

I could see by the set of her lips and the narrowing of her eyes that she wanted to argue with me. That wasn't happening, mainly because I wasn't going to stick around to listen. I had work to do.

Max was still standing in the foyer when I returned, his coat on and everything. He looked uncomfortable, and a pang of guilt hit me at the way I'd abandoned him.

"Sorry. I should have brought you back with me," I said.

"No, it's fine. This is your house. I'm just a visitor."

"Okay, well, let's go. We've got a lot to do."

Chapter 11
Graveyard Dirt

Gage:

I grabbed my jacket and we went outside. The mist hung over everything, a gray, wet curtain hiding any details more than twenty or so yards away. The gloominess of it matched my mood perfectly.

I paused at the car. "You sure you want to do this, Kincaid? You don't have to."

"I want to help. Besides, Freiberg was right about the karmic connection, and that includes anyone involved in the ritual. If I'm going to be karmically connected to this thing anyway, I might as well make sure you do it up right."

We slid into the front seats.

"I don't think I get what you mean by karmically connected," I said as I turned the ignition.

"You're using information Adam gave you, plus like I said the rest of us are going to be involved in the ritual itself. That makes us ethically and energetically bound up with your ritual. So anything that goes wrong will affect whoever participates, either directly or indirectly by providing information or tools."

"I see." I pulled out of the drive. "Will it affect Nova?"

"Karmically, no, I don't think so. That's because it's not something she's participating in voluntarily. But she will be affected energetically, no matter what happens. That's the point of the operation."

"Just one more reason to get it right."

Max hauled out his smart phone. "There's a pioneer cemetery not far from here. Okay, you'll want to go up to White Oak Road, turn west, and go about one and seven tenths of a mile to get to the cemetery."

"How do I get to White Oak Road?"

"It's about four miles north on this road. You'll be taking a left."

"I'm not a complete idiot," I said dryly. Even I could tell where west was, especially since I had a compass direction indicator on my dashboard.

"Just drive, Dalton."

I grunted. The roads out here were narrow, winding country lanes, not freeways, but I gave the car as much gas as I thought I could get away with. Fields dotted with enormous, gnarled trees and little clumps of sheep and cows passed by in a blur. I saw a few farmhouses that reminded me of Brad and Marie's place, some of them with falling-down wrecks right next door, as if their ancestors had built a new house and left the old one standing. But the new houses were already fifty and sixty years old at least.

"I've been wondering. How long have you lived in the area?" Max said.

"A few weeks."

"Whoa. I figured this was where you came to escape Hollywood."

"I bought the house so I could be near Nova."

He leaned against the window. "You have got it bad."

"She means everything to me. That's why I can't fuck this up."

"We'll do everything we can." Max nudged me with his elbow. "Seriously. Everybody likes Nova. We'd help even if we hated you."

"Careful with those warm fuzzies," I said. "You're making me blush."

The ritual couldn't be conducted until the dark of the moon, which was in a few days. This delay drove me apeshit crazy, but according to Freiberg and Max, it was crucial to the success of the ritual, so I wasn't going to try to fudge it. All the details had to be correct. I owed it to Nova.

White Oak Road wound up into some hills on the west edge of the Avery's Crossing area. We passed small vineyards and hobby farms as we penetrated more deeply into the hills. It seemed to take forever and I was beginning to think we'd passed the pioneer cemetery we were looking for, when Max pointed.

"There it is. Turn."

I pulled into a lane so narrow the tall grass on either side brushed against the car doors. "Are you sure?"

"Yeah. I saw the gravestones."

The car crept forward, the grass making soft brushing sounds against its body. Through the mist, I could make out the shape of one of those enormous, spreading trees, its bare branches twisted into weird patterns. Other trees and shrubs were clustered throughout the open space of the cemetery; I could see the tops of their branches. But only the huge one really stood out.

The road widened enough for a gravel pull-out. A small, weathered sign made of wood announced that this was White Oak Cemetery. I parked the car and we got out. The mist came down more thickly now, almost turning into full-fledged rain.

"Come on." I strode through a small mowed area in the tall grass and into the cemetery itself.

Someone had cut the grass here within the last few months. It was only slightly overgrown, not the jungle-like thicket that bordered the road. Rows and clusters of headstones and monuments spread away from us in three directions, some of them shiny and relatively new-looking and others dull, mossy, broken.

"Where do we go? Is there something in particular we're looking for?" I said, scanning the area.

"Not really. Just walk until you feel it's the right place."

Most of the graves were covered with sod. Would it be right to dig through the grass to get to the dirt beneath? It seemed disrespectful, so I started wandering, heading for the trees and bushes. Maybe there would be some bare ground beneath them.

Max followed me silently. We were alone, and most of the graves were at least fifty years old. Not too many people came out here, I guessed.

It felt peaceful, yet I also felt something watchful in the air. Maybe it was only my imagination, powered up by our mission and the clinging mist. But I kept wanting to turn around and see if someone were spying on us.

Max gained on me and then took the lead. Off to our left, someone picked out a soft tune on the guitar. I turned my head, peering through the misty air. A dark figure sat on of the larger black granite headstones, his dark head bent over his instrument, his feet in their glossy black dress shoes braced against the stone. How had he gotten up there? It seemed like a difficult place to perch.

Something about him seemed familiar to me, but I couldn't place him. Obviously, it wasn't Jeremy. Jer had been a blond and this guy had dark brown or black hair. His black suit fitted closely, a European cut rather than the boxy American style.

Hold on. A black suit? He wasn't smoking a cigarette, but he could easily be the smoking man. What the hell was he doing here? What was with the guitar?

He lifted his head and looked right at me. An icy finger seemed to trace the length of my spine. The dude smiled at me.

I couldn't return the smile. My head turned more and more as I continued walking up the hill. Max, ahead of me, didn't seem to notice the man in the black suit.

The suited man nodded once. Then he bent his head over his guitar again and began to play another tune. I thought about what Max had said—that I should just go up to the guy and ask him what he wanted.

Kincaid was losing me, though. While I'd dawdled, staring at suit guy, he'd been charging up the hill. He was already in the trees. I didn't want us to get separated, but I also didn't want to yell out for him to stop.

I glanced back at the suit guy. He'd vanished. The headstone where he'd been sitting was vacant. Nobody was on the open field portion of the cemetery at all, except a crow hopping over the wet ground. How had he disappeared like that? There was no cover anywhere, unless he was crouched behind the headstone where he'd been sitting.

It didn't look quite big enough to hide a grown man of his size, though. Nope, it was like he'd truly vanished into thin air.

I'd grown up in the shadow of The Deal, yet I felt completely out of my depth here. My mother and I had never explored the occult. We'd only done our best to avoid the subject, and now that I was grappling with it directly, the bizarre events that continually confronted me made me wonder if I was losing my mind.

"Gage, you coming?" Max hollered from the top of the hill.

"Yeah. Be right there." I turned my back on suit guy's headstone. Whatever or whoever he was, it would have to wait. I had some graveyard dirt to collect.

I caught up with Max in a dash up the slippery grass of the hill. Big, old trees and overgrown shrubs covered the whole crest of the hill, with graves huddled at their feet and almost obscured by all the plant growth and the clinging mist.

We rounded a cluster of rangy bushes and came upon a small house-like building that looked startlingly familiar. Only it wasn't red. Someone had painted it a dull buff color, with no difference between the body color and the trim. I stood and stared at it.

"What's wrong?" Max said.

"I've seen this before."

He tucked his chin down as he stared at me. "Seriously?"

"Yeah. I had a dream about it. I was building it in the dream, and I painted it red."

"Interesting." He walked right up to it and peered in the window.

"I thought Nova would like it. That's why I made it red." I tagged along behind him, although I didn't look in the window. Something about the small building made me uneasy.

"Hey, look at this." He pointed to a sign fixed to the siding.

I peered at it. The sign explained that this building was known as the Sexton's Tool House and had originally housed, in addition to gardening tools, the corpses while their graves were being dug. The hair on the back of my neck stood up at that.

"Corpses, huh?" I muttered. Jesus.

"I thought they usually laid people out at home in the front parlor," Kincaid said, frowning.

"Maybe some people didn't have room. Besides, it says here they kept ice in here to keep the bodies from rotting too fast. Why the fuck would I dream about a place like this?"

67

"I don't know." He shook his head. "Only that it's connected with death and so is hell."

"This place is giving me the heebie-jeebies, I don't mind telling you."

"Yeah, I don't like it much either. Let's get what we came for and go."

We turned away from the creepy little building and wandered off to another clump of shrubs and trees, which sheltered an odd little memorial made of gray stone. It looked kind of like those fancy mausoleums some of the bigger cemeteries have, complete with pillars and an elaborate little roof, except it was only about two feet tall. Like a mausoleum for dolls or something. The ground around it had no grass, only fallen leaves and a few acorns.

"This looks good." I crouched down to scoop some of the damp soil into my hand.

"Declan Stanhope," Max said. "He was only twenty-nine when he died."

I grunted and stood up. "Thanks, Declan. We appreciate it."

"You have good instincts." Max dug in his jeans pocket and withdrew a dime, which he carefully laid at the foot of the little memorial.

"I do?"

"Yeah. Thanking the dead. It's also traditional to pay for any soil you remove from a grave by leaving a silver coin."

"Hm. Maybe if this acting thing doesn't work out, I can have a career in the dark arts."

And according to the devil himself, my acting work was real. I wasn't the cheat and the fraud I'd always believed myself to be, since The Deal had mostly been in my mom's head. The devil just liked jerking us around, I guess, pretending he'd made a deal with her just to see what she'd do.

Max sent me a sharp glance. "You kid, but good instincts are essential in this work. Always listen to your gut and your heart. They can save you when your rational mind hasn't got a fucking clue what's really going on."

I took a deep breath as we headed back down the hill, trying to release some of the tension. "Okay. I'll start by saying that corpse house or whatever it is gives me some major bad feelings. Way beyond it being a way station for dead bodies."

We reached the corpse house again and gave it a wide berth, the wet grass soaking the hems of our jeans.

"In fact, ever since we got here, I've felt like someone was watching us."

"There's always some heavy energy in a graveyard," he said, "but I know what you mean. This place almost feels haunted."

I glanced at him. He seemed at ease despite the creepy topic of conversation, his hands in his pockets, gaze traveling across the graves and landscaping in a relaxed kind of way.

"Remember that dude we saw on the side of the road on the way to Seattle?" I said. "The one you said wasn't human?"

"Yeah?"

"I saw him here, on the way up the hill. He was sitting on top of a gravestone, playing the guitar."

Max frowned, his black brows drawing down harshly. "Whoa. We need to find out what he is and what he wants."

"Yeah. But not here."

"No. Not here."

We reached the car. Max seemed as relieved as I was to shut the doors on that creepy graveyard, turn on the heat and the radio, and drive away.

Chapter 12

Corpse House

Gage:

The mist was as thick as ever when I left Brad and Marie's farm that night. Coupled with the darkness, it completely cloaked my surroundings and seemed to press in on the car in a wet, dark embrace. Wisps of fog floated up and over my windshield like ghosts. Which reminded me of the cemetery Max and I had visited earlier.

I'd been in a damned hurry to get away from there this afternoon. Now, I had the urge to go back and see what it was like at night. A stupid idea right on the face of it—at the least, I could trip and break a bone on a dark, wet night like this.

Of course, on second thought, that sounded like my mom talking. Or maybe my insurance agent. I was insured for a fuckload of money, and he and Cindy would have fits if they knew I was thinking of risking my precious self.

We'd done some divination to find out who or what suit guy was, but we hadn't really turned up anything conclusive. Marie seemed to think he was a good guy. I didn't think so. He seemed too much like a creeper. And since the divination hadn't worked out and there was nothing more for me to do at the farm, I decided to get gone.

Marie had told me to chill, but I couldn't do it. I left her place just as restless as I'd been when I got there. We had the graveyard dirt and we were going to use my blood for the ritual, plus Marie and Brad already possessed the asafoetida and galbanum. Apparently, those were herbs and they were fairly standard magical supplies.

That meant there was nothing for me to do but hang around and wait. I'm not much good at waiting.

I took the turn onto White Oak Road, barely visible in the misty darkness. I couldn't have cared less about the insurance. If I killed myself, my rates couldn't go up, now could they? Besides, I'd go to hell and then I could be with Nova.

That wasn't the true reason I headed for the graveyard, though. I couldn't put my finger on the real reason; it was one of those nagging urges that you know are going to drive you nuts unless you give in to them.

Max had said I should listen to my gut and my heart, hadn't he? And both gut and heart were pushing me toward the cemetery.

There aren't any streetlights in the country. Very few houselights, too. That left me only my headlights to illuminate my way. It's amazing how dark it can get when you don't have the city lights to brighten things up, something I'd always taken for granted as a city boy.

The dark reminded me pleasantly of Nova's cabin, even while it creeped me out.

I found the gravel pull-out and parked the car. With the headlights out, I could see almost nothing at all. It was so dark I couldn't even see the end of the hood. The rain shut out the stars and the moon, if there even was a moon. I'd never been very aware of that kind of shit, but even I could tell there was nothing to see tonight. Just blackness.

I rested my skull against the headrest. Why had I driven out here? It was too dark to do much of anything.

A picture of Jeremy's ghost sitting on the bed and playing guitar flashed into my head. "I wish you were here," I muttered.

He'd probably tell me I was crazy to care so much for a chick when there so many others out there I could have. But he would never have abandoned Nova to her fate, any more than I would.

When I'd fallen in the river, drunk and stupid with drugs, Jeremy's ghost had appeared to Nova and directed her to the bank so she could pull me out. She hadn't realized he was a ghost until he disappeared on her. If he could do that, he should be able to show up here and advise me.

Nothing happened, though. Idly, I started to hum a tune. It was the song I'd played at Marie and Brad's, the one I'd written for her. Without the guitar part, it didn't sound as good, but I didn't care. Nobody was here to listen.

Get out of the car.

The voice came from inside my head, but it didn't sound like me. It sounded like Jeremy.

I stopped singing and looked around, hoping to see him in the back seat. No-one was there.

Get out of the car. Go for a walk up the hill. Find the corpse house.

"You want me to walk around in a graveyard after dark?" I muttered under my breath. "And visit the corpse house? Seriously, dude?"

I got the impression of laughter. Either I was nuts, or my best friend wanted me to take a walk in the graveyard. And it was just like him to laugh at me over my reluctance to go.

I leaned over and popped open my glovebox to get my flashlight. "This is crazy. But I'm doing it."

Now to see if I could find my way with just this tiny beam of light to guide me. My feet slipped on the wet grass as I strode into the cemetery. Cursing, I struggled to keep my balance. Wouldn't it be hilarious if I fell and broke my neck out here? Yeah. Hilarious.

I knew the area I wanted was roughly to my left, so I headed in that direction.

The corpse house was a lot more difficult to find in the dark. As I bumbled around, getting tangled in some bushes and banging into headstones, I wondered if anyone would notice my car sitting there. People didn't usually take kindly to those who frequent graveyards at night. But it was so dark that nobody would see it unless they knew exactly where to look.

The black silhouette of the corpse house reared up in front of me. I shined the beam of my flashlight on it, waiting for the nasty feelings I'd had before to creep up on me. They hovered at the edges of my awareness, but it was much less intense than before.

Wasn't that odd. You'd think it would seem even more eerie at night.

Now that I was here, I wasn't sure why I'd come. Yes, the corpse house was exactly where Max and I had left it. Okay. Now what?

I moved around the side. It had a stone block as a front stoop. No overhang. My boots clumped dully over the hard-packed earth as I walked to the door. Of course it was locked—no-one would leave something like this open at night—but I put my hand on the doorknob anyway. And it moved.

Okay. I'd been wrong. It wasn't locked.

I paused as the door creaked open just a sliver. To go in or not to go in. It couldn't be all that interesting in there, right? Just one room, I imagined, with maybe a cellar where they'd kept the ice in huge blocks, waiting for a body. On the other hand, why not?

I pushed the door open all the way and went in, the door squealing shut behind me. My flashlight beam swept back and forth slowly, showing dusty floorboards, peeling plaster on the walls, thickly cobwebbed window sills and filthy glass. Garden tools stood propped against the wall or hung from hooks.

I was right. There wasn't anything in here, really.

Except a table. The center of the room was taken up with a big, wooden table with thick, square legs and a metal-clad top. I froze with the flashlight beam centered on that table.

They must have put the corpses there.

Why did whoever was responsible for this place keep the corpse table? The house I could see. It probably had historical value. But that table?

It's got historical value, too.

Yeah. I knew people in Hollywood who'd pay enormous piles of cash to have such a morbid thing in their house. Think what a conversation starter it would be.

I played the flashlight over the floor again. There was a square trapdoor off to one side, which I imagined led down into the cellar. Where they'd kept the ice.

My skin crawled as I turned back toward the door. Whatever I'd thought I would find here, it seemed to be absent.

I opened the door and stared out at the view of the cemetery. It was too dark to really tell, but the plant life outside seemed different somehow than it had been when I entered. Bigger. Thicker.

Weird how I hadn't noticed how heavily overgrown this place was on the way in, or how tightly the branches crowded the house. I pushed leafless twigs out of my face as I made my way back to the open space of the cemetery, twigs I didn't remember from the trip in. But the open space never came. The underbrush cleared away quite a bit, yet all that did was make the column-like trunks of the epically huge trees more obvious.

Had I gone the wrong way? Maybe I should turn around and try another route, because this didn't look familiar at all. But something kept driving me forward.

I walked beneath the canopies of some evergreens that were so big they looked like they belonged in Middle Earth, and finally found my way to the entrance. A wrought-iron fence surrounded it, and on the other side I could see the tightly spaced houses of a suburb.

The fuck? Where had that come from?

White Oak Cemetery was in the middle of farmland. There weren't any suburbs anywhere nearby at all. So where the hell was I?

The smart thing would be to turn around and go back. But my heart kept telling me to move forward, so that's what I did. I left the cemetery behind and entered the suburban neighborhood ahead of me.

The houses were strangely empty-looking. None of them had cars parked in front, even those without garages. I wouldn't expect much activity so late at night, but there weren't even any porch lights. No traffic noise, either.

It was like this place was isolated somehow, drifting somewhere far away from human civilization.

The prickling on the back of my neck returned. Was someone watching me? When I glanced around, of course I saw nothing except more empty-looking houses with blank windows. I kept going, turning a couple of corners without knowing why except it seemed like the thing to do.

An apartment building rose up ahead of me. It was one of those nondescript places that cater to college students, a big dark-brown building with a covered second-story walkway like a cheap motel. Only one apartment had any lights on; just like the larger neighborhood, this building seemed largely abandoned.

I took the concrete stairs up to that walkway. The units I passed all had cheap, aluminum-frame windows. Dark windows. The doors were just as crappy, just brown slabs all beaten up and gouged from decades of hard use.

At the third door from the end, I paused. This was where the lights burned, their glow seeping out around the drawn curtains inside. My heart started hammering crazily in my chest. Why was I here? What would happen if I rang the bell?

Something would change. I didn't know what it was, but I'd come this far and I wasn't going to turn around until I found out why I was here. I rang the bell.

Chapter 13
Don't You Know Me?

Gage:

That old, brown door opened so fast it was like she'd been standing on the other side waiting for me to ring.

Nova.

My breath caught. Yellow light flooded out of her apartment, casting her face in shadow. But I could still see her, so clearly it hurt. The elfin, slightly pointy chin, the high cheekbones, the perfect little nose.

She gazed up at me with a faint crease between her beautiful brows, her golden-brown eyes troubled but not afraid. "Hello?"

Her voice. It seemed like forever since I'd heard it.

"Nova," I said, gazing into her eyes. "What are you doing here?"

Was this hell? It didn't seem very hellish, but then I'd never visited the underworld before, so what did I know.

She frowned, showing no recognition. "I'm sorry. Am I supposed to know you?"

Cruel fists clamped around my heart and throat. Oh, God. No.

For a moment, I couldn't speak. She didn't know me. Didn't remember me.

"Gage," I said thickly. "It's me, Gage."

"Gage? I don't know anyone named that."

"Baby, don't you recognize me?" Stupid of me to hurt over that, but I did. I had an icy rock lodged in my throat and another, bigger one in my gut.

"No. I'm sorry. I don't know you."

I stared at her as all my words left me. Something about the transition from our world to this one must have damaged her memory. Or maybe *he* had taken it deliberately, although I couldn't understand why he'd do that.

She wore skinny jeans and a long tunic. Her brown hair was loose around her shoulders, and as usual she wore no make-up. She looked so beautiful, so perfect, my whole body ached to hold her and I almost reached for her. But I didn't want to frighten her.

If I scared her, I could lose her again. That was more than I could bear. I forced myself to remain still, to avoid threatening her in any way.

"Can—" I cleared my throat as I prepared myself for rejection. "Can I come in?"

Shit. So much for not scaring her.

"Okay." She stood back to let me come inside.

That was weird. If she didn't recognize me, why was she allowing me in her apartment? But nothing about this was normal, and she didn't have her memory so maybe she didn't know any better than to let a stranger in her place.

I glanced around her living room, which didn't match the rundown exterior of the building at all. This place was ten times better than the little hole she'd been renting in Avery's Crossing. She had posters on the white walls and a colorful red and light-green throw rug over the beige wall-to-wall carpet, plus two blankets draped over her couch, even though she could only have been there a few days.

The faint, homey smell of some kind of savory dinner still hung in the air. And there was music—soft, indie folk-rock playing in the background. A couple of thick textbooks sat on the top of a sleek, modern coffee table.

Someone wants her to feel at home.

And I was reasonably sure who that someone was.

"So, what did you say your name is again?" she said, smiling hesitantly at me.

"Gage Dalton." I couldn't smile back. My lips just wouldn't make that upward curve.

"And you think you know me?"

"I do know you. For months now."

Those lovely golden eyes of hers narrowed as she stared at my face. "Are you sure I'm not just someone who looks like the girl you know?"

"Yes, I'm sure." I had to fight past the obstruction in my throat. "Your name is November Daye Pennyman, right?"

Her lips parted and her eyes went wide. "Yes. It is." Then she scowled. "But you could have done research to find that out."

"You love art. Your parents want you to be a doctor but you secretly want to be an artist. You have all kinds of drawings on the walls of your parents' cabin, and you made all of them."

Her gaze went from suspicious to something so intently focused on my eyes I felt like she could see inside of me. "Nobody knows that."

"I do," I said. "Because we were there at the cabin together. You don't remember, but we were together."

Nova shook her head, retreating a step. "This is too bizarre."

"I know it's weird and unexplainable. But I'm here because I've been looking for you. You shouldn't be here."

Her head tilted slightly to one side. "What do you mean by that?"

"I mean..." I paused, searching for a way to tell her what was going on without sounding crazy. "You disappeared. We live together and you just disappeared."

She reached up and pressed the tips of her fingers against her lips. "Why don't I recognize you, then?"

"I don't know." I took a breath and tried to calm down. "I've been looking for you."

"You have?"

"Yeah." My throat closed up again. I swallowed. "Yeah, I have. I was afraid I'd never see you again."

Nova shook her head. "I don't understand."

"I know, baby. But this world is not where you belong."

She raised her straight, dark brows. "This world? What does that mean?"

I waved my hand at her apartment in general. "This world. This place. Neighborhood. Whatever you want to call it."

"Are you saying this isn't—" She broke off, frowning. "I don't think I understand what you mean."

How did I explain it without sounding like a dangerous lunatic? If I sounded too weird, she'd just reject me and everything I told her. I wracked my brain for a way to communicate that wouldn't have her wishing she had a tranquilizer dart and a straitjacket waiting for me.

"Look, haven't you noticed anything strange about this place? About your life lately?" I said in a low voice.

She gave me a wary look. "Maybe. But that doesn't prove anything."

"Have you talked to your parents lately?"

Her gaze became even warier and she turned her body slightly away from me. "No."

"I can't really tell you what's going on because I'm not sure myself. But I know something is wrong. I know you're not supposed to be here."

"You're starting to scare me." She backed up another step.

"I'm sorry. That's the last thing I want to do. I just want you to know that this—" I gestured to her general surroundings again. "This isn't normal."

I hated the way she was looking at me, like she thought I might hurt her. God, that stung. I would never lift a finger against her, not ever under any circumstances, but she didn't know that. Not anymore. She didn't remember me.

"Let's not talk about that," I said.

"Okay." Nova shifted her weight from one foot to the other as her hands came up to grip her elbows. "What do you want to talk about? The weather?"

She wanted to make small talk? I wasn't even sure I remembered how to do that. Talking was not why I'd come here. I wanted to grab her and make a run for it, but she'd probably fight me if I did that. She might get hurt. I had to ease her back into this whole Gage and Nova thing.

"Uh...what have you been doing lately?" I said. Casual. Make it casual.

"Oh, you know." She gave a shrug. "The usual. Studying, mostly."

"Studying? What are you studying?"

Her stare turned downright suspicious. "I thought you said you knew me."

"In our—when we were together, you'd quit pre-med and were studying art. Mostly watercolor painting."

"I was?" She looked more baffled than pleased by this information.

"Uh huh. You were. What are you studying now?"

"Pre-med. I'm taking micro-biology this term."

"How's that going?" I leaned my ass against the back of her couch.

"Really well. Much better than it ever has before, actually."

Given the weird emptiness of her neighborhood, I doubted the existence of the classroom, but maybe I was wrong. Either way, I wanted to know more about this strange half-world she'd been living in.

"That's good," I said. "Can you show me your classroom or lecture hall or whatever it's called?"

Her gaze darted back and forth across her nondescript, plush beige carpeting. "Um...yeah, I guess so. But it's really boring."

"Maybe you can tell me what building it's in and I'll just drive by. I'd love to see where you're spending your time."

"It's in Ingram Hall," she said, fixing me with that suspicious stare. "I don't know why you'd care about that."

"Because I care about you," I said, struggling not to touch her. I wanted to, so bad. Just to feel her skin under mine. But I couldn't scare her.

"I noticed as I came over here that this neighborhood is kind of different," I added. "It almost seems like nobody lives here."

"It is kinda empty," she admitted, plucking at the hem of her tunic. "Or maybe everyone just likes to keep their houses dark at night."

"Can you give me directions to your science building?" I said.

The truth was that I didn't think she really had any classes at all, or if she did they were completely illusory. I wasn't sure if *he* was making her hallucinate classes or simply giving her false memories of having been to class. Was there a difference, anyway?

Given the deserted neighborhood she inhabited, it seemed likely there was no Ingram Hall. But I couldn't come right out and tell her that or she'd probably freak out and maybe even decide I was there to attack her. I wanted her to realize it on her own.

I took a slow step toward her.

She didn't back away like I'd expected. She wasn't having normal reactions to me at all. I put my hand out, so gradually, until I could touch her shoulder. She stood there and allowed it, just watching me, apparently unafraid.

Then her hand came up and covered mine, skin to skin. I closed my eyes.

"You do seem familiar now," she said in a low voice. "But I still don't remember you. That's so weird, isn't it?"

"Yes, it is."

She moved closer to me. I could feel the heat of her body now. Her free hand reached out and touched the front of my jean jacket.

"You're all wet," she said.

"It's raining outside."

"Take off your jacket." She started to unbutton it.

I opened my eyes and watched her. "Nova, if I asked you to take a walk with me, would you do it?"

She finished unbuttoning to stare at me again. "Maybe. Why do you want to go on a walk?"

"There's something I need to show you."

She studied me intently, her gaze lingering on my eyes, my hair, my jaw, and finally settling on my lips. Her hand reached higher, all the way to my face. Her fingertips felt like feathers, they were so light and soft.

"Is it all right if I kiss you?"

"Of course it is," I said hoarsely.

She went up on her toes and pressed her lips briefly to mine. The whole encounter had such a dreamlike feeling that part of me didn't believe it was really happening. I set my hand in the small of her back and drew her against me as I bent my head to hers.

Our bodies touched from my lower chest to my hips. Our lips clung together. After a second's pause, Nova moaned and grabbed onto me, her mouth attacking mine. The deprivation and fear of the last days seemed to ignite a matching blaze in me, because I grabbed her too. Our tongues mated, hot and wet, as my other hand cupped her round little ass, squeezing and massaging her.

I wasn't thinking about getting her back to ordinary reality anymore. All I could remember was how much I wanted and needed her.

My hands slipped under the hem of her tunic to meet her smooth, warm skin. She trembled and sighed into my kiss, so I moved upward toward her breasts. Some part of her must have remembered me or she wouldn't have let me do all this touching.

My fingers met the soft bottom curve of her breast and I realized she wasn't wearing a bra. My cock pulsed frantically against the tight denim of my jeans as I traced that luscious curve. She arched up a little, in invitation.

I cupped her and she sighed again. When I brushed my thumb across her hard little nipple, she whimpered. She really wanted this.

My cock was almost painful now. "I want to see you," I whispered.

She pulled away, just far enough to yank the tunic over her head, her eyes glazed with desire, her lips full and parted. Damn, she was so beautiful.

I lifted one sweet breast to my mouth and suckled her and she grabbed onto my skull, holding me to her as if I might try to get away. I had my other arm around her waist, bracing her as I continued to suck and pull at her nipple and her whimpers gave way to frantic cries of pleasure.

She was so hot she was driving me crazy. I switched my attention to her other breast, which she pushed eagerly into my hand. There was no doubt in my mind that she wanted this, wanted me. Even if she didn't remember our relationship, her soul still recognized me.

Her hands roved across my shoulders and back before she started tugging at my clothes. She pushed my jacket off me and then started with my T-shirt. I let her lift it up to bare my chest and belly, even though it meant I had to abandon those beautiful breasts of hers.

She pressed her face to my naked skin, then her lips, kissing and licking me everywhere.

I grabbed the waistband of her jeans, fumbled at the button. She took over for me, her hands trembling as she yanked at button and zipper. Finally the jeans lay on the floor and she was completely bare except for a pair of plain white panties. I got on my knees and pulled the panties down to her ankles.

Then I buried my face between her legs. She gave a squeak of surprise. I shoved her thighs apart to get better access. She buried her fingers in my hair as I licked her, one long swipe full of the tangy, salty taste of Nova. She pushed her pelvis forward as if begging for more.

All her reactions to me were so natural and unrehearsed that everything she did was a turn-on. It was all her, all real, none of it an act.

"Sit." I pointed at the scruffy old recliner next to her.

She obeyed. I lifted one of her legs to the arm of the chair, spreading her out for me. Then I got to work.

God, I'd missed this. The taste of her, the little helpless noises she made, the way she squirmed under my attentions. My cock continued to twitch, demanding attention, but I wanted to make sure Nova had everything she needed before I satisfied myself.

She came apart with my face between her legs, her fingers pulling my hair, her voice yelling my name. I groaned, kissing the soft skin of her inner thighs over and over before I rose to take her.

The chair was too low for me, so I threw one of her blankets on the carpet, then drew her down to the floor and ripped my fly open. She didn't even hesitate, just opened her legs for me, reached for my cock to guide me into her. I almost fell apart when she touched me.

Her hand on me felt so damned good. I groaned, clenching my teeth and pinching my eyes shut, fighting to hold onto my control. I needed to come inside her, not all over her belly like a teenager with his first girl.

She brushed my tip through her soaking wet folds and I groaned again. "Baby. God, you feel so good."

She moaned, her hips surging upward toward mine. I sank into her and we both cried out. Nova felt like heaven every time I entered her, but this was different. More intense, almost sharp, almost painful. I needed her so much more than I'd never needed her before.

She wrapped her legs around my hips and pulled my head down for a kiss. Her tongue plunged into my mouth, taking me as I took her, and it was so hot I almost came right there.

With a harsh groan, I took up a brutal rhythm of thrusts that she met with eager pushes of her hips. We were both moaning as we moved together, our mouths devouring each other, desperate and insatiable. I couldn't have stopped at that point even if I'd wanted to.

She screamed against my mouth and her nails dug into my skin, causing sharp shocks of pain that sent me over the edge. I didn't want to come yet but I couldn't stop myself. I shuddered and shook in her arms as agonizing pleasure savaged me and I emptied myself into her. Vaguely I felt her shuddering, too, and her nails continued to rake me, the pain only intensifying my orgasm.

The stunning waves of pleasure subsided, slowly, as I continued to shake on top of her. She wrapped her arms tightly around me and pressed kisses to my face and neck.

"Nova," I said. "God, I love you." *I love you.*

She didn't answer with words, but she kept kissing me.

Because I couldn't stay inside of her forever, I withdrew from her body, reaching up to her couch for the throw blanket that lay draped over one arm. I arranged it over both of us and tucked her into my side. She went willingly, laying her head on my shoulder and draping her arm over my chest.

"Do you remember me now?" I said lazily.

"I'm not sure."

"Maybe we should do that again. It might help."

She laughed softly. "I think we should."

81

I gave her narrow shoulders a squeeze. "I've missed you so much. You don't know how hard it's been, baby."

She tilted her head back to look at me. "You know, I think I've missed you too, even though I didn't know anything about you. I kept feeling like something was wrong. Like there should be someone here with me, and now you're here and that feeling has gone away."

My throat and chest seemed to swell up again, making it hard to talk, but this time it was happiness and not despair. "I'm glad." I nuzzled her cheek. "I love you, Nova. So much."

She sighed, snuggling against me. "I feel...I can't find words to say how I feel."

"It's okay. You don't have to say it back."

She'd already told me, in Avery's Crossing, and I hadn't been able to reciprocate. I had a lot to make up for.

"It's so weird that I feel like I know you and obviously I trust you or we wouldn't be here together like this," she said. "But I can't remember you."

"Maybe you will. Eventually."

"Yeah." Her small palm stroked my bare chest. "I hope so."

We were laying together on the floor, the scent of sex rising around our bodies, the drowsiness of afterglow pulling me down into sleep. But there were some things I needed to get straight before anything else happened. Just in case we were pulled apart again.

At the moment, I felt like everything I said and did was just in case.

"Nova, how do you feel about kids?"

She raised her head, giving me a perplexed stare. "Kids?"

It wasn't the kind of thing you usually bring up right after having sex with a woman for the first time. For her, this was our first. So I was probably freaking her out right now, but I needed to know, because if we got out of this devil problem alive, I wanted to make our relationship permanent.

"Yeah." I gave her a little smile. "Do you want them?"

"Sure, yeah, I do. Not right away, though. I'm a little young to be a mom, I think."

I rubbed her back. "Kids are good. Waiting is good."

She smiled back at me. "So we agree? Is that what you wanted to know?"

"Partly. I've also been thinking about fame and whether that's important to you."

"Fame?" She looked even more baffled than before. "Why would I care about that? Are you planning to become famous? Become a reality TV star, maybe?"

She gave me a teasing nudge.

"No, not reality TV." Boy, she really didn't remember who I was. "But...if I were famous, would you care if I retired? If I became just another guy?"

"No." She tilted her head, her hair sliding across her shoulder. "I think fame would be a burden, actually. It might be a relief to give it up."

"Some people get a huge charge out of it. They love having other people watching them, following them around."

She made a face. "Yuck. Not me."

God, she was too perfect.

"Come here." I pulled her down again, so she was tucked into my side. "I think maybe we make a good couple."

"Yeah? Me too."

"If I were famous, like a Hollywood star or something," I said, stroking her hair, "I'd try to keep my family out of the limelight as much as possible. Keep my private life private."

"I think that's really wise."

"Yeah?" I bent down and kissed her, a long lingering kiss that made my blood catch fire again.

Long afterward, we lay still together in a haze of more afterglow. I couldn't seem to string more than two thoughts together in a row. My body felt heavy and replete with satisfaction, her soft warmth perfect against my side.

"Gage?" Nova said softly. "I'm sorry I forgot you."

I got all choked up again at her apology. "It's not your fault. It's this place."

She snuggled in closer. "What about this place?"

But I didn't answer. A drugging haze of sleepy relaxation came over me. I was supposed to get her out of here, supposed to take her away. But I was so sleepy. I just wanted to rest my eyes for a few minutes.

Chapter 14
Off-Kilter

Nova:

My bedroom seemed too quiet and too empty. I lay in my double bed and stared at the white popcorn ceiling, awash in the weak gray light of morning, and tried to figure out what was wrong. I normally woke up alone, so that couldn't be it.

My alarm clock glowed red on the bedside table. As usual, there was virtually no sound from the rest of the apartment building. Everything was quiet as a tomb.

A glance around the room told me nothing. It looked the same as always—inexpensive but stylish minimalist dresser, pale blue and white horizontally striped curtains, matching comforter, mirrored closet doors half open to display my limited wardrobe. Everything was right where I'd left it.

Gage.

Along with his name, a vivid image flashed into my mind. A tall, muscular man in my arms, his beautiful face gazing down at me, blue eyes dark with desire, brown hair tumbling over his forehead. I shivered as a memory of extreme arousal powered through my body.

We'd made love—had sex, that is. Passionate, hot sex, so hot I hadn't stopped for one second to consider birth control or even whether having sex was the right thing to do. In that moment, it had felt like the only thing to do.

Was that real? Had it actually happened, or was it one of my crazy dreams?

It couldn't have been real. I wouldn't let a stranger into my apartment and then have sex with him. Okay, I had let Declan in—and had thought it was odd at the time—but we hadn't done anything more than talk and bake cookies. I certainly hadn't stripped naked for him.

Nope, Gage was just a dream character. That was a bummer, actually. I'd liked him a lot. A heavy sigh of disappointment escaped me. Life would be better if he were real.

I love you.

He'd said those words—in my dream—and I'd believed him. But that's what happens in dreams. You can do and say all kinds of bizarre stuff and it all seems perfectly natural, until you wake up.

This was one dream I wished hadn't ended. I was awake and I wished I could go back to sleep, just in case I could find my way back into the same dream. I would find him again and we would be together.

My stomach growled fiercely, though. Right now, I needed either tea or coffee. And maybe some breakfast.

I got out of bed and discovered I was naked. Another unusual detail, because I always wore pj's to bed. I grabbed my blue waffle-weave bathrobe and padded barefoot down the beige-carpeted hallway toward the kitchen.

To get there, I had to pass the living room. That was where it had happened. I walked slowly into the living room, moving as if I'd fallen into a trance, staring at the carpet. We'd made love on that floor, in front of the couch.

It was just a dream, Nova.

But my throw blankets were all over the place. All over the floor, to be precise, as if left there after we'd had sex on them. Frowning, I bent to pick them up. Could I have been sleep-walking last night? Could I have tossed the blankets on the floor as part of my dream?

I threw them back on the couch and then I saw it. A denim jacket in a heap at the foot of one of my chairs. An equally large gray T-shirt lay next to it. The jacket couldn't be one of mine—too big for me and besides I didn't own a denim jacket. My heart pounding in dread and excitement, I went to pick it up.

It was so huge I knew it definitely belonged to a man. Did this mean—oh my God, had Gage really been here last night? But then, I'd— I'd really had sex with him. He'd really said he loved me, not to mention all those other things he'd told me.

You shouldn't be here... You disappeared.

I lifted the jacket to my face, pressing my nose into the interior. It smelled like him, the spicy natural scent of a young, healthy male. My whole body instantly reacted with a flood of achy yearning as some of the details of the night before came back to me.

Now that I'd allowed myself to believe it had really happened, I could feel the slight soreness between my legs. Obviously, my pussy had gotten a workout.

He'd done things to me, made me feel things I'd only fantasized about. I wanted him again, now. Right now.

If only he were here.

He'd left me without saying a word. Why had he done that? Was it one of those morning-after regret things? But he'd said we knew each other and that he loved me. Not before he'd gotten into my body, either, but afterward when he'd gotten what he wanted and we were laying together. He'd been so tender with me, so sweet.

And then he'd simply disappeared. He hadn't even left a phone number, or taken mine.

The denim crackled as I hugged it to my torso. There was something in the pocket. Feeling a twinge of guilt for invading his privacy, I reached in and drew out a piece of folded paper.

It felt like good-quality sketch paper. I unfolded it and stopped, shocked into stillness by what I saw. Someone had sketched a portrait of me, in graphite. There was a signature in the bottom right hand corner. I peered at it and my mouth went dry.

Nova Pennyman. That was my signature.

I didn't recognize the drawing, but it looked like my work. And that was definitely my signature. How was any of this possible? Gage had a drawing of me, apparently a self-portrait signed by me, in his pocket. He knew me, but I didn't know him. He claimed to love me.

What the hell was going on?

This was only the latest bizarre development in a whole series of them, not to mention the general weirdness of my neighborhood. The lack of traffic on the streets. The tomb with Declan's name on it. Something was wrong in my life and I needed to figure out what it was.

Today was Monday. I had three classes plus a four-hour shift at work this evening. I ought to be rushing around getting ready.

Call in sick.

That would be irresponsible of me. And I might lose my job if my boss found out I'd called in when I wasn't really sick. I couldn't afford to lose that job.

But this situation I was in, the strange events in my life...it demanded an explanation. How could I placidly go on with school and work while I had these questions in the back of my mind?

My life was so freakishly out of kilter that I couldn't wait any more to figure out what was happening to me. Something was very wrong.

Was I crazy? Hallucinating? Or had I somehow found myself in the midst of real events I simply couldn't explain? I needed answers.

If my classes had to suffer, so be it. Maybe I'd make enough progress that I could make my shift at the Unique Boutique tonight.

Some hot oatmeal and two giant mugs of coffee with cream and sugar fueled me up to investigate. Bundled up in jeans, a wool peacoat and floppy beanie, I left my apartment determined to turn up something, some kind of clue that would help me understand.

I stood on the outdoor walkway in front of my apartment and scanned my building. I smelled the pungent scents of the boxwood and juniper bushes planted around the building. The iciness of the winter air bit right through my peacoat, making me wonder if I should go back inside and put on something warmer.

No. No more delays.

I scanned the parking lot. There were only two cars parked there, one of them mine. Who the other belonged to, I could only guess. Declan? Someone I hadn't met?

My immediate neighbors were a complete mystery to me. The only one I'd met so far was Declan.

It's not that I expected to become buddies with all my neighbors, but I'd never even caught a glimpse of these people and I'd been here at least two months. That could not be normal. Where was everyone? Didn't they ever go to the supermarket or take their kids to the park?

Most of them were probably at work right now. But there would be signs of occupancy in their apartments. Welcome mats. Open curtains, windows I could look through. Something.

You're being a major creeper.

Yep, and I didn't care. My problems were bigger than that.

As I turned toward the stairs, movement at the corner of my eye caught my attention. I looked to my right at the parking lot. Someone was down there, and it wasn't Declan.

I gripped the cold black metal of the railing and stared. It was a man, standing right in the center of one of the parking spaces. He was slim and dark-haired, and he wore a black suit with no overcoat. He was smoking a cigarette that gave off a huge amount of smoke. I could smell it from here, an odd, spicy-sweet scent that seem more like gingerbread than tobacco.

My hands tightened on the railing until they hurt. I'd seen that man before. But where? When?

He looked wrong, though. Maybe it was only the visual effect of all that smoke, but he almost seemed more gray than black. He almost seemed transparent, like a ghost, and he was supposed to be solid.

He turned his head and gazed directly at me. Then he sauntered over to the sidewalk and disappeared behind an overgrown juniper.

I shivered, and not from the winter cold. That man was the first person I could remember seeing in the neighborhood besides myself and Declan, and I couldn't really count myself. Did he live here? He didn't fit in very well.

Then I scoffed at myself. Fit in? How could he fit in to a neighborhood that had only two other residents? But it wasn't an upscale kind of place. The buildings were mostly worn down, needed paint jobs and new landscaping, and that wasn't the kind of neighborhood where the men wore perfectly fitted suits.

Run after him and ask him where he lives.

Ha. No way. Something about that guy gave me a major case of the creeps.

Nope, I was going ahead with my original plan to snoop around my building and that was it.

I started with the apartment next to mine. My knock on the unadorned, flat brown door received no answer. I rang the shabby little bell and still got no answer. There was no welcome mat, either, just plain concrete outside the door, and the curtains were closed. Thick dust and rain spatters clung to the glass. Apparently, no-one lived in this unit.

Okay, on to the second place.

That apartment didn't have anyone home either. When I peered in the window, I found it just as dusty and cobwebbed, along with a generous sifting of dead flies. I couldn't see anything because it was too dark inside. I tried the third and the fourth, only to get the same result. The door of the fifth apartment swung open when I knocked on it.

Standing in the outdoor air, I stared at the dark sliver of room revealed. "Hello?" I called out. "Anyone home?"

Still no answer. I pushed the door open a little wider and peeked inside. The living room, laid out in the same pattern as mine, appeared to be empty. No furniture at all, just a carpeted floor and bare walls. The carpet and paint color matched those in my own unit.

Maybe whoever had rented this one had moved out and forgotten to lock the door behind them. But what about those other places?

I retraced my route along the hall, trying each door in turn. Some were unlocked. All of the unlocked ones contained rooms empty of furniture. In fact, none of them showed signs of ever being occupied. The carpet all looked perfectly smooth and unmarked, and had that chemical smell of new carpet. And when I flipped the light switches, nothing happened. No electricity.

This was weirder than I'd imagined.

They've renovated the place and just haven't filled the building. A lot of vacancies doesn't mean anything nefarious is going on.

Maybe so, but I was going to find out more about this building. Like did anyone live here besides me and Declan? And shouldn't the electricity in the whole building be on, even if some units were unoccupied?

I continued my search. It didn't take me long to discover that every single apartment unit was apparently empty except for mine. Every single one. Hadn't Declan said he lived in one of these? Or had I assumed, simply because he'd said he was a neighbor?

If he didn't live in my building, then where did he live?

A tiny voice in my head whispered that when he went home, he went under that small memorial I'd found in the cemetery. The one with his name on it.

Chapter 15

Torn Away

Gage:

Hard, pale light filled the room. I was cold. Extremely cold, and sore. My body hurt all over.

I blinked and rubbed my eyes. What the fuck? This wasn't Nova's living room.

The floor beneath me was hard and cold. Wooden. Dusty. I raised my head and looked around. Where...?

Holy shit. I was inside the corpse house. It looked different in the daylight, but I recognized the peeling plaster on the walls. And when I looked behind me, I saw the chunky legs of the table.

I forced myself upright, my head pounding right along with my heart. My shirt and jacket were gone and my jeans were still unzipped, as if I hadn't moved at all since taking Nova in my arms and falling asleep. But she wasn't here. The small room held no-one but me and it smelled of rot and mildew.

With a low groan, I got to my feet. I zipped my jeans. My shirt and jacket were nowhere to be seen and my flashlight was missing too. How had I gotten back here?

I needed to get to Nova as quickly as possible. I strode to the door and yanked it open and stopped, dumbfounded. This couldn't be the same place I left the night before. Where were all those huge trees? Where were all the bushes?

They were gone. What I saw now looked exactly like the cemetery Max and I had visited during the daylight, the one in the mortal world. The one outside of Avery's Crossing. Wherever Nova's apartment was, I knew where it wasn't. It wasn't here.

I slumped against the doorjamb. I'd lost her again. The self-portrait she'd drawn was in my denim jacket pocket, so I'd lost that too. How could I have been so stupid as to fall asleep? I should have hustled her out of there immediately.

My head slammed back against the jamb. "Damn it," I said out loud.

What had I been thinking? How could I allow myself to fall asleep? Jesus, I'd lost her again and this time I might never get her back. What if she were stuck in that horrible in-between place forever?

"Gage!"

I opened my eyes at the masculine shout. Several people approached across the sodden grass of the cemetery—Max, Adam, Marie. My mom, dressed in jeans and a sweatshirt. She was even wearing running shoes, which she must have borrowed from someone because to my knowledge she didn't own a single pair of athletic shoes.

What the hell was she doing here? I didn't want her around.

I closed the door of the corpse house—er, Sexton's Tool House—and came down the single stone step. They rushed up to me, surrounding me with worried faces and questions.

My mom's voice rose shrilly over all the others, making me wish I were deaf. "Gage! We've been looking everywhere for you! We thought you were dead!"

Max clapped me on the shoulder. "Where the hell have you been, dude? And where's your shirt?"

"Here. I've been here. I don't know where my clothes went."

He gave me a look of utter bafflement. "For two days?"

"What?" Now I was just as baffled as he was.

"Yeah. You've been gone two days."

I shook my head. "No. That can't be right. I left Brad and Marie's and I decided to come here for a while." I glanced at my mom and decided to censor my story. "I must have fallen asleep in that little house. I didn't wake up until this morning."

"You fell asleep in there?" Max said in a disbelieving tone.

"Yeah. I must have. That's where I woke up."

Adam and Max just stared at me. They glanced at Marie and went back to staring at me.

I flicked a glance at my mom. "Let's talk about this later. Right now I need food."

"Food is a great idea," Marie said firmly. "Let's go to a pancake house. Max, let him borrow your jacket."

Without a word, Max slipped off his jacket and handed it to me. He wore a flannel shirt underneath, so I guessed he was warm enough.

"Thanks." I slid into the jacket. He and I were pretty close in size, and it fit fine.

My mom threw her arms around me. "I'm so glad you're alive. Oh my God, I thought someone had gotten to you."

I patted her awkwardly on her back. "I'm okay, Mom. Everything's fine." Except it wasn't, of course.

We still had the ritual, however. Maybe we could rescue Nova that way.

***

Nova:

Declan showed up just after I decided to pause in my investigation of the downstairs apartments in order to break for lunch. He wore a heather-green pullover sweater and jeans, a nice outfit but not the kind of thing you'd wear if you were the manager of a bank. Not even in Avery's Crossing. Besides that, it was eleven o'clock in the morning, an unusual time for a banker's lunch.

He came sauntering up the sidewalk outside my building, giving me one of those big, sunny smiles of his. "Hey, Nova. What're you doing down here?"

"Just having a look around," I said.

"Oh, yeah? I hope you're not breaking and entering."

I looked into his eyes and saw only a teasing twinkle, nothing accusatory. So I smiled back.

"Is it breaking and entering if they're empty?"

"I don't know." He glanced at the nearest apartment door. "Probably, since you're not the owner."

"Well, then it's a good thing the owner doesn't know."

Declan's smile became a frown, the corners of his mouth turning down. "Did you really go inside?"

"I don't think you want to know. I was about to have lunch. Would you like some too?"

"Sure. Yeah, that would be great."

We walked up the concrete stairs in companionable silence, but when I glanced over my shoulder at him, he looked troubled. His frown was still firmly in place.

"I didn't hurt anything," I said, getting my key out of my pocket.

"I didn't think you had."

"Then what's the problem?" I opened the door.

"Nothing. I'm just worried about you."

"Worried? Why are you always so worried about me, Declan?" I held the door open so he could go inside.

"I'm not *always* worried," he said with a quizzical glance at me. "But it doesn't seem like a good idea to break into empty apartments."

"Would it be better if they were occupied?"

"No. That's not what I meant," he said.

I closed the door but didn't bother locking it. I was starting to think there weren't any people around to lock out.

"Nova, is everything okay? You look different."

"I do?" I threw my coat on the couch and went into the kitchen.

"Yeah," he said, following me. "You look pissed off."

"Hmm." I got out bread and sandwich fillings. "Now why would that be?"

"I don't know." He leaned against the cheap, brown laminate of my counter top and regarded me with that same puzzled frown. "Why don't you tell me?"

"Where do you live, Declan?"

"Huh?" He gave me a blank stare.

I made a vague sweeping gesture with my whole arm. "All the apartments are empty except this one. So where do you live? I thought you were in my building."

"I don't remember saying that."

"You said you were my neighbor. In an apartment building, that usually means you're in the same building or complex. But you're not. So where do you live?"

He straightened, pushing off from the counter. "Nearby. You know. Around."

"Around? So what does that mean? Do you camp on the streets?"

He flushed, the first time I'd ever seen his face change color. "No, I don't camp out."

"Well, where's your place? Maybe we can have lunch there for a change. And speaking of lunch, aren't you off kinda early?"

His green eyes narrowed. "What are you implying?"

I shrugged. "I don't know. It just seems a little early for a business lunch hour."

"Did I do something to offend you? Tell me what it was so I can fix it."

"No. You haven't offended me." I unscrewed the lid on the mayo jar.

"Then what's wrong? You seem like you're angry with me."

I sighed. A big, shoulder-shaking sigh. "Declan, something is really off about this neighborhood. And us. Don't you think it's weird that nobody lives in this building except me? Don't you think it's weird that nobody ever seems to be home in all the houses around here? Don't you wonder about that?"

"Not really. No." But he raked his fingers through his blond hair, making me wonder if he was being completely truthful.

"Well, I do. I can't stop thinking about it. And I had a visitor last night."

His dark-gold brows pinched together. "A visitor? I thought you said there weren't any other people around."

"He's not from around here," I said, watching him carefully. "His name is Gage Dalton. Do you know him?"

"No. Should I?"

"I don't know." I reached up and pinched an eyebrow with my thumb and forefinger. "I don't know anything anymore."

"So who is this Gage fellow then?"

This Gage fellow. What an oddly old-fashioned phrasing. Sometimes Declan sounded completely modern, but then he'd throw in some anachronistic expression that made him seem like a relic from some other age.

"He said he knows me," I said. "He thought I should know him. He said--" I dropped my gaze for a moment, studying the vinyl floor that pretended to be tile. "He said he loves me."

"What?" Declan growled. "Where is he? I want to talk to him."

My head snapped up and I stared at him in shock. "What? Why?"

"He's got no business coming here and molesting you that way."

"He wasn't molesting me," I said firmly. But my cheeks flushed with heat, betraying me.

I didn't consider what Gage had done to me molestation because I'd wanted it. Still did. But the fact was we'd been intimate, and I didn't even know him. Or if I did, I didn't remember it.

"Nova?" Declan stared at me, his face changing from indignant, even angry, to sad as his eyes began to tilt down at the corners. "What happened between you and him?"

I pressed my lips together. "That's really none of your business."

"It isn't? I thought—"

"We're friends."

He made an angry slashing motion of his hand. "You let me kiss you."

"Yes, I did. That doesn't give you the right to tell me I can't see other men."

Until now, I wasn't even sure how Declan felt about me. I mean, I knew he was attracted, but I didn't realize he felt territorial. This was a new phenomenon for me—a man jealous over me.

"Are you going to see him again?" he said, his voice sulky.

"Probably. But that's not the point here. I want to see your house or apartment. The place where you live."

"No." His voice had turned flat, his green eyes secretive. "That's not possible."

I folded my arms over my chest and gave him my sternest scowl. "Why not?"

He merely shook his head.

"Tell me. I promise I won't freak out."

He gave me a look so full of anguish and fear that I wanted to take him in my arms, just to comfort him. "Because I can't remember where it is."

"You can't remember or you don't want me to find out?"

"I can't remember. I swear it."

I finished making sandwiches, although my appetite was long gone. Declan might be hungry.

"Don't you think it's suspicious that you can't remember your own home?" I said as I pushed a plate in his direction.

Declan hung his head. "Yeah. I guess it is."

"Help me figure out what's going on here."

He stared at me as if by looking at me he could make me change my mind. I just stared back. If he didn't want to help me, I wouldn't try to force him. I'd go by myself, the way I'd originally planned. It would be less lonely with a companion, though.

He blew out a heavy breath. "Hell. All right."

Now we were making progress. "I'd like to look inside the houses around here."

"You don't start small, do you?"

I grinned. "I started with the apartments. Those are small. Now it's time to move on to something larger."

Eventually, we'd have to head back to the cemetery, but I was going to leave that for later.

Chapter 16
Ritual

Gage:

There were no visible stars in the sky. Rain pattered down all around us, bringing out a moist, green scent that would have, in better days, made me happy. Somewhere in the distance, coyotes went into a frenzy of yipping and high-pitched howls. The only light we had was a kerosene lantern sitting on the altar, to be replaced by candlelight when we started.

I wore the heaviest jacket I owned, black leather with chains. In the pocket, I carried a pair of Nova's panties, the ones she'd been wearing before she was taken. They still had the scent of her body on them, a link to her that we could use to help power the spell.

The ritual had to take place either outside or in an underground location, like a cave, cellar, or basement. Brad and Marie had allowed us to set up a pavilion on their land, out of sight of the house and ringed around with a line of rock salt so thick it would take days to rain away. We hauled our equipment out to the site and then sat around a hibachi waiting for the astrologically perfect moment to begin.

I didn't pretend to understand all that crap, but it was in Freiberg's book and I meant to follow the ritual to the letter. No mistakes. The outcome was too important.

The weather had not chosen to cooperate. We huddled beneath the gigantic rented awning we'd set up to get out of the rain, but it was cold enough to see our breath rising in little clouds anytime someone talked, coughed, or breathed. Everyone's noses had turned pink long before the sun went down.

"Your temple would have been perfect for this," Max remarked to Adam.

The blond gave him a dirty look. "No way I'd let anybody do something like this in my house."

"No?" Max grinned at him. "I thought you were a master of the dark arts."

"Yeah, and I didn't get that way by calling up all kinds of infernal shit I couldn't handle. You'd best believe I'll be doing every purification I know after this is over."

"Me, too," Marie said. "We all will. We don't want anything from the rite to follow anybody home."

Their words made me feel like icy little worms were wiggling all through my guts. Even if this thing worked and we got Nova back, it could still go wrong in so many ways. What we were doing—opening up a gateway to hell—was incredibly dangerous. Some might even say stupid.

Okay, anybody with a brain would say it was stupid. Yet Marie, Brad, Max, and Adam were all here helping me, just because they couldn't stand to allow an innocent woman to suffer.

Adam turned to Max. "Where's your girlfriend, by the way?"

"Caroline is at home."

Adam's blond brows rose. "Why is that?"

"Because I don't want her mixed up in this shit," Max said, scowling.

"Oh, I see. You won't let your girlfriend get involved, but you want me to host this thing in my basement?"

"You don't have a girlfriend. Or any kids either," Max said, stretching his legs out with an insolent glance at Adam.

"How the hell do you know?" Adam said. "Maybe I have a dozen girlfriends."

"Like I said..."

"Boys, quit fighting." Marie handed Max a mug of something with steam coming out. She was always taking care of us with food and drink.

"Adam, you want some hot cider?" she said.

"Sure. Thank you."

I didn't blame him for not wanting a ritual like this one at his home. I wouldn't allow it either. Marie and Brad claimed they had full confidence in the wards placed on their house, but I noticed we were out in a field and not in their basement.

"Gage, you want some?" she said.

"Aren't we supposed to be fasting?"

"Yeah, but you can have a little something to drink. Besides, I put something in it to enhance our abilities here tonight."

Freiberg stared at her suspiciously. "What did you use?"

"Mugwort. Just a drop of tincture. You'll be fine."

He gazed at the contents of the mug she'd handed him and sniffed. "I can't smell it."

"Of course not. I put spices in to cover it because it's not very tasty. You don't have to drink it if you don't want it."

"I know that," he snapped.

Brad turned from whatever he was doing at the altar to stare at Freiberg, who turned red.

"Adam," Max said. "If this is too much for you, you don't have to stick around. It's not your fight."

"It's not yours either. It's Gage's, and I'm staying."

Everybody was staring at Adam now and I could see it made him uncomfortable. "He wants to make sure we don't fuck it up, since we're using his book for the instructions."

"I understand that," Marie said. "And I don't blame you, Adam."

"It's not just that." He rubbed his left brow. "I knew someone who did a similar ritual once. I never saw him again." He gave a sigh and shook his head. "I know you're pretty experienced, but I'm not sure you really understand what you're getting into here. This shit can go so wrong you'll be haunted by it for the rest of your life. And I'm not speaking metaphorically here."

Marie sat down in the empty chair next to him. "We do understand that. But what should we do? Should we forget about Nova? Just let the devil have her?"

He shook his head, looking miserable and not saying anything. I couldn't figure out if he was afraid for himself or for us. Or maybe for everyone, because if we accidentally let something evil out into our world, things could get ugly for the whole earth.

Did I want to be responsible for that? No. Of course not. But I couldn't abandon Nova. I wouldn't do it. Ever.

"None of you need to be here," I said. "I can take care of this alone."

"No, you can't," Max said. "It's too big for one person."

I met his level gaze. "Maybe, but I don't want anyone else taking any risk. This situation is my fault and it's up to me to make it right."

"Honey, it's safer for everyone if we help you," Marie said. "So don't think you can scare us away. We're doing this. At least, I am. Anyone who doesn't want to be here should leave now, because it's about time to start."

"I'm in," Adam said. He glared at Max and Brad. "Don't even say it."

"Okay." Max shrugged. "I'm in too."

"You know I am," Brad said.

Adam had used flour to draw a huge, elaborate circle on the ground under the awning, with strange shapes and symbols around and inside it. The altar stood in the center of the circle. We took up pre-arranged positions at the perimeter of the circle, one at each of the cardinal directions. Marie had assigned me west, because it was the traditional direction of the afterlife or underworld, according to her, and I was the one seeking for Nova.

We'd rehearsed this, but not enough to please me. I had a cheat sheet in my pocket so I wouldn't screw up my lines.

I stood in my place and watched Marie and Adam as they walked around the circle intoning a bunch of words I didn't really understand. They'd translated all of it for me earlier and I knew the gist of it but I couldn't follow word for word because it was in a mixture of Latin and Greek.

Their voices sounded strange to my ears. They weren't talking in any normal sense, but they weren't singing either. It was a kind of chanting, but with only one pitch, the vowel sounds all drawn out and exaggerated.

The tones seemed to hang in the air and vibrate in a way that ordinary human voices didn't. I could feel a tingling in the air, a heaviness, that I'd noticed before when something paranormal was about to happen. But this was more intense than anything I'd experienced in the past.

They finished walking the perimeter of the circle. Marie picked up a brass bowl from the top of the altar and brought it to me. She met my eyes. I nodded and drew the knife I had ready, unsheathing it. We needed human blood.

Marie held the bowl under my hand as I slashed myself across the palm. The blade was so sharp I hardly felt it bite into my skin until the cut was already made and blood welled from my body and dripped into the vessel. Then sharp, burning pain erupted all along the cut.

Adam wrapped it in a bandage and secured it for me. He, Brad, Marie, and Max were all chanting more Latin and Greek now, while I stayed silent and focused on keeping pressure on the wound in my hand.

Marie took the bowl with my blood in it to the altar. She picked up a little paper bag, spoke some words over it, and dumped its contents into the blood. Graveyard dirt, the stuff Adam and I had gathered from the cemetery.

I stood at least two yards from the altar, yet I could feel the power surge as the dirt met my blood. The air almost hummed with it, pressure building and pushing against my skull. The chanters' voices changed pitch, went slightly up the scale. I could feel something watching us from outside the circle, although I couldn't tell what it was.

Marie carried the bowl back to me. I took it from her hands and almost dropped it. The thing tingled against my palms. It felt icy cold, even though my blood had been hot when it left my body.

Marie and Adam resumed their original positions. I turned and faced the west, the direction of the dead. Glancing down at the blood-dirt mixture, all I could see was a moist, black substance, like mud. But it was no ordinary mud.

I swallowed. Sticking my finger into that mess didn't seem like a pleasant idea. But this was what we needed to power the gateway that we were trying to open between us and Nova's location.

I dipped up some of the mud with my forefinger. It tingled fiercely against my skin. Gritting my teeth, I crouched down to mark the ground. With my free hand, I brought out my cheat sheet.

"Gates of Hell, I command you to open for me. Open and release your prisoner, November Daye Pennyman." I tried to make my voice match what I'd heard from Adam and Marie.

At the same time as I said the words, I copied the symbol of the gateway onto the ground using the blood-dirt mixture. The hum in the air became a low throb, a beat I could feel but not hear. It grew harder and faster with each stroke of my finger, each flourish of the symbol I added.

I completed the symbol. Nothing happened. The mud just sat there on the ground, like regular mud, nothing magical about it. That is, the throbbing continued, but the gates didn't appear.

Shit. No. This couldn't be. It had to work.

I glanced over my shoulder at the others. They were staring at my symbol expectantly, their faces tense with the energy of the ritual. Okay. Maybe...

A low buzz came from the ground in front of me. I whipped my head around. The symbol now glowed a deep, dark red. A little breeze, hot and sulfurous, drifted out of it.

"Holy shit," I whispered.

Standing, I backed up a pace. The symbol's glow continued to brighten and expand, until it seemed to stand away from the ground like a separate entity. The whole circle vibrated now. A hot wind gusted from the symbol, blowing my hair back from my face and billowing my jacket.

The ground beneath our feet rumbled. The symbol rose and hovered in front of us like a doorway.

"November Daye Pennyman!" I hollered. "Come forth!"

Suddenly, the symbol disappeared into a portal of flame, of fire in the shape of a gate or door. Through the flames, I could see shapes moving, black silhouettes that could be people...or something else.

I yelled for Nova again as I put my hand in my pocket and grabbed her panties. They had her energy all over them, so they should help to connect me with her.

One of the black shapes approached us. I took a step forward. Was it her? It looked small enough to be her, but I couldn't tell. "Nova?" I said.

The shape paused.

"November Daye Pennyman, come forth," I repeated.

The view through the flames shifted, swinging around like the view through a moving camera. I saw a living room. Beige carpet, white walls, brown couch, red and pale green accents. It looked like Nova's place.

Two people sat on the couch. They were staring at me. The view drew closer. I saw her staring at me, her golden-brown eyes wide with fear. Nova! But what was she doing with another guy?

He was some tall, blond dude and he had his arms around her, the bastard. What the hell did he think he was doing?

They both looked terrified. Nova clung to him. She held onto him like he was the one she loved and trusted, and that felt like a spike to my heart.

"Nova!" I yelled as my pulse raced.

I saw her lips move. She might have said my name. Sweat broke out all over me. Her small body leaned forward, toward me, and I reached out for her.

"Nova, come on! Come through the gate."

She shook her head, her eyes wide with fear.

"Please, baby! Come on! I'm right here."

The blond dude grabbed onto her even more tightly, like he'd never let her go. Who was that guy? Was he a demon? Another trapped soul? Whoever he was, he had no business trying to keep my girl from me.

I took a step toward the gate. The heat of it beat against my face and the stench of the sulfur made me gag. Sweat rolled freely down my body beneath my winter clothes.

"Nova, I love you," I called. "Come here to me. Come back to me."

Out of the corner of my eye, I saw a slender black shadow slip through the gate into our world. Oh, shit. Not good.

"We don't have much time," I said. "Nova, come on. You belong here. Please, come now."

She said something to the blond guy. He shook his head and tried to hold onto her. She pushed his hands off and stood up. Took a step toward me.

Nova was coming to me.

"Yeah! That's it, baby!"

The gate crackled. Flames burst past its edges, flickering into our world. The rectangular shape of it faltered, and the symbol reappeared for an instant before the gateway resumed.

Nova paused on the other side, her eyes round, hands in fists at her sides.

"Baby, come on!" I yelled. She had to do it now.

The symbol flashed in front of our eyes again. I saw Nova shaking her head. I took another step toward her. Someone caught me by the arms, holding me back.

"Let me go!"

Whoever it was didn't answer, and he didn't let me go. I struggled against him as Nova's image wavered eerily through the flames. His fingers bit into my arms like shackles. My feet slipped on the wet grass and mud of the field as I fought his hold. What was wrong with him? He was keeping me from going to her.

The gateway crumpled completely, leaving only the hovering symbol glowing red against the sky.

It flickered and winked out. Only blackness now. The darkness of an ordinary field on an ordinary night in winter.

I screamed in rage, flailing against the idiot keeping me from her. Fuck! Fuck no! Our stupid fucking ritual had almost worked and then I'd lost her again. How many times would I have to lose her all over?

"Gage!" Max hollered in my ear.

So it was him. I sagged in his arms, hoping he'd drop me so I could sweep his feet out from under him. Fucking prick. He had a girlfriend, and here he was keeping me from mine.

"Gage, stop," Brad said. "You can't help her right now."

He grunted as I twisted my body, trying to get rid of him. My feet scraped against the heavy mud. I growled like an animal, but they kept their hold on me no matter what I did.

They both had me, Max and Brad. I'd thought it was just one man, but I now realized I had one on each arm. And they still had trouble keeping me down.

Adam came around in front of me. I kicked at him. Part of me knew I was behaving like an idiot, but the rest of me just wanted to hurt something. Anything.

Nova was gone. I'd lost her again. I might never get her back now, because what other recourse did I have? I'd used the only tool I possessed, and it had failed.

"Gage, you have to stop before you get hurt," Adam said. "You can't help Nova if you get hurt."

"Fuck you!" I screamed it so loud it ravaged my throat. "I can't help her anyway. I lost her! What can I do now? Huh?"

"We'll figure something out. Stop fighting."

I couldn't do that. I could never stop fighting for her.

Chapter 17
Aftermath

Nova:

The gate of fire collapsed in on itself, shutting Gage away from me. My legs dropped out from beneath me as if the muscles had been cut. They simply lost their ability to hold me up.

I screamed. I didn't remember opening my mouth, but terrible noise came out of me, an animal screeching that went on and on. My fingers dug into the plush carpet all the way to its backing.

I'd lost him. Why hadn't I run through that gate the instant I'd seen it? I'd been too afraid, too weak, and now he was gone. I might never see him again.

Heavy male arms closed around me. A deep voice murmured against my ear. I couldn't make any sense out of his words. All I could think was that Gage was gone, again, and I couldn't get him back.

The gentle, golden light from my accent lamps, light that had seemed so cozy and inviting before, now looked weak and pathetic. The darkness outside my windows pressed in on me, cold and heartless, keeping me from the man I loved.

"Nova." It was Declan. Declan was here. "Nova, it's all right. You're all right."

"No, I'm not!" I wailed.

"Yes. You're all right. You're safe."

"No!"

He only hugged me tighter. "Yes. You're safe. I'm here. No-one will hurt you."

"You don't get it! I want him back!"

"No. He's dangerous. He's—"

I punched him on the arm. "Don't say that."

"Nova, you saw what just happened. That was—I don't know what it was. But I think we can say it isn't safe or normal."

"He's Gage. I love him."

"Shhh." He leaned back, drawing me up against his body, pulling my head down against his green sweater.

I let him hold me because I didn't know what else to do. I couldn't keep fighting him. He was way too strong and I'd never win a fight like that. Besides, he wouldn't hurt me. He just didn't understand.

If I hadn't been with Gage, if I hadn't known real passion, I might have been satisfied with Declan. He was a good guy, and very attractive. His well-muscled frame felt good against me. But he wasn't the right man for me.

The right man had appeared in a gate of flame and then vanished. What did it mean?

A sob broke free from my throat and then I couldn't stop crying. I hardly knew Gage. I could only remember one encounter with him, and although it had been beautiful and ecstatic, it didn't quite explain my agony at losing him.

Yet I couldn't seem to stop crying. Declan held me against his chest and patted my back, a little awkwardly, like he wasn't sure he was doing it right. I shouldn't take advantage of him this way. He might take it as romantic encouragement, and that wasn't fair to him.

I choked back my sobs, shuddering, wiping my eyes. "I-I'm sorry."

"Don't be. That was an extremely upsetting thing to witness."

That statement startled a short laugh out of me. "Yeah, it sure was."

"I'm glad you're still here."

I wasn't. I wanted to be with Gage, and I was more convinced than ever that's where I belonged. This strange half-world I occupied along with Declan wasn't real, or if was real then not in the usual sense. It was set apart somehow from the mundane world we'd thought we lived in.

"Nova? You didn't want to go with him, did you?" he said in a low, concerned tone.

"Yes," I whispered. More than anything.

Except my fear had kept me from going to him. The flames had scared the crap out of me. How do you walk through a gate made of flame?

Gage would have done it. I could see he meant to cross over into this world, and he would have if those guys on his side hadn't grabbed him and held him back. If they hadn't interfered, we'd be together now.

"You don't mean that," Declan said.

I twisted in his arms, glaring through tear-swollen eyes at him. "Yes, I do. I love him. I should have gone with him but I was too scared and now I'm stuck here."

His mouth turned down. He looked so hurt I almost wanted to take back my words, except they were true and I wouldn't deny them.

"I'm sorry, then," he said. "I should have let you go."

"It's not your fault. I was too afraid. I'm a coward."

"No, you're not. You're the bravest girl I've ever known."

I sighed and rubbed my eyes. "Declan, do you even know any other girls?"

"Of course I do."

"No, you don't, because there aren't any other people here. We're the only ones, remember?"

"I know girls from my hometown," he said with wounded dignity.

"Oh? And where is that?"

He dropped his gaze. "I'm not sure."

"Yeah, because we're stuck in this otherworld where nothing makes sense and we can't remember important stuff from our own lives."

He pulled his chin down with a dubious air. "Do you really believe that?"

"Yes. I really do. Don't you?"

"I don't know." He lifted a hand to comb his fingers through his hair. "It's such a peculiar idea. I can't quite bring myself to accept it."

I didn't want to hurt him, but I needed an ally here, someone to help me figure out what was really going on, and Declan was the only person available. So I had to get past his resistance, even if it pained both of us, and convince him of the need to understand what was happening to us.

I moved out of his embrace to sit beside him on the floor. "Do you know how old-fashioned you sound?"

"I do?" His brows crimped together.

"Yeah. The way you talk is really old-style." I wrapped my arms around myself as a chill set in.

Declan pulled my crimson throw blanket off the couch and handed it to me. I wrapped the soft, fluffy fabric around myself, wishing it were Gage's arms instead.

"I'm not sure what you're getting at," Declan said.

I sighed and hitched my blanket a little higher. "I think you might be a ghost."

He stared at me blankly. Then he laughed. "Come on, Nova."

"Seriously. There's a monument in the cemetery with your name on it. And you talk like a guy from a long time ago. And you can't remember where you're from."

He shook his head. "I'm a manager at a bank. Ghosts don't work."

"Do you really have a job? Can you remember what you did there today?"

"Of course. I've told you all about our customers."

"Yeah, but I mean can you remember what you did today? Not just funny stories, but the boring day-to-day stuff, like logging into your computer in the morning. Sending routine e-mails. That kind of thing."

He leaned against the couch in a slouchy way I suspected was meant to make both of us think he felt relaxed about this conversation. I wasn't buying it. His jaw was working back and forth, for one thing. A sure sign of tension, if I ever saw one.

"I remember..." He paused and frowned. "My office. It has a red leather wingback chair in it."

"Okay. Do you have a computer?"

He looked at me strangely. "Computer?"

"Do you even know what that is?"

His frown deepened. He lifted his hand to his forehead, rubbing as if he suddenly had a headache. "Yes. I—it's a—"

"Declan, you're not from this time."

"That can't be true. I feel like I belong here."

"Of course you do. I did too, at first. But my memories are all wonky, like I can remember what I do here in the apartment clearly, but anything I've supposedly done at work or school is all fuzzy. I'm pretty sure that part isn't real at all. Whatever put us here has tried to make it seem as natural as possible, but he didn't fill in all the blanks." That made me wonder why.

Who or what had put us here? Why hadn't he/they/it created a more detailed world? Did he want us to figure it out eventually?

"I don't believe in the supernatural," Declan said.

"Even after you saw that flamey gate thing? You still don't believe?"

He gave me a pained grimace. "It was pretty convincing, wasn't it?"

"Yeah. Because it was real. This place?" I waved my hand at my apartment. "It's not real. It's some kind of dream or illusion or something."

"But why? What's the purpose of all this?" He glanced around my apartment, bafflement plain on his face. "Why would someone do this and how would they accomplish it?"

"I don't know. I think if we both got all our memories back, we'd understand."

We sat there on my carpet for a minute, staring at each other. Declan looked a little lost. Damn. I didn't want him to be a ghost, and I hated that I had to try to convince him he was. For one thing, what if I were wrong? For another, it was an awful thing to realize about yourself and I hated to do that to him. But we needed to know the truth.

"Maybe I'm a ghost, too," I said.

"I don't think so," he said, meeting my gaze squarely. "If you were, why would this Gage fellow come for you?"

"I don't know. Maybe you're right."

"And maybe you are too." He shook his head and grimaced again. "I don't want to believe it. I don't want to be dead."

"I know. It sucks, huh?"

He laughed ruefully. "Yes, it certainly does. But I need to know if it's true. Will you go to the cemetery with me? I want to see this memorial of mine."

***

Gage:
My bed, the one I ought to be sharing with Nova, was warm and soft. I could still smell her on the sheets, because I'd refused to wash or change them. I didn't want to lose one of the only parts of her I still had.

Last night, we'd wrapped up the ritual with a binding spell to seal the escaped spirit into the circle. It had taken almost as much energy as the original ritual had, and I was wiped out. And I still didn't have Nova. All that work and risk for nothing.

Downstairs, people—male, from the sound of it—shouted at each other. I groaned and pried my eyes open. They were so fucking loud their noise had come right through my closed bedroom door and awakened me.

I glanced at my clock. Nine in the morning. Fuck. It was too early for me after what I'd done last night, and besides, where the hell were Ted and the other security guys? They should be down there taking care of the problem.

Or maybe they were the problem.

I slid off the mattress in my skivvies. Whoever it was would get an eyeful because I had no intention of dressing up for those fuckers. What were they doing at my house so early, anyway?

The thought that it could be paparazzi flitted through my sleep-deprived brain. Could one of the photogs have tried to get in the house? Nah. Who would be that stupid? They knew the rules and they all had telephoto lenses. Who needed breaking and entering when you could spy on people through your camera?

Of course, we did have the house shut down pretty tight with shades and curtains, making it much more difficult to get a good shot.

I stumbled down the stairs. Now I could hear the voices more clearly.

"Sir, Mr. Dalton is sleeping," Ted rumbled. "You'll have to come back at a better time."

"Do you know the meaning of a search warrant?" An unknown male voice. "Let us in or Mr. Dalton will have bigger problems on his hands than waking up too early."

Holy shit. The cops were here.

I strode through the foyer, all my sleepiness gone. Ted stood with his bulk jammed in the opening of the front door, his meaty hand tight around the wood, fury and apprehension in his stiff posture.

"It's all right, Ted. I've got it."

He turned, his brown eyes tight with misery. "Are you sure?"

"Yeah, of course I'm sure. They're cops with a search warrant."

He shook his head. "Okay. But I don't like it."

Neither did I. That wasn't the point. You didn't say no to cops with a warrant unless you wanted to look guilty as fuck.

I grabbed the doorknob and opened the door wide. Two middle-aged guys in cheap gray suits, one African-American and one white, stood on my front porch, watching me and Ted with cynical eyes. Their gazes flicked over my near-nakedness yet betrayed no reaction.

The black guy had unusual, light-green eyes, and the white guy was one of those red-heads whose skin is almost as red as his hair. Neither of them looked like they were the easy-going kind.

"What can I do for you?" I said, as pleasantly as I could manage.

"I'm Detective Bryant," the black guy said. "And this is Detective Koslowski from the Benton County Sheriff's office. We have a warrant to search your house and grounds, Mr. Dalton."

"Can I see it?"

He handed me a sheet of paper. I'd never seen a search warrant before, so I wasn't completely sure what I was looking at, but it seemed legit.

"Okay." I handed it back. "You got ID?"

Bryant and Koslowski, their movements practiced yet edged with impatience, brandished Benton County sheriff badges at me.

"Ted, can you have Cindy call in and make sure these guys are who they say they are?" I said. "In the meantime, come in."

"You know why we're here," Bryant said, his words more of a statement than a question.

"Why don't you explain it to me," I said.

"We need to ask you a few questions in regard to the disappearance of Nova Pennyman." Bryant walked into my foyer, followed closely by his partner.

Of course, I'd been expecting a visit from the police. I kept the dismay off my face as I nodded.

"Let's go into the family room and talk," I said, leading the way.

Ted hovered in the doorway between family room and kitchen, talking on his smart phone, presumably to Cindy, or maybe to the Benton County Sheriff's office. The cops sat down in the orange club chairs Nova loved so much and insisted on calling "persimmon", and I took a seat on the couch. Koslowski pulled out a voice recorder and set it on the coffee table between the officers and me.

"How would you describe the relationship between you and Miss Pennyman?" Koslowski said.

"We're lovers. Boyfriend and girlfriend." I carefully avoided looking at Ted, or anywhere that wasn't Bryant or Koslowski.

"Is this a committed relationship?" Bryant said. "You do have a reputation as a ladies' man."

Talking about my feelings wasn't natural to me and frankly I didn't think my love for Nova was any business of the police. But saying so would only make me look guilty, so I hid my discomfort behind a careful screen of calming thoughts—playing scales on my guitar, watching snow fall.

"Nova and I are exclusive with each other," I said. "We love each other."

Bryant nodded. "And when was the last time you saw Miss Pennyman?"

"On Tuesday night at one o'clock."

"And did you argue at that time?"

"No. We were having a great night." One of the best of my life.

"Describe the events of that evening for me," he said, his face betraying none of his thoughts.

"Uh...we made love. We talked for a while. Then she fell asleep. I was hungry so I came downstairs for a snack. When I went back to the bedroom, she was gone. The bed was empty." That, of course, was mostly true. I couldn't exactly explain that I'd really gone downstairs because I overheard my mother crying over something Lucifer had said to her.

"Did you search for her?" Bryant said.

"Yes. Everywhere. I couldn't find her."

A faint frown marked Bryant's forehead. "When you say everywhere, what exactly do you mean?"

I meant the otherworld. Hell. But I couldn't tell him and Koslowski that.

"The whole house," I said. "The garage. The grounds. She wasn't here."

"Did you call her friends?"

"No. She doesn't have many friends. She had a falling-out with a couple of them."

"I see." Bryant tapped out something on his tablet. "So you didn't tell anyone?"

"No. I thought maybe she'd gone out for a while and that she'd come back."

"Did she take a vehicle?"

"No." God, that sounded bad.

"So you thought she'd gone out for a walk at one o'clock in the morning?"

I suppressed a wince. "I didn't know what else to think. She seemed happy with me before she fell asleep."

He and Koslowski exchanged a glance.

"Do you have a life insurance policy on Ms. Pennyman?" Bryant said.

"What? No. Of course not. Why would I do that?"

"No reason. Just a routine question," he said, watching me carefully.

"I would never hurt her." I let a little hurt into my voice. "I love her."

"I'm sure you do." Koslowski stood. "If you don't mind, we'll have a look around."

"Sure. Look anywhere you want." I refrained from adding that they wouldn't find anything incriminating. A remark like that might inspire them to an even more thorough search—not that I had anything to hide.

"I hope you don't mind if I make myself some coffee," I said, getting up.

"Not at all. Koslowski will go with you."

I glanced at the red-head. "Okay."

Did they think I'd run?

"I'll go with Officer Bryant, if that's okay," Ted said.

I sent the cops a questioning glance.

Bryant shrugged. "You can come along, just don't get in my way."

I went into the kitchen, pretending I wasn't naked except for a pair of boxers. Koslowski tagged behind, saying nothing. That was fine. I didn't want to talk to him anyway.

It took me a few minutes to get the coffee ready to brew. I had to grind the beans and heat the water before I could put everything in the French press Nova preferred to the Keurig Cindy had bought for the house. I had to admit, French press coffee was pretty damn good.

It would taste a hundred times better if she were here to enjoy it with me.

"You want a cup?" I said to Koslowski.

"No thanks." He took up what I thought of as the bodyguard pose, arms crossed over his beefy chest, face blank.

He might be guarding me, but it wasn't for my benefit. I puttered around with the coffee for a minute before pouring myself a mug of black. Thank God my mom was still sleeping off her latest binge upstairs, because if she'd been down here this would be an even bigger clusterfuck than it already was.

Of course, we still had a good chance Bryant would wake her, rummaging around up there.

Koslowski's expression never changed. He never gave any indication he realized I was almost naked. He just stood there like a big, ugly statue. I let him stare. There was nothing for him to see, since I hadn't done anything wrong.

Well, that wasn't exactly true. I'd done plenty wrong by drawing Nova into my fucked up life. But my bad decisions had nothing to do with the law, and I sure would never deliberately harm Nova.

I took my coffee to the table and sat down with it. The sound of Bryant's and Ted's clomping footsteps came from upstairs. I didn't even glance up at the noise. Keeping your cool was vital in situations like these.

But if they did find something they thought was suspicious, they might take me to jail. I didn't care much about my own skin, just that I couldn't do anything to help Nova if I was stuck in lock-up.

You can't do anything to help her anyway. She's beyond your help.

But I didn't really believe that. There had to be something I could do; I just had to figure out what it was. And jail time would put a major kink in that plan, so I had to stay out, for her sake.

Eventually, Bryant and my security guy clumped back down the stairs and into the kitchen. Ted's jaw looked tight, his thin lips even thinner than usual. Bryant glanced at Koslowski and gave him a subtle head-shake.

"I'd like to have a look in your garage, as well as the first floor of the house," Bryant said.

I nodded. "Go ahead. Take your time." Hurry the fuck up and get out.

Ted followed him as he continued his search. I wondered what in particular they were looking for. A body? Blood? Signs of a fight?

Koslowski continued his inscrutable staring. He had that move down pat. Probably a lot of people had broken down under that stare and told him all kinds of shit they later wished they hadn't. I just sat there and contemplated my coffee. One hundred percent Arabica beans, dark roast.

You know what? I wished the cops did have some kind of supernatural investigative ability, because then they might actually be of use. They might be able to help me get Nova back. As it was, they were only in the way. Ray Pennyman hadn't done his daughter any favors when he'd reported her missing, but he didn't know that.

It seemed like it took forever for Bryant to finish up. He gestured to Koslowski and they marched off to the foyer to confer. I didn't look at Ted. I gazed into my coffee, and when that got too boring, I looked at my hands. Looking anyplace else would probably trigger a search in that very place, and I didn't want to encourage the cops to linger.

Bryant came over, his light eyes stern. "I didn't find anything, but I'm still keeping an eye on you. Don't leave town."

"I wouldn't think of it." I raised my brows. "Is that all for now?"

"Yes. We'll be in touch, Dalton." He glowered at me before rejoining Koslowski and leaving my house.

I slumped a little against the chair back. Shit. Fuck. Police involvement was not good.

This only turned up the pressure for me to get Nova back, and right now I had no idea how I was going to do that.

Chapter 18
Memorial

Nova:

Rain drizzled down out of a pewter-colored sky as Declan and I started out the next morning. I'd let him sleep on my couch under the red throw blanket, because I didn't want to make him go out there in the dark and cold alone. I wasn't in love with him, but I liked him a lot and the idea of him wandering in the dark only to disappear into his grave just made my chest hurt. Maybe Gage and I could help him get free.

Could you resurrect a ghost? I had no idea. What would he use for a body? The one he had, the real one buried beneath that memorial, wouldn't be much use. Or maybe he was like me, stuck here even though he'd never really died. Maybe no-one was buried under his memorial.

This place was damned confusing. I glanced up at him as we left my building and walked into the neighborhood. His head was down to keep the rain out of his eyes, but what I could see of his face looked grim. Lost, just as he'd been last night.

"I'm sorry," I said.

"Don't be sorry. It's not your fault." He looked ahead, ignoring the rain that beaded in his hair and on his blond brows.

"Yeah, but I didn't have to make you do this."

He glanced at me sidelong, his smile wry. "You aren't making me do anything. This is my choice. I want to know."

"Okay." I stuck my gloved hands in my coat pockets. "I just hope we find out something useful."

He nodded but didn't say anything. We walked in silence to the graveyard, the rain falling softly all around us. The scent of fresh soil and green growth pleased my nose. It smelled so real. Whoever or whatever had done this to us was incredibly powerful if it could create an illusion so believable.

The grass in the cemetery was wet and slippery. The stones seemed wreathed in gray veils as we made our way up past the corpse house. I gave it a wary glance as we skirted it, but there weren't any creepy ladies inside it today. Or if there were, they were staying below the windows and out of sight. Good for them.

Declan's memorial looked even more forlorn than the first time I saw it. The accumulated oak leaves, the moss, the sad little inscription with his name on it all seemed so lonely today.

He stood and stared at it, his hands stuffed in his jeans pockets. I waited for him to say something. Big splats of rain dripped off the mossy branches of the overhanging tree, occasionally hitting me on the head.

Declan took a step beyond the path, into the space of the grave itself. He leaned down and rested his hand on the top of the memorial.

"This is mine," he said. "But I'm not dead."

"You're not?" I wondered if the stress of seeing his own memorial had broken him.

"No. I remember. I remember this date." He pointed to the birth date. "But the death date...I don't remember that at all."

"That's probably because you were dead," I said gently.

He gave me a sharp glance. "I don't think so."

"Declan—"

"Are you dead?" he said with vehemence.

I blinked. "No. I'm not. Why?"

"How do you know?"

"Uh..." How did I know? "Well, I don't feel dead."

"Neither do I."

"And Gage told me I wasn't. He said Lucifer took me as payment for Gage's debt."

"I think something like that must have happened to me." He traced the lettering on the inscription. "I was taken here bodily."

"But wouldn't that have been one hundred and seventy years ago? How can you still be alive after all that time?"

"I don't know. Maybe time works differently here. Maybe there is no time."

"If Gage gets the gate open again, I want you to come with me," I said. "Come back into my world."

"I'm not sure that's a good idea."

"You can't stay here by yourself."

His mouth twisted. "It seems I've been by myself for almost two hundred years."

"All the more reason to come with me."

Another sidelong glance. "Your darling Gage won't like having me around. Where would I live? I don't belong in your world."

"We'd find a way. You're my friend and I care about you. I don't want to leave you here."

His lips tightened. "We'll see. First we have to find a way to send you back."

Yeah. How were we going to do that? I didn't know how Gage had gotten here in the first place, so whatever mechanism had allowed him to visit me wasn't available to Declan and me.

Information would help, though. Knowing who we'd been before we arrived here, for example.

"I wonder if it would help for us to try getting our memories back first," I said. "Then we'd know more, right?"

"Probably."

"Does this place look familiar? Do you think you ever came to a cemetery like this one when you were alive? I mean, when you were in your own time?"

He overlooked my slip-up, gazing thoughtfully around the graveyard. "Maybe. The trees are too big. I don't remember anything so overgrown. Some of these monuments and stones look familiar, but none of them are especially unique. Stones like this could be found in any American graveyard." He paused, his face taking on a more intent expression. "That little tool house, though. That does look familiar."

"Tool house?" I said.

"Yes, the tiny house-like building you hate so much."

"Oh. The one where I saw a ghost. That's a tool house?"

He lifted his shoulders. "I'm pretty sure it's where they kept the sexton's tools, so he could keep the grounds tidy. They also laid out the bodies there during the hot months. They would keep ice in the cellar and bring it up when there was a death to keep the body from rotting. Don't people do that anymore?"

"No. We have artificial refrigeration now."

Declan gave me a really strange look. "Do you?"

"Yeah."

"Hmm. Well, I may remember that tool house. Everything else, though...I just can't tell."

***

Gage:

Cindy and I stood at the front windows, the ones flanking the front door, and watched Detectives Bryant and Koslowski as they wrapped up their search and returned to their plain black Crown Victoria. Thank God they were finally leaving. Of course, they didn't find anything suspicious but that hadn't seemed to convince them of my innocence. I had the feeling they were waiting, biding their time until I incriminated myself.

"Do you think they'll watch the house?" Cindy said. She'd come down just in time to see them walk out the door.

"I don't know. I hope not, because I'm going out."

She gave me a glance of alarm. "I don't think that's a good idea."

"I have to go. There are things I have to take care of."

"I can do it."

I laughed ruefully. "No, you can't. This is something only I can do. Don't worry, I'm not going to skip town. I'm not an idiot."

"I know that." She sounded snippish.

I gave her a long look. Her normally perfect hair stuck out in a dozen different directions and her makeup looked smeared, like she'd put it on without looking in a mirror. She wore a pair of jeans, a faded and oversized blue sweatshirt, and a pair of fuzzy slippers with owl faces on the toes.

"I hope the cops didn't wake you," I said.

"No. But I wasn't ready for visitors either."

"Sorry about that."

She waved off my comment. "Not your fault. I just hope they don't come back."

"I hope they don't need to. I have to find Nova."

Cindy peered up at me, her face filled with more concern than I'd ever seen in my own mom. "If you needed help, you'd tell me, right? You know you can tell me anything."

"I do need help. Nova is in trouble."

"What kind of trouble?"

I didn't think Cindy would understand. On the other hand, she'd been around me and my mom for a lot of years, so maybe she'd picked up a thing or two.

"Has my mom ever told you about The Deal?" I said.

Her slim shoulders hitched up. "I've heard you two mention it now and then."

"She made a deal with the devil. My soul in return for my career."

Cindy gave a snort of laughter. Her carefully manicured hand came up to cover her mouth as her eyes crinkled in amusement. I just stared at her, waiting for her to get the fact this wasn't a joke.

She saw my unamused face and her grin faded. "You actually mean that."

"Yes, I do."

"How old were you?"

"Ten."

She shook her head. "Gage, you were just a kid. Maybe you misunderstood something. Maybe it was a bad dream."

"It wasn't a dream. Go wake up Mom and ask her. Anyway, it turns out you can't bargain with someone else's soul, and Lucifer took Nova instead of me. Just to make me miserable, because apparently that's what he does."

Her eyes narrowed on my face. "You're telling me Nova is in hell."

"I'm not sure that's where he took her. But yes, she's in Lucifer's possession."

"I hope you didn't say that to the cops."

I shook my head with a roll of my eyes. "I'm not an idiot, Cindy."

"Of course you're not. I didn't mean it like that."

"Okay," I said. "Good to know. Look, I've gotta get some clothes on and get going."

"Where?"

"You don't want to know." I turned toward the stairs.

"Yes, I do." She caught me by my forearm. "Where are you going, Gage?"

"To a cemetery, okay? I'm going to try to get in touch with Nova."

She lost all color in her face. "I thought you said she wasn't dead."

"She isn't. But she is in hell. I contacted her once, through a local cemetery, so that's where I'm going. Don't tell anyone where I am, all right? Unless it's Adam Freiberg, Max Kincaid, Marie or Brad. Anybody else, tell them you don't know."

Cindy shuddered. "A cemetery. That's ghoulish."

"It's all I've got."

Chapter 19
The Key

Gage:

It was the third time I'd been to the White Oak Cemetery and it was starting to look familiar to me. The rain gave it a damp smell and the required creepy effect, most of the headstones lost in gray mist. It looked so classic, it could have come right out of an old horror movie.

I left my car in the usual spot and made right for the corpse house. I needed to come up with a better name for that place; "corpse house" made my skin crawl and Sexton's Tool House didn't really encompass the weirdness of the place. Anyway, no pretty name would take away the skin-crawling nature of a building used to keep corpses cold before they could be buried.

There was no getting around the general nastiness of that building. Yet that was where I had to go.

In Nova's world, this part of the cemetery had giant trees, evergreens and deciduous kinds with no leaves because of winter, rising up like the pillars of some huge building. Here, the trees were small until you got to the crest of the hill, where Freiberg and I had gathered the graveyard dirt.

And it was quiet. The only sound I could hear was my own breathing and the squishing of my brown biker boots over the wet ground. All I needed was a few crows cawing and flapping their wings to make the horror-movie setting complete.

My hair began to stick to my skull from all the water in it. A cold droplet ran down the back of my neck and under the collar of my black leather moto jacket. My stomach churned as I grew closer to the corpse house and I wondered, once again, if my idea would work.

It had to work. Otherwise...

I glanced around to see if there were any other people nearby to see me go into the building. Nobody was within sight. My muscles tight with anticipation, I climbed the stone step and turned the doorknob. And it opened.

I let out a relieved sigh. At least no-one had come by to lock up yet. With a quick glance around the room, I noted that nothing seemed different from the last time I'd been there. I shut the door behind me.

Now what? I guessed I'd have to wait at least a few minutes, and there was nothing to do in here but twiddle my thumbs. I strolled over to the table that took up the center of the room and leaned against it with the intention of relaxing for a while.

The metal of the table top seemed even colder than I'd expected, the kind of cold that gets under your skin and all the way into your bones. I had a sudden mental flash of a female body lying there, dressed in her Sunday best, her bell-shaped skirt hanging over the edge of the table, her flesh bluish-white and stiff looking. I flinched and removed my hand.

Was that a real vision or just my imagination? There was no way to know for sure, but since Freiberg had told me to trust my gut, I wouldn't be putting any of my body parts against that table again.

My idea was to wait for a little while inside the corpse house and then leave, in the hope that when I left I'd be in Nova's world. I didn't know how long the waiting period should be. I hadn't been in it very long the first time, so maybe I could go now.

I licked my lips nervously. Took a deep breath. The air inside the house smelled just as strongly of dry rot as the other time I'd visited. I reached out and opened the door.

My stomach dropped about twenty feet. Nothing. Not a damn thing. The view was exactly the same as when I'd come in. I was still in Avery's Crossing.

I shut the door and leaned against the wall. "Damn it, Nova. How am I going to find you?"

Naturally, I got no answer.

* * *

Two homemade apple pies courtesy of Marie sat on my kitchen counter, the scent of cinnamon and apples filling the whole room. Their golden-brown crusts gleamed. Ordinarily, I'd be fighting the urge to dig into one of them immediately instead of waiting until we'd eaten the main dish, but tonight I was too focused on my failure to rescue Nova to enjoy food.

Because of her, my kitchen was stocked with real food I might actually serve to guests. This came in handy when Marie, Brad, Max, Caroline, and Adam had all showed up at my house, Marie with those apple pies. She was like the proverbial Earth Mother, taking care of everyone in her orbit.

The apple pies sat on the kitchen counter, making everyone's mouth water. My security guys were hanging out in the upstairs office, being professional, while the rest of us took up the kitchen and family room. My mom hadn't emerged from her lair in hours, and I was hoping she'd stay hidden a while longer.

"I have the drums and my guitar in the car," Brad said to me as he lingered near the coffee.

"Oh, yeah?" I said it casually so as not to encourage him much.

That was the same thing I'd done with Max, when he'd offered to accompany me. I hadn't believed he could really play and I'd been wrong. He was actually pretty good. Maybe I was being unfair to Brad as well.

"I thought we could all use a little distraction tonight," he said.

"Yeah." My shoulders slumped. "I'm not sure that's possible."

"You'll get her back," he said with a sympathetic look. "I know you will."

"How?"

"Saw it."

I raised my brows without saying anything.

"A dream," he clarified. "This morning."

"And all your dreams come true?"

"Just the good ones." He smiled. "Don't give up, Gage. We'll get her back."

"I still don't know how."

"Neither do I. But we'll figure it out. I think a breakthrough is coming soon."

I blew out my breath. "God, I hope so."

Nova had made some spaghetti sauce in volume and frozen it. That was what I'd heated up for dinner, along with some pasta and one of those salads you buy at the grocery store in a bag. It was the best I could do.

I brought the drained noodles to the table and set them next to the sauce. "Everything's ready."

"How are you?" Max said as he came up beside me.

I shot a sidelong glance at him. "I'm surviving."

"Heard you tried the corpse house again."

"Yeah. Didn't work."

He clapped me on the shoulder. "Keep trying. I have a feeling that corpse house is the key."

"So do I. That's why I went there. But I don't think it'll work."

"You've got to think positively," he said. "I know it's hard. But if you don't try, then what?"

"I didn't say I was giving up."

Everybody was treating me like—I wasn't sure how to describe it, but it was starting to irritate the shit out of me. I didn't want to be the fragile dude who needed hugs and encouraging words. I wanted to be the frigging hero. I wanted to be the one who stormed the gates of hell and stole Nova back where she belonged.

The helplessness of being stuck on this side, of not being able to reach her, grated on every last nerve.

I sat down at the white-painted banquette with its abstract upholstery in shades of cream, gray, and orangey-red to match the family room. Nova loved the way the house was decorated, which pleased me because I'd bought it to please her. But she wasn't here to enjoy it.

"This is a lovely house," Marie commented.

"Thanks."

"Did you have it professionally decorated?"

"It came that way." I poured myself a generous glass of red wine. I wasn't supposed to be drinking. I'd promised Nova I wouldn't do that shit anymore.

"So, Max, you didn't bring Fred tonight?" I said, just to distract myself from my morbid thoughts. Not that talking about a dead guy was all that uplifting.

"No. He was busy," Max said with a grin.

"What's he doing?" Caroline asked.

"I think he has a girlfriend."

Her brown eyes widened. "No way. Really?"

Max shrugged. "I'm not sure. He was acting kinda mysterious about it."

"Can ghosts have lovers?" I said, thinking of the blond dude I'd seen with Nova.

"I think that depends on the ghost." Max reached for the sauce pan. "Fred is the most alive ghost I've ever met."

"Do you know what makes him that way?"

"Me, I think." He shook his head. "He's always felt like he had to take care of me, since he's my ancestor. Now we're close and I don't know. I guess he doesn't want to move on yet."

"I wish we could bring him back," Caroline said wistfully. "He died too young."

"Yeah. But if we could do that, we could bring back Carter." Max glanced at her, his face suddenly sad.

Who was Carter?

Max met my gaze. "My little brother. I accidentally shot him when he was three."

"Holy shit." What an inadequate response, but I didn't know what else to say.

"Yeah." Max bent his head over his food.

Caroline put her arm around his waist and leaned her head on his shoulder. He looked down at her. Then he pressed a kiss to the crown of her head.

I had to turn away. I couldn't watch them together. It was too hard, when all I wanted to do was put my arms around Nova and I didn't know if I'd ever see her again.

"This is great sauce," Marie said.

I winced. "Thanks. Nova made it." And that put a stop to the conversation.

The rest of the meal was quiet, with everyone lost in thought. We finished up and reconvened in the family room, where I'd already laid a fire. I was getting pretty good at the fire thing for a guy who'd never burned anything but cigarettes until a few months ago. But that skill wasn't going to save Nova.

Chapter 20
Reservoir Of Power

Nova:

I'm sitting with Gage in an enormous living room, or maybe family room, decorated in a casually glamorous style that reminds me of something out of a shelter magazine. There's this fireplace with a thick, primitive wooden mantel and a gray stone surround that goes all the way to the cathedral ceiling. A fire burns on the hearth. A real one, made with wood, not one of those gas things you turn on and off with a switch. There's a faint scent of woodsmoke in the air.

We're cuddled up together on a luxurious white couch and he's playing with my hair. I look up at him. He's never told me he loves me, but I can't interpret the tenderness in his gaze any other way.

"You don't have to stay here with me, you know," he says softly.

"Why wouldn't I stay?"

His mouth curls up on one side in a wry half-smile. "Your mom and dad. Your dad hates my guts, Nova."

"So? I'm not with you to please him."

He cups my face, his powerful hand gentle on my skin. I love that gesture. It makes me feel so cherished. "Baby, I don't want to come between you and your family. I'm not worth it."

"That is bullshit," I say firmly. His mom and her stupid behavior—selling him to the devil? Really?—have totally messed up his view of himself. "Of course you are. I said I love you and I meant it. I'm not going back on that just because my dad is being a jerk."

His thumb rubs back and forth along my cheekbone. "Okay. It's up to you."

"Do you want me to go?"

"No," he says, his blue eyes darkening. "If I had my way, you'd stay with me forever."

Forever is a long time. Does he really mean that, or is he being poetic? I'm not sure.

"Well, I'm not going anywhere. You went to a lot of trouble to convince me to move in here and I'm not leaving now."

He laughs a little. "Good. I'm glad to hear it. Your dad's gonna be pissed, though."

"He'll just have to deal. I'm a big girl. He got over my living in the cabin, and he can get over this. Besides, once he gets to know you, he'll love you as much as I do."

He gives me a skeptical look. "Sure."

"You don't believe me now, but you'll see."

He pulls me onto his lap. I struggle, but only in a token kind of way, just so he doesn't take my cooperation for granted. His big arms lock around me and hold me to him and I loop my arms around his neck as he kisses me.

His lips. Oh, my God, his lips. They always feel so perfect, soft and firm at the same time, warm and a little wet and utterly erotic. The way he tugs at my lips with them, the way his tongue sneaks out and licks me, the way he always seems to know whether to be gentle and sweet or rough and desperate.

I moan into his kiss. Tonight, it's gentle and sweet. Coaxing, caressing, suggesting. He tastes like apples.

His hands stroke up and down along my back, and then he reaches for my ass. He loves to touch me there, and I love it too. There's just something about those big, warm hands on my butt that turns me on every time.

He's hard as rock under my crotch, the bulge in his jeans pressing in just the right place on my body. I grind down on him and we both moan. His hands grip my ass mercilessly.

"Gage, what about—whoa. Sorry, man," says an embarrassed-sounding male voice.

We jerk apart and turn to see Ted retreating into the hallway. I bite my lip and turn back to Gage. He's laughing with his eyes, his shoulders shaking.

"You think that's funny?" I whisper.

He chokes. Grins. "Yes."

"We should go upstairs. Get some privacy."

He does that quirky eyebrow thing. "Why? I want to fuck you right in front of the fire."

I blush. "There's a fireplace in the bedroom."

"So conventional." He grins at me. "Fine. We'll go upstairs and do it in the bedroom like normal people."

"Normal? You're anything but normal," I say, and jump off his lap before he can stop me.

He gives a ferocious mock growl and comes at me, so I leap away with a squeal and run for the stairs, Gage at my heels. All the way up the stairs, I'm giggling and gasping for breath at the same time.

He could have caught me in a flat second, but he lets me stay ahead of him all the way into the bedroom. He throws the door shut, grabs me around the waist, and tosses me on the glamorous black and white bed. I bounce a couple of times. He flicks a switch on the wall and moody accent lighting comes on in black metal and crystal sconces on the walls. Then he pounces on me.

"I'm going to eat you alive, little girl," he growls, and pretends to bite my neck.

I burst into more hysterical giggling. I sound like a brainless idiot and I don't even care. I'm laughing, breathless, and aroused simultaneously, my legs wrapped around his narrow waist.

Gage raises his head, laughing too, that gorgeous smile I could never resist from the first day I met him. Then his eyes darken and his mouth descends on mine, and we're lost in ecstatic desire again.

Then, darkness.

***

Suddenly, I found myself alone. I moaned, my body aching with unspent desire, and pushed my hips against the bed. My hand reached for Gage, but he wasn't there anymore.

What?

My eyes popped open. I lifted my head and looked around to find myself back in my own twin bed in my little apartment. I'd been dreaming again.

Or had it been a memory?

The black and white bedroom. I remembered that. There was a lovely crystal chandelier and a bench with zebra-striped upholstery. The master bedroom in the house Gage had bought in Avery's Crossing so he could be near me. He'd convinced me to move in with him.

That room with the huge stone fireplace, too. That was the family room. My parents had visited us. We'd talked in the family room, and my dad had been incredibly rude to Gage.

My mind flooded with a cascade of hundreds of images. Me living alone in my parents' cabin in the Cascade Mountains. Going down to the river and finding Gage floating there, unconscious, snow falling all around us. Me hauling him out, taking off his soaked clothes, warming him, desperately hoping he would live.

Pain savaged my head as an invisible vice clamp seemed to bear down on my skull.

I saw him trying to convince me he really was the famous movie star Gage Dalton. I saw him kissing me for the first time. I saw him leaving me in a helicopter, flying back to his life in L.A.

The headache intensified, combining with surges of nausea to make me groan and clutch my skull.

He'd returned to Oregon after a couple of months away from me. That was when he'd bought the house in Avery's Crossing, just to be in the same town where I lived. And he'd told me all about The Deal, the bargain his mother had made with the devil for his soul in return for an amazing career in Hollywood.

The Deal. That was why I was here. I remembered it all now. Gage had told me he loved me. Then Lucifer had decided to take me, since he couldn't legitimately take Gage's soul. Of course, he couldn't take mine either, because I hadn't offered it to him. All he could do was take my whole body and stash it here, in this weird illusory world. I guess he thought Gage would be more miserable if he took me than if he put Gage here.

I sat up in bed, shivering, my arms wrapped around me. Would Lucifer keep me here indefinitely? Would I remain, decade after decade, like Declan, never aging?

Gage loved me. I didn't have to wonder or guess anymore. He'd come out and said it.

I needed to get free. Had to find a way back to him.

If that gate of flames ever opened again, I'd be through it in an eyeblink. No hesitation. But how to get it to open?

***

Gage:

Even the fire in the fireplace couldn't cheer up a room without Nova in it. She ought to be here. The black night hung over me, only slightly impeded by the walls and window glass of the house. It wanted in. I could feel it.

I leaned against the wall where the kitchen met the family room and watched my new friends milling around the big open space of the sitting area, their faces carefully neutral. They seemed like they were trying to hit the perfect note between too happy for the circumstances and so glum they'd depress me even more than I already was. The cheerful colors in the room did nothing to raise my mood; all they did was remind me of my missing girl.

"Care to play a tune for us, Gage?" Brad said as he chose a spot on the couch.

"Sure." Anything to get my mind off my problems.

I'd been playing a lot lately, every time I had a spare minute. I wasn't sure why, just that it seemed to help me. And the guitar I'd come across in L.A. seemed to call to me. Every time I glanced at it, I had the urge to play.

I'd found the instrument in an alley behind an occult store during the time I'd been trying to stay away from Nova. After finding out that the clerk in the store had no idea how to help me weasel out of my mom's deal with the devil, I'd left and taken a shortcut through the alley only to stumble on a homeless guy with a very fine guitar. He'd insisted I take it, and I'd been playing it ever since.

The strangest thing about that homeless dude was that he'd called me G, a nickname only my dead friend Jeremy had ever used for me. And for an instant, he'd seemed to have Jer's eyes, blue instead of brown.

I picked up the guitar from its spot next to the couch and messed around with it, making sure it was in tune. Only this guitar was always in

125

tune. Whenever I touched it, a small voice inside me said it wasn't an ordinary musical instrument, which was just plain crazy. Have you ever heard of a magic guitar? No, I didn't think so.

"What would you like to hear?" I said, glancing around at my friends.

"Anything you want to play," Marie said.

So I started at random with the first piece that popped into my head. It was Spanish influenced, nothing like the bluesy stuff I used to play with Jer. Nova loved it, though.

Damn. Everything I did, said, saw, or played reminded me of her. I couldn't get away from her, yet I couldn't be with her either.

"I can't match that," Brad said when I finished.

I shrugged. "I can play something easier if you want."

Max grabbed my doumbek. "I'll play along, if that's okay."

"Sure." Whatever. He was pretty good.

I started a ballad, another favorite of Nova's. If I couldn't get away from her, I might as well wallow in it, right? Everything reminded me of her. It was like her spirit had infused the house and even me, so if I couldn't be with her physically then at least I could feel some connection through the music.

I pictured her in that apartment of hers, maybe sitting on her couch, wrapped in her fluffy red blanket, listening to me play. Maybe some part of her could hear me. Maybe she would know how much I loved her.

Sappy shit, I know. That's what happens when you fall in love. You turn into a pile of mush.

I didn't even care anymore if I was sappier than a bottle of maple syrup. I was over worrying about my man-card. I just wanted my girl back.

"I think you've got something here," Adam said when we finished our second song. He hadn't talked much all night.

"What's that?" I said.

"This music. It's connecting you to her."

"Yeah, I know."

He shook his head. "Not just emotionally. Psychically. I could see the chords."

"The what?" I said with quirked eyebrows.

"Chords. Psychic connections. Energetic connections that look like lines or chords between you and her. They're really strong." He looked at Marie. "Did you see them?"

She nodded. "Yeah. I did. Gage, I think he's right. Maybe you can establish an even stronger connection with Nova if you keep playing."

I rested my arm over the body of the guitar. "I've been playing constantly for the last few days and nothing's happened yet."

"You don't know that," she said. "Keep trying."

I peered at her. "You really think this could bring her back? It doesn't seem like it would be enough."

"You're giving up?" She sounded so very disappointed in me.

"No. I'll never give up," I said, straightening my back. "But music seems so soft. I want to do something real, something that will make a difference."

"Dude, I just told you it's making a difference," Adam said, irritation plain in his voice. "You're not really listening."

He was right. I was whining. If I wanted to save Nova, I had to use any tool I could get, no matter how odd it seemed to me.

I bent my head over the guitar. "Okay. I'm listening now."

"That instrument isn't a regular guitar, is it?" he said. "Can I touch it?"

"Sure. Go ahead."

He leaned forward and reached out his hand. The bizarre thought that he'd dirty it flashed through my mind. At the last instant, I pulled the guitar away. "On second thought, no. I don't want you touching it."

He dropped his hand with a glance at Marie. "Okay. I think he's charged it."

I raised my head to stare at him. "I've what?"

"Charged it," he said, meeting my gaze head-on. "You've poured so much of your own energy into it that it's become a kind of magical tool for you, a reservoir of power. And you don't want me to touch it because that would muddy the energy."

The Secret Rites of Necromancy was the book where we'd found the ritual we'd used to try to get Nova back. It belonged to Freiberg, and he'd been adamant that neither Max nor I could touch it. At all. Not even with gloves on.

"Like how you didn't want me touching your book?" I said.

"Exactly like that."

I dragged my fingers over the smooth wood of the instrument. "I have no idea how to use this thing. Magically, I mean."

And then I did. What if music was the key to making a connection to Nova? If I took the guitar to the cemetery, took it right into the corpse house and played Nova's songs, maybe that would open the gate again.

I'd been singing in the car the one time I had managed to go through the gate in the cemetery building. Playing the guitar in the corpse house itself ought to be even more powerful.

I stood. "I've gotta go."

Chapter 21
Come With Me

Gage:

I parked the car in my usual spot at White Oak Cemetery and got out, half expecting to find Suit Guy sitting up there somewhere, playing his guitar or smoking. But the only sound was the frogs, and they cut out when I slammed the car door, leaving silence. The air smelled only of rain and fresh dirt and fir trees.

I pulled the flashlight out of my jacket pocket and turned it on. Then I hauled my guitar case out of the back seat and slung it over my shoulder. The rain had stopped for the time being. The air felt cold, though, and smelled almost like snow. Playing wouldn't be easy in this weather, with my fingers stiff from the cold.

I headed into the cemetery. The place was starting to feel like a second home. Tombstones loomed out of the mist as I wound my way up the hill toward the corpse house. I still hadn't come up with a better name for the place, and I hoped I wouldn't need one. With luck, this would be my last visit.

The corpse house reared up out of the darkness behind its shrubby screen, looking even creepier than it had the last time I'd seen it. I thought of the image that had come to me then, of the woman's body laid out on the table, and my hand hesitated as I reached for the doorknob.

No-one is in there. They don't use this place anymore. It's just here for historical reasons.

I grasped the knob and tried to turn it. The thing refused to move. Locked.

Shit. I tried again, but it was most definitely locked.

I had to get inside. The portal that had opened via the corpse house was the only success I'd had in reaching Nova.

Maybe there was another door. I prowled around the outside of the building, training my flashlight on the side of the house, looking for a second entrance. There were windows on both the front wall and the two sides, but only one door.

I had no idea how to pick a lock. This left me with only one option: break a window.

With my flashlight trained on the ground, I searched for a rock I could use as a weapon. The long grass and weeds seemed to cover everything, hiding any rocks or useful debris under matted leaves.

After prowling around for a while, I got frustrated and gave up on the rock idea. Instead, I removed the guitar case from my back and took off my leather jacket, wrapping it around my arm and right hand. Then I smashed my fist through one of the side windows. The crash and glassy tinkle of breaking windowpane destroyed the silence of the night. I reached through the hole I'd made and unlatched the window, then pushed up the sash.

I slipped back into my jacket and slung the guitar case over my back. Then I stuck the flashlight in my jacket pocket. Gripping the sill in both hands, I dragged myself up and over the edge.

My shoulders barely fit through the window. I wriggled, going head first into the darkness of the corpse house, my guitar banging against the window frame and the bottom of the sash. Fuck. I couldn't get the damned thing through this way and I was in an awkward position, hanging on my belly over the window sill.

I reached up and grabbed the case with my left hand. With my right, I fumbled to un-clip the strap. The window sill dug painfully into my gut.

The dry-rot smell of the house filled my nostrils as I pinched the release on the strap clip. The case slid down my back, trying to escape my hold on it. Clamping down hard with my left hand, I hauled it over my shoulder.

The neck of the case caught on the window sash. "Fuck," I muttered, bending at an even greater angle forward to make room for the thing and causing the sill to dig so deeply into my gut I could hardly breathe. I should have taken the guitar out of the case before I'd tried to come through the window.

Another yank brought the case over my head. It slipped out of my grasp and banged to the floor. I cursed again at the thought of the damage the guitar might have suffered from that fall. If it was broken ...

I slithered the rest of the way through, putting out my hands to break my fall and hoping I wouldn't cut myself on the glass. I needed my hands in good condition so I could play.

My knees hit the dusty wooden floorboards with a thump. My head came forward and banged into one of the legs on the table, sending pain crashing through my skull.

"Jesus," I growled, clutching my head in one hand.

I switched the flashlight on. The bluish light caught on dozens of tiny shards of glass littering the floor in front of me. I gathered myself, got to my feet, dusted off my hands. They seemed free of broken glass at least.

The only place to sit was either on top of the table or on the floor, and there was no way I'd sit on that table. So I found a glass-free spot on the floor and unbuckled my case. I took out my guitar. My fingers were stiff from cold and from punching out windows, so I rubbed them together for a minute to warm them up.

The stink of dry-rot was oppressive in here, lightened only a little by the open window and the fresh air coming in. I'd always hated the smell of old buildings that were shut up all the time, like this one. It made my skin crawl.

I cleared my throat. "Okay, Nova, this is for you."

My first song was the first thing I'd ever played for her, back at her parents' cabin when we were snowed in. She'd been so surprised I could play. I smiled as I thought of the way the music had soothed her, helping her through the worst of the nausea caused by the stomach flu we'd both contracted.

The cold air and old smell of the corpse house seemed to fade away as I focused on Nova. Her golden-brown eyes, her elfin face and beautiful smile became more real to me than the dusty floorboards under my butt or the blocky legs of the ugly table rising up a few feet away from me.

Segueing into the next piece, I could almost see her sitting cross-legged on the couch in our family room, her dark hair sliding into her face as she listened to the music. I wanted her to sing along with me someday. I'd promised her I'd consider performing as long as she accompanied me. In my mind's ear, I could hear her soft voice as she sang along with me.

The first two songs had really been a warm-up. Now that I was in the groove, I switched to one I'd written just for her. The words made my voice catch with longing, but I pressed on because I had to finish. I needed to sing these songs for her.

The energy in the air around me shifted as I sang. It seemed warmer somehow, the cold less biting on my nose and fingers. Even the dry-rot smell seemed to lessen until by the end of the song it was almost gone.

The last notes faded. Had I made the connection? I couldn't tell without opening the door.

I returned the guitar to its case and slung the case over my back. Flashlight in hand, I walked to the door. The lock was a simple deadbolt, which I undid.

My hand rested on the doorknob. When I opened it, I would know if I'd succeeded. My heart burst into furious pounding and my palms began to sweat.

No sense in hesitating.

I opened the door.

The cathedral-like trunks of huge trees rose up ahead of me, all wreathed in thick white fog. I let out a huge breath of relief. I'd done it. This was Nova's temporary world.

Then my heart took up its pounding rhythm again. I was going to see her, touch her, hold her. I was going to have my Nova back again.

I started running.

Thick fog seemed to wrap itself around me as I plunged into the cemetery from the corpse house. The ground under my boots felt uneven, slippery. I ran, raced, as fast as I could force my body to move.

The air smelled wet, even wetter than it had in Avery's Crossing. There was something heavy about it, something that reminded me of death, although it was clean and free of exhaust fumes and other human odors. Wet dirt and rock, the deep kind from under the surface of the earth; that's what it smelled like. It reminded me of the stink of an ancient crypt I'd visited once in Ireland.

Maybe that smell was a warning. I hadn't noticed it the other time I'd been here. I didn't care anyway. I was going to Nova and that was all that mattered.

Tall grass and overgrown bushes tangled in my jeans and dragged at my boots. I stumbled, went down in the wet grass with a heavy grunt of pain. My left ankle hurt, but I clambered to my feet anyway.

When I put weight on my left foot, a stab of pain shot up into my calf. I hobbled forward, almost but not quite running, slowed down to an infuriatingly snail-like pace by the injury. It wasn't going to keep me from her. Lucifer could cut off both my feet and I'd still keep going, running on the stumps to get to her.

The huge, ancient trees that loomed over me felt like sentinels, only I wasn't sure if they were trying to keep me out or keep others in. The bizarre thought came to me that they were truly watching, and the fog was watching too. But they didn't move to stop me, so I kept on running.

I reached the suburban part of her world. The houses crouched in the shadows cast by the orange streetlights, just black hulks with no light of their own. They seemed watchful, too. Probably just my imagination. At the moment, I felt as if everything around me had eyes and ears and none of it wanted me here.

The streetlights made pools of orange light down the length of the street ahead of me. In the shadows, houses crouched silently, their driveways empty of cars. None of them had any light at all—no outside lights, no indoor glow from behind curtains or shades. Just darkness.

The houses were a mix of older places, probably built in the twenties and thirties, all the way through newer stuff from the nineteen seventies. Some of them were charming, mostly the really old ones, but many were nothing more than rundown, run-of-the-mill ranches with no particular style. The yards were full of overgrown bushes and weedy grass, everything damp with the mist that also clung to my hair and clothes.

The only sound came from the thud of my boots on the concrete of the sidewalk. No traffic noise. No barking dogs. No wind or raindrops or any other noise. Just my footsteps.

The concrete of the sidewalk was a lot easier to traverse than the cemetery grass. A lot less slippery, even though it too was wet from the fog and rain. I panted, mostly from the pain of my leg, as I jogged along the street, trying to remember where I'd found her apartment building.

That spreading lump of a juniper bush at the corner ahead looked familiar. I turned right at the juniper and ran another block. There. Her building's parking lot, which held only two cars. I wondered if one of them was hers.

The building, too, was dark except for a single window on the second floor. That must be her unit. It looked like the right one. Did no-one else live in her building?

She must be so lonely here all by herself. Of course, she had that blond dude to keep her company and I hated that idea. He might have tried to take my place.

If he had, he was going to be disappointed, because I was taking it back. Taking her back.

I dashed across the parking lot, empty except for two cars. Although these two cars existed here, I could hear no traffic noise from other vehicles. Just like all those houses and apartments that seemed unoccupied. It was like the place had been abandoned, as if all the residents had simply gotten up one morning and left, with only Nova staying behind. Except I was pretty sure the whole place had been conjured up just for her benefit.

At least that cosmic asshole hadn't put her in hell proper. It was the only thing I could be thankful for at the moment.

My ankle hurt like a sonofabitch by the time I got to the concrete stairs that led to the second-story outdoor hallway. I grasped the metal railing and hauled myself up, step by painful step, my feet clunking against the concrete. Fuck. When I got to her place, I was going to have to beg for an ice pack before I could rescue her. This was less than heroic.

I stumbled along the hallway to the apartment with the lights on. Yes, this looked like the right place. I'd made it. I banged on the door.

There was no answer. I banged again. Still no answer.

I pressed my ear to the door but heard no sound from inside. There was a shabby little doorbell on the right side of the door, its metal frame dotted with the dark brown paint used on the building's siding. I pressed it.

132

"Coming!" Her shout came faintly from somewhere in the apartment.

It sounded like Nova. Part of me didn't really believe I was going to see her, but that had definitely sounded like her.

I waited impatiently, drumming my fingers against my thigh, glancing around to see if anyone else was watching. Just because I hadn't seen anyone else here didn't meant they weren't around. Maybe they hid when strangers came by. But I didn't see anyone. No movement of any kind.

She unlocked the door. I turned to face it, my heart racing, my throat suddenly dry. This was it. Finally.

The door opened. Nova stood there in the light, looking up at me, her eyes round with wonder. "Gage?"

I nodded, my throat tight. "Yeah."

"You came back!" She threw herself at me.

I caught her as her arms wrapped around my neck and she gave a little hop to pin her legs around my waist. Laughing, I grabbed her ass to support her. My ankle yelped, but I ignored it. She pulled my head down and captured my mouth in a fervent kiss.

She tasted so good, so Nova. I could tell she'd had a glass of wine with her dinner. And she smelled the same as always, her hair sweet with the vanilla scent I loved.

"I can't believe you came back for me," she murmured, pressing kisses all across my jaw.

"Of course I came back. I love you."

"I thought I'd lost you. When I didn't go with you—I was so afraid—"

"Baby, I knew you were afraid. That whole night was pretty freaky."

She slid from my grasp until her feet touched the concrete, but she kept her arms around me. "I know. But I should have trusted you. I should have gone with you."

"It doesn't matter. Get your shoes and jacket and come with me now."

She nodded. "Okay. I'll be ready in a sec."

I stood in the doorway, holding the door open while she stuffed her feet in a pair of running shoes and grabbed a wool coat I didn't recognize. I was afraid that if I closed the door on her, I'd lose her again. Or if I went inside, I wouldn't be able to get out again. Who knew how this crazy place worked? All I wanted to do was get her back through the corpse house and into the mortal world.

She stuffed a red beanie on her head. Then she looked up at me with wide, startled eyes. "Declan."

"Who?"

"My friend, Declan. You saw him when you tried to rescue me before."

I frowned, thinking the name seemed vaguely familiar. "The blond dude?"

I didn't like him. At all. And I hated the delay he was causing us at the moment.

"Yeah. He's trapped here, just like me. We have to get him, take him with us."

"No." I shook my head, fighting back a territorial growl. "Nova, we don't have time."

Her mouth and eyes all turned down at the corners and her hands twisted together. "But he'll be stuck here, maybe forever. He doesn't deserve that."

"Probably not, but I'm not going to risk your life for him. I can't do that."

Her eyes were starting to glisten. Was she going to stall so long we'd get stuck here permanently? "He'll be all alone when I go."

I rested the back of my head against the door in frustration. "I can see you care about this guy."

"He's been really great."

She probably knew him better than she knew me. After all, she didn't remember our life together, so lately Declan had taken up a lot more of her time. Maybe she wanted to be with him as more than friends.

"Is he more important to you than I am?" I said, hating how jealous I sounded.

Her eyes went wide again. "No. No, it's not like that. I just don't want him to suffer. I'd feel the same way about any friend."

I shoved my fingers through my hair. I wanted to relax about this and not act like a caveman, but my nerves were jumping with the need to get her to safety. "How much do you know about him? How do you know he's like you? Maybe he's a demon or something, sent to distract you."

Her forehead creased. "I don't think so. He's never tried to do anything threatening. And there's a tombstone in the cemetery with his name on it."

My mouth dropped open. "Holy shit. Declan Stanhope? Is that it?"

"Yeah. How did you know that?"

"His memorial is where I got the graveyard dirt to do the ritual that opened up that gate on the night I tried to rescue you."

She pressed her hand to her mouth. "Wow. What do you think it means?"

"I don't know. But I do know we need to go. I don't want to hang around here any longer than necessary. The last time I did that, we got separated, remember?"

"Yeah." Nova frowned. "But Declan doesn't deserve to get stuck here. We can't leave him just because you're jealous."

My heart felt like it was wearing concrete shoes. "I'm not jealous. Okay, maybe I am, but I'm just trying to protect you."

Please, please let her agree with me. Please don't let her delay so long we couldn't get back to the real world.

She looked up at me with those pleading brown eyes and I crumbled a little bit.

"Do you know where he lives?" I said, knowing I was going to regret asking.

"No. He couldn't tell me."

"Then how can we find him? How do you get in touch with him?"

"I don't. He just drops by all the time." She huffed a frustrated-sounding breath. "You must think I'm crazy."

"No, I don't. It's this place. But Nova, if you don't know where to find him then how can we take him with us?"

"I don't know." She looked like she was going to cry. "I can't stand the thought of abandoning him."

"Jesus." I shook my head. "We've got to go, babe. I never want to wake up without you again."

She nodded, tugging at her beanie. "I know. I get it. That morning after we made love, I thought you were just a dream at first, when I woke up in my bed all alone. And then I started to remember all kinds of stuff about the cabin, and you coming to Avery's Crossing for me and buying the house."

I took a step into the apartment, keeping the door open with my right hand. "You remember all that?"

"Yes. I remember it all." She gave me a sad smile. "You told me you loved me right before Lucifer showed up."

"Yeah, and we've gotta get out of here before he shows up again. Do you have what you need?" I held my free hand out toward her.

"Yep. I think I've got everything." She glanced around. "My purse. Where's my purse?"

"Baby, you don't need that. You have a purse at home."

She frowned again, looking baffled. "I do?"

Something told me she hadn't quite grasped the fullness of what had happened to her. "Yeah. It's in the foyer closet."

"My God." She rubbed her forehead. "This is so bizarre. Sometimes I feel like my mind is breaking."

"I know what you mean. Come on, now. We've got to hurry."

She glanced around her apartment again, something reluctant in the way she looked at her temporary crib. Her shoulders moved up, then down in a huge sigh. "Okay. Yes. Let's go."

Thank God. I put my arm around her as she came out onto the walkway and shut the door behind her. We didn't bother locking it.

"You brought your guitar," she said, glancing at my back.

"Yeah. It's how I got here."

"Really? That sounds like a story."

"Uh huh. I'll tell you when we get home."

We moved off down the hallway, me limping slightly. I didn't want to favor the bum leg too much because that would slow us down.

Nova studied my leg. "What happened to you?"

"I slipped running over here. Wet grass."

"You should have let me put an ice pack on it and give you some aspirin."

"Nah." I squeezed her shoulders and grinned at her. "No time."

It seemed to take a lot longer to go down the stairs than it had to climb them. My ankle burned and screamed every time I put weight on it and the stairs made way too much noise with our combined weight. My stupid ankle was making this rescue much too drawn out and noisy, but there was nothing I could do about it now.

"Nobody else lives around here, do they?" I said as we left the parking lot.

"Not as far as I can tell. I went around the neighborhood one day trying doors."

I glanced at her, startled. "You did? It could have been dangerous."

"Yeah, but nobody was home. Anywhere. Declan and I are the only two people here. It's so weird and creepy." She shivered in my embrace.

The fog seemed to close in as she spoke. I could almost feel a watcher somewhere in the gauzy darkness. There shouldn't be anyone to watch, as abandoned or empty as the neighborhood was. Yet I sensed someone, some awareness marking our presence.

"I'm glad I'm taking you home," I said.

"Me too." She wrapped her arm around my waist. "I missed you so much."

The thought of her wandering this eerie neighborhood, trying to see if anyone was home, made me sick to my stomach. The things that could have happened to her...what if Lucifer had planted demons here?

Come to think of it, why hadn't he? If he'd wanted to, he probably could have created a much more detailed illusion for her. She could have lived here for months or even years without ever suspecting something was wrong.

Maybe he wanted her to start suffering, feeling lonely. Who knows? The mind of the devil probably isn't something a human can understand.

"I haven't done anything except look for ways to get you back since the night you left," I said, glancing at a little bungalow on our right. I could just make out the shape of the front porch through the fog as we passed it.

"Really?" She gave me an adoring smile and it didn't even embarrass me. It made me feel all warm and mushy inside, though.

"I was obsessed."

"How did you get here?"

I slid my arm from her shoulders and took her hand instead, limping as fast as I could manage. "Through the cemetery. There's this little house thing. I call it the corpse house."

"You came through *that?*" she said in a voice of horror. "That place gives me nightmares."

"I know, right? But that's how I got through that other night, when we made love. So I kept going back, hoping it would work a second time." And we'd have to do it again, because that was the only way home.

She grimaced. "Yuck. So I have to go in there, huh?"

"It'll be okay. It's not that bad. Plus I'll be with you." I only hoped it would work again. Otherwise, we'd be trapped here in this lonely, foggy half-world full of empty, watching houses.

Nova laughed, her voice full of nervous excitement. "Don't worry, I'm not losing my nerve. I'd go through a dozen corpse houses to get home."

I recognized one of the worn-down ranch houses I'd passed on the way in. Beyond it, there was only darkness. No more streetlights, just shadow. The blackness of the night had a grayish cast to it because of all the fog, and I couldn't see any detail ahead of us. But I knew where we were.

We were almost there now. So close. So damn close.

"When we get back, I'm going to take you up to our bedroom and not let you out for at least a week," I said.

"Good." She grinned up at me.

"I'm glad you're on board with that. And then we're going to get married."

Whoa. I hadn't actually planned to say that. The idea had been knocking around in my head for a while, but I hadn't even visited a jeweler yet. My big mouth. Nova deserved a better proposal than that lame-ass slip of the tongue.

She gaped up at me. "Huh? Seriously?"

It was too late to take it back, and besides I'd never do that. I met her gaze and held it. "Yeah, seriously."

"You just proposed to me on the edge of a graveyard."

I looked up and saw the black wrought-iron of the graveyard fence, the points sticking up like spears. Beyond that, everything was dark and ominous-looking, with the trunks of those epically huge trees rising up out of the fog.

She was right. We'd been closer than I'd even known. We'd made it to the edge of the cemetery and I hadn't even noticed. I'd been too busy thinking of everything I wanted to do with and to her when we got back.

"I'm just that romantic," I said, winking at her and trying to ignore the continuing sensation of being watched.

"You should write a book."

I bent down and kissed her on the forehead before pulling her into my arms. Her body fit perfectly against mine. "I know this is a weird place to propose, and I don't have a ring yet, but I don't want to wait. Will you marry me?"

"Are you sure that's what you want? You'll be tied down."

I took her face in my hands. "You know I don't care about that. I want to be tied to you. I love you and I want to live the rest of my life with you. Is that what you want too?"

"Yes." She leaned up to brush her lips over mine. "I want to be with you. I want to be your wife."

"I love you, Nova."

She squeezed my hand. "I love you, too, Gage."

We entered the cemetery through an opening in its wrought-iron fence, our feet squishing on the muddy grass. With Nova next to me, it even eerier it had earlier. Before, the Unseen had seemed to watch me as I ran toward her. Now, I could almost feel its fingers on the back of my neck. The fog moved, wisps and curls of it coiling around our legs.

I took out my flashlight so we could see where we were going. We were doing this, sentient fog or not. There was no way I'd back down now.

"I finished your songs," I said, mainly as a distraction from the nasty atmosphere.

"You did? Can I hear them?" She swung our clasped hands back and forth.

"As soon as we get home."

"That's so cool. I can't believe you wrote songs for me."

"I had to pay you back for the pictures."

We were talking softly, as if we didn't want to wake up the people sleeping in the nearby houses. Except there weren't any people sleeping nearby. Just empty space, and that Declan dude, wherever he was.

A pang of guilt shot through me at the way we were leaving him behind. Maybe he really was a human, trapped here in this not-quite-dead, not-quite-living world the way Nova had been. If so, we were doing a shitty thing in leaving him. But I couldn't sacrifice my chance to save Nova just to help someone when I wasn't even sure whether he was a demon or a person. I couldn't do it.

"Your friend," I said as we headed into the bushes that surrounded the corpse house. "This Declan guy. We'll come back for him."

She shot me a wide-eyed glance. "You'd do that?"

"Yeah. I don't want to leave an innocent dude in a place like this. But I've got to get you home first."

Chapter 22
Games

Gage:

The corpse house was hidden in a bank of fog so thick I could barely tell where it was supposed to be. Only the dark shingles and angles of its roof showed over the top of the white, and even that was mostly lost in the shadows of the giant trees all around us. I squeezed Nova's hand to let her know we were almost there. Almost to safety.

She looked up at me and smiled. Soon, we'd be back in Avery's Crossing. We'd go back to the house and drink some hot tea or whatever Nova wanted. We'd talk and laugh because the danger would be over. And then we'd go upstairs and make love until we were too sore to move.

Our feet made low squishing, slipping noises on the slippery mud and grass and dead leaves. I smelled the same odor I'd noticed before, when I'd come through. That crypt smell. It was stronger here, in the cemetery, and especially by the corpse house.

A shiver crawled up my spine. That smell bothered me. But I wasn't going to stop now, or even slow down. If anything, the stench made me want wish I could burst into a dead run and if it hadn't been for my twisted ankle, I would have.

"Not long now," I whispered as I stepped onto the stone stoop and grabbed hold of the doorknob. I let go of Nova's hand to do that.

As I opened the door, I swung my flashlight beam ahead to illuminate the interior. The beam fell upon a man. I stopped short and Nova bumped into me with a gasp. She shrank against my side.

The man—it was him. Lucifer. Not a man at all. His pale hair and eyes looked nearly colorless in the bluish light of the flashlight. He was leaning up against the table, his arms crossed, a smirk on his face. Chills raced all over my body.

"You didn't think I'd really let you go, did you?" he said.

"Yeah, I did."

He laughed. "Gage, you still don't understand how this works."

Sick rage boiled up inside me. I loathed him with a fire I'd never felt for anyone before. Rage and despair choked me, stole my voice. I stared at him, grinding my teeth, wishing I could tear out his throat with my bare hands.

He grinned. "You look so disappointed."

"Let me go," Nova said, staring at him, trembling in my embrace. "You've had your little joke. It's time to let me go."

"But I like having you here."

140

"So what? You know I don't belong here and you have no claim over me. Let me go home."

He tapped his forefinger against his chin. I recognized that gesture from the night he'd taken her from me. Arrogant prick.

"I see no reason why I should let you go," he said. "You've provided me with hours of entertainment. What am I going to do without you?"

"Torture some poor souls in hell," she said. "Isn't that your job?"

"Actually, it isn't. My job is to test people for God. But never mind that. You're here because of a deal Gage's mother made. I accepted that deal in good faith and now I find I'm about to be cheated of my profit. I don't think that's fair. Do you think that's fair?"

"Yes," she said. "I do. You know the deal is false. You always knew. Quit playing games."

He pouted. Like, literally stuck his lower lip out. "You're ruining my fun."

"Poor baby." Nova took a step toward him.

"Don't!" I caught her elbow and tried to yank her back.

"What's he going to do to me? He's already made me a prisoner."

"I don't know and I don't want to find out," I said. I glowered at him, wishing once again that I could destroy him somehow. "What do you want from me? Take something from me, not her. She's innocent."

"And you're not?" he said with a mocking smile.

"What do you want? Name your price."

Lucifer cocked his pale head and studied me, his gaze traveling from my head to my boots and back again. Once again, just like the other time I'd met him, I got that sensation of cold fingers crawling over my body. There were more of them this time. They seemed intent on feeling out every nook and cranny of me. I gritted my teeth, fighting the urge to rub my hands over myself.

"Do you know how to play that thing?" he said, nodding toward my guitar.

I bit back an impatient growl. "I think you know I do."

"Such confidence." He grinned suddenly, and I didn't like the expression on him. "Play me a song."

"Huh?"

"I want a song. If it's good enough, I'll let Nova go."

"That's it? You just want me to play one song and you'll let Nova go?" I said, un-slinging the case.

"Hmm." He tapped his finger against his chin again. "Now that you mention it, that does seem too easy, doesn't it? Let's make it more challenging."

Nova shook her head at me, her brown eyes suspiciously moist. "No, Gage. Don't do it. You can't deal with him, you know that. He can't be trusted."

"What else would you have me do?"

"Leave me here. I'll be okay." She sounded brave, but I could see the fear in her eyes.

"No fucking way. I am not leaving you here. Don't ask me to do that." I unbuckled the case and drew out the guitar. "Do we have a deal?" I said to Lucifer.

"First, let me hear you play something," he said, staring intently at the instrument.

"All right." I should have been scared shitless, but just as when he showed up in my family room, I wasn't afraid. Just pissed off. I wanted him out of our lives.

I slung the strap of the guitar over my shoulder and played the intro to "You See Me", Nova's first song.

As I played, I glanced at Lucifer. His pale face went even paler. He stared at my guitar in what looked like horror.

"Where did you get that thing?" he said.

"I found it. Why?"

"Get rid of it. I don't want it here."

"I'm not throwing it away," I said. "No. You wanted me to play and I'm playing."

"Not with that thing. I can't have that object in my realm." He reached for it. At the last instant, he snatched his hand back as if simply being near the guitar had burned him. "Fine. Keep it. But you can't play it for her."

"Why not?" I snapped. "You're playing one of your fucking games again. I should have known you'd have no honor."

Lucifer drew himself upright, with every appearance of being deeply wounded and offended by my statement. Either he was a much better actor than me, or he was really insulted.

"I am not going back on my word. I simply despise the sound of that thing." He gestured at my guitar. "It is out of harmony with this place. If you want to play for Nova's soul, you'll need a different instrument."

I looked at Nova and rolled my eyes. "Fine. What guitar would you like me to play?"

"I'll provide one for you."

"With actual strings?" I said. "A real guitar that makes real music?"

"Of course. And there's one other thing." His glass-clear eyes glittered in the low light. "You'll play not just for me but for all the denizens of hell. If you can calm them, you'll win Nova. If not, then I'll keep her with me. Is that clear?"

"You want me to do what?" I said.

Nova shouted "no!" at the same time.

Lucifer merely grinned. "I believe you heard me. But just to clarify—I'll bring you into hell. You will play an instrument of my choosing. If you can successfully stop the inhabitants from their constant moaning, screaming, crying and retching, then you may have your girl. If not, then I will keep her."

"You must be crazy," I growled.

"Perhaps. Do we have a deal?"

I didn't trust him. He was probably hiding something from me. "How long do I have to make them quiet?"

His gaze lifted up and to one side, as if he had to think about that. "Let's say for the duration of one song," he said.

"One song? How do you define a song?"

His grin sharpened. "You're getting better at this. Shall we say, all known verses plus any refrain?"

"Once through," I said. "No more than that."

"Done."

I gritted my teeth. I still didn't trust him. Not for a half second. "How do I know you won't cheat?"

Lucifer lost his grin. His pale brows came down. "I never cheat. I don't need to."

"You're just the soul of honor and chivalry, is that it?"

His grin reappeared. "Yes, pretty much. Do we have a deal, then?"

I blew out all my breath. "Fine. Okay. We have a deal."

"Nova will stay here," Lucifer said. "While you accompany me to hell."

"Gage?" Nova grabbed my hand.

"No," I said. "She comes too. I don't want to be separated from her."

"I'm afraid this is non-negotiable. She stays here or the deal is off." Lucifer shrugged. "Take it or leave it. Either way, I get your girl."

Fuck. That.

"Fine. Nova, wait here. I'm sure this will only take a few minutes."

"What if time runs differently there?" she said, clinging to my hand. "What if you get back and I'm an old lady? I couldn't stand that."

"I give you my word," Lucifer said. "That won't happen. The events in hell and the time in this place will run concordantly. I swear it."

I shoved my fingers through my hair. "Jesus."

"Please, Gage."

"Baby, what choice do we have? He's not going to let you go unless I do this thing."

She raised a trembling hand to her eyes and wiped away a tear. "Okay. I'll stay here. But—"

"You must stay inside this building," Lucifer said. "If you leave, Gage won't be able to find you ever again. Do you understand? You must stay here."

She nodded slowly. "Yes. I understand. I'll stay in this building while I wait."

He gave her a benevolent-looking smile that was as false as a celebutante's eyelashes. "Good girl. I like you, Nova."

"Can we just get this over with?" I said, un-slinging my guitar. "Here, babe. Keep this safe for me, would you?"

***

Nova:

One instant, Gage and Lucifer were standing in the corpse house with me. In the next instant, they were gone and I was alone. I clutched the guitar to my chest, the flashlight gripped precariously in my other hand.

It was too quiet in here. The only sound I could hear was my own breathing. No frogs. Too cold for crickets. There weren't even any owls or coyotes. Or wolves. I would have taken a couple of wolves howling as company over this deathly silence.

I blew out a breath. The air inside the little house smelled stale, like dry rot and mildew, and I hated that smell. I could almost taste it, the stench was so strong. I'd rather be outside with the gravestones than in here, in this creepy little room with its even creepier table.

What was that table for, anyway? I couldn't figure out this building. It was too small for anyone to live in and besides there was only the one room. No fireplace, no kitchen of any kind. This was not and had never been a home.

So what was it? I wasn't sure I wanted the answer to that question.

Oh, yeah. Declan had told me they used to keep bodies in the cellar. On ice. Lovely. I supposed they displayed them on that table in the middle of the room, for relatives to come and see them before the burials.

Ugh. I was shut inside an otherworldly, semi-historical morgue or funeral home.

Suddenly, the face of the woman I'd seen in the window came back to me. I shuddered. What if she returned? What if she'd never left?

Oh, God. I so did not want to be here. I wanted Gage. Now. But he was busy saving my skin, so I had to be a big girl and get through this trial by myself.

Don't go outside, Lucifer had said. Or I'd be lost forever.

Okay, fine. I wouldn't go outside. I'd stay in here, because I sure as hell didn't want to be lost forever.

What did that even mean? Never mind. I didn't need clarification.

I slumped against the wall, as far away as I could get from that nasty table. Slowly, I sank to the cold, hard floor. There had to be some way to pass the time while I waited.

The guitar bumped against my hip. I hugged it to me, arranging it on my lap. There was no way I'd ever be as good as Gage, but I could play a few songs. That would distract me from my fears and with luck would make the time pass more quickly.

Setting the flashlight upright on the floor next to me, I positioned my fingers for the first chord, lifted my right hand to strum. An odd sound caught my attention, like a soft, low scrape.

I turned my head, peering into the shadows in the corners of the room. "Hello?" I said, like one of those idiots in a typical horror movie.

As if the thing that's coming for you is going to stop and make conversation.

Naturally, there was no answer except another of those scraping noises, mixed in with an eerie rustling sound. Scrape ... rustle ... scrape ... rustle ... scrape. It sounded like feet shuffling or dragging over the floorboards. The flashlight flickered.

Sweat broke out all over my body. "What do you want?" I said, my voice all thin and weak.

Scrape ... rustle ... scrape ... rustle ... scrape...

The flashlight flickered again and went out, leaving me in utter blackness.

Holy shit. I pressed my back against the wall as my heart rate zoomed off the chart. Whatever that thing was, I couldn't leave the building to get away from it or I'd be lost. I'd never see Gage again. But I couldn't just sit here and wait for whatever the thing was to get me.

"Nova?"

I gave a violent start. The voice sounded high and girlish, but it wasn't a child's voice. It was more like a teenager who thinks she needs to sound sweet and cute.

"Go away." I clutched the guitar to my chest again, like a shield.

"Nova? Are you there?"

Oh, God. Oh, God.

I shook my head so hard my hair flopped around. "Go away. Leave me alone."

"Nohh-va," the girlish voice sang. "Nohhh-va. Are you there? Come out, come out, wherever you are."

Maybe she—it—couldn't see me. I scooted my butt along the floor to the left, in the opposite direction from the voice. The scraping and rustling sounds followed, slowly, unevenly. As if she couldn't quite make her feet work correctly.

I swallowed through the dry knot in my throat. *She's just a ghost. She can't hurt you.*

Except I had no idea if that was true, especially in this place. Ghosts might have a lot more power here than in the normal world.

"Nohhh-va," she crooned. "Why are you hiding from me? I only want to play."

I scooted farther to my left. "I-I don't like playing."

"Yes, you do." She followed me.

If only I could see what was going on. Except then I'd be able to see *her*, and I wasn't so sure I wanted that.

"He said you would play a game with me," she said in her childlike voice.

That high-pitched, wispy tone gave me the creeps almost as much as the scraping sound of her ghostly feet. There was something so wrong about it.

"He lied," I said, scooting a couple more feet to the left.

"No, he didn't." She almost sang the words.

Gage's guitar bumped against the floorboards as I scooted away from her again. We were going to go around and around like this. I could tell.

Please get back, Gage.

My silent plea didn't do me any good, of course. Gage couldn't hear me and had no idea what was happening to me. I only hoped he was doing all right wherever he was.

Hell. That's where he is.

If he could survive a trip to hell, then surely I could stand up to a sweet-voiced girl ghost.

Chapter 23

Hell

Gage:

I blinked and the corpse house was gone. Along with my flashlight, my guitar, Nova, everything else I knew or cared about. I sat on the stone floor of an immense cavern of some kind. At least, I thought it was a cavern, although I couldn't see the ceiling or even the floor, although it resided just underneath my ass.

I gazed around myself, trying to make sense out of what I saw and felt. Violent, searing heat, for one thing. The air smelled just as I'd thought it would—it stank of sulfur, like a hundred million rotten eggs. Lucifer and I were perched on a rocky outcropping, poised over what seemed to be a black pit of nothingness, except there were beings suspended in the pit.

Monstrous beings. One seemed to be mostly an enormous mouth full of lava or molten metal. Human figures writhed in the heat of whatever filled the creature's mouth, their faces contorted with horror. I shuddered and recoiled from the sight.

"Gives you pause, doesn't it?" Lucifer said. "At least, I can tell it does for you. Me, it doesn't really affect. If anything, I find it satisfying."

"You are sick."

He smiled pleasantly, although the warmth never reached his eyes. "Do you think so?"

"Yes, I do. No offense, but there's something wrong with you."

"And yet I am essential to the shape of the universe."

Uh huh. Forgive me if I doubted that.

"Do you have a guitar for me or not?" I said, keeping my gaze away from the horrific sights in front of me.

"Impatience is such a human trait." He reached behind himself and drew out a guitar from the shadows. "Here you go. See what you can do with that."

I took the guitar from him. It was a super-glossy black with red accents, big like my own. I ran a fingertip over the sound-box.

So... hell. I was in hell, but not as a permanent resident. Never thought I'd be able to say that.

The place was exactly what I'd expected, and nothing like I'd expected. It was dark, for one thing, in spite of the flames I saw flickering everywhere. The fire seemed to give off tremendous amounts of heat but very little light. And there was noise. So much noise— screeches, howls, agonized screams, and underneath it all a deep, dark muttering that seemed to come from the place itself rather than any one of its inhabitants.

I stared out at the pit. In spite of the darkness, I could somehow see each and every one of the beings suspended in it. Some of them were beasts, bizarre creatures that could never exist in the ordinary world. And some of them looked human.

The weirdest thing was that the humans couldn't seem to see each other. Even those who floated within an arm's reach of another person behaved as if alone. They never looked at each other, never tried to speak to each other, and certainly didn't touch. It was as if they were blind to the other humans, yet they looked at the demon-creatures with more terror than I'd ever seen on a human face.

A man who looked about my own age drifted close to a monster with an enormous, distorted head that looked something like a crocodile's and a body like a horse. The human shrieked, flailing his arms and legs as if he thought he could swim away from the crocodile-horse thing. Of course, it was no use. He drifted closer and closer no matter how hard he tried to escape.

I clenched my hands against my sides, unable to look away from the unbearable sight. The poor fuck just couldn't help himself no matter what he did. Some kind of current had him in its power, drawing him toward the crocodile-headed creature.

When he drew close enough, it opened massive jaws filled with teeth the size of kitchen knives, and clamped down on his torso. His gurgling scream filled the air and made me shudder. I wanted to howl too.

This place was like a Hieronymus Bosch painting come to life, horrible and riveting and nauseating. I couldn't even imagine being stuck here for eternity.

Was this really the destination of people who did bad shit in their lives? Was this a fair punishment? How much evil did a person have to do before he deserved something as awful as what I'd just witnessed?

"Amazing scenery, huh?" Lucifer said in a pleasant, conversational tone.

I turned my head to stare at him. "How could anyone deserve what I just saw?"

He tilted his head. "Feeling sorry for the sinners, Gage?"

"Just answer the question."

"It's not so much a matter of what they deserve. It's more a matter of what they've created for themselves."

"I don't understand."

"I know." He grinned at me.

I hated that grin. "So you're telling me that the people who end up here have created this?"

"Not exactly."

"Of course not. Do you ever just answer a question straight, or do you always have to sidestep and evade?"

"Of course I do."

I narrowed my eyes. "Which one?"

He grinned again. "All of them. Are you ready to play?"

"I need a mike," I said.

"They'll hear it. Just play."

I settled the guitar on my knees. It was a dreadnought style, like my own, except this one had that glossy black body and red accents. Not very imaginative, right? Black and red, just what you'd expect Lucifer's guitar to look like. He should have made it pink with sparkly unicorns or some shit.

I grinned at the thought and gave the strings an experimental strum. Perfectly in tune, just like mine. That must be the way magical guitars worked.

"Something funny?" Lucifer said.

I glanced at him sidelong. "Nope. Just enjoying a beautiful instrument."

"Ah." His pale eyes betrayed nothing.

Sometimes when the dude looked at me, he reminded me of a shark. I'd seen them, live ones, in aquariums. Their eyes have this glassy coldness, a complete lack of expression, that makes them seem even scarier than they already do. It's like there's nothing and nobody home except the urge to kill.

Now, maybe that's not true for sharks. Maybe they have a ton of emotional depth and we humans just can't see it because their faces are impossible for us to read. And maybe it's not even true for Lucifer. But I can tell you that it feels true. That bastard feels colder than absolute zero.

I cast my gaze out over the pit and all the hapless souls floating there. The horrific noise, which I'd managed to mentally block for a few minutes, slammed down over me like a killer wave and I shuddered and broke out in a sweat. What if I couldn't do it? What if I couldn't calm them down at all?

I mean, I wasn't a real player, a real musician. I was just a hobbyist. I didn't even perform for anyone except a handful of friends. What the fuck made me think I could pull this off?

I was going to lose Nova forever.

All my life, I'd been a fake, a fraud. Everybody thought I had the juice, the talent or skill or whatever it takes to succeed. And the whole time, I'd known I was just a fake. I'd never, not once, really known what I was doing as an actor.

There had been so many times I'd wanted to run. To just change my name, hide somewhere nobody knew me, and pretend to be normal. Hell, just be normal. Because I wasn't anything special and I knew it. If only the rest of the world would realize that, but they were all fooled because of The Deal.

Every movie I'd done, I'd had to pretend I knew what I was doing. Pretend I knew how to make a character come alive, when really all I did was memorize lines and do what the director told me to do. Like a trained dog.

Music had been something private that I did only to please myself. It wasn't even important enough to call it a sideline. I didn't take it that seriously. I mean, I practiced, sure, but only for the pleasure of it.

So now I was supposed to pull some kind of magical musical ability out of my ass? I was supposed to soothe the savage breast with my glorious playing? I closed my eyes. Nova and I were both completely fucked, and all because of my overconfidence.

The Deal was bogus all along. You succeeded on your own merit, according to Old Nick there.

True. He had told me that, with a certain delight in the fact that my mom and I had contorted our lives around the idea of this Deal when it was fake the whole time. It might as well have been real, though, for all the damage it caused us.

"You gonna play that thing or just cuddle it all night?" Lucifer said. "Not that I care. The longer you delay, the more likely that Nova will end up staying with me."

Fucker.

My eyes popped open. Right in front of me, in the pit, a demon creature hung suspended in mid-air. It looked a lot like a monstrous frog, except it had wicked-looking claws on its webbed feet. Its huge frog-mouth hung open and inside it was filled with what seemed to be molten metal. I'd seen a similar creature when I'd first arrived.

The surface of the metal glowed orange and yellow, with a few darker spots where it had cooled. There were human figures partially submerged in that metal. They looked crisped, blackened by the heat, yet not dead.

Duh, of course they were dead. But they were still conscious, here, of their pain. Their faces and limbs twisted and writhed in agony, and just like those other humans I'd seen, they didn't seem to be aware of each other.

I had to soothe that? Impossible.

What choice is there? Either play something or give up on Nova.

Yeah. That was my choice. Try and fail, or give up and fail.

I wished Nova could hear me play this. At least then she'd know how I felt about her. I'd said the words, but this was different.

I played a simple tune I'd done a million times, just to get a feel for the instrument. It seemed stiff, the notes flat, without depth.

Glaring at Lucifer, I said, "you gave me a piece of crap instrument. You're not playing fair."

"Who said I had to play fair?" He grinned that shark-like grin.

There was no way I could make magic with this thing. I scowled at the guitar. I was going to fail. Who could respond to music coming out of this? It looked expensive, but either it was cheaply made or it was just a dud. Or maybe Lucifer had created an inferior piece on purpose to screw with me.

Problem was, I didn't have a choice. This was the guitar I had to play, or else give up on her forever. And I couldn't do that; I couldn't give up.

So I'd play, no matter how wooden and crappy it sounded. I'd make it an offering for her. Even if I lost her, this would be my offering to her, the last thing I would ever say to her.

Quit being such a maudlin bastard and play the damn thing.

"Nova, this is for you," I whispered, and began to play.

Chapter 24
Soothing The Damned

Nova:

Gage was gone and I was alone with a ghost. I couldn't see anything at all. Only blackness, pressing in against my eyeballs. But I could hear.

The scraping, sliding noise came again, drawing closer and closer and closer. I caught my breath, struggling not to scream like a fool. I'd handled Jeremy's ghost with ease, and I'd faced down that thing that had attacked me in my art building, so why was I being such a freaking wimp over this? What's-her-name was just another ghost, right?

Easy peasy. I could handle myself around ghosts.

She whispered my name again and I bolted. I crawled on one hand and both knees, my right hand clamped around Gage's guitar. No way was I letting go of the guitar.

"He promised me you'd play," she whined.

A rustle of cloth followed, as if she were dressed in very full skirts. I scrambled a few more feet in the thick blackness of the little building, cursing the flashlight that had abandoned me.

Or maybe her ghostly presence had stolen its light. I didn't know and really it didn't matter. I just wanted the damned thing back and fully functional.

"Nohh-va," she sang out softly.

I was thoroughly sick of the sound of my name in her voice.

"Shut up," I snapped, scuffling a little farther away from her.

"That's not very nice."

I slammed my shoulder into something hard on my right. A grunt of pain and shock escaped me. I reached out and touched the wall, felt cool plaster and wood. The wood felt like—yes, it was vertical—the molding around the doorjamb. I'd found the door.

"I just want to play," she said.

She was so close now. So close that I could smell the sickly sweet stench of death on her. I pinched my nose shut, but not before the odor made me gag.

My hand traveled along the cool, smooth wood of the door. Up and up until I found the knob. The hard brass felt like heaven under my hand. I had the way out. I could escape.

Thank God. I was going to get out of here, away from her. My spirits rose in a giddy surge.

I turned the knob.

No. You'll be separated from Gage forever if you leave the building.

Shit. Shit. Lucifer had said if I left this building I'd be stuck in his half-world forever. I couldn't leave. No matter what happened.

I stopped, my hand still clasped around the cold brass. Behind me, she shuffled closer, her skirts softly rustling, the stink of rotting flesh drifting up from her like some kind of disgusting perfume.

"Nova? Don't you want to play with me?" she said, her voice plaintive.

Cold, damp fingers brushed my cheek. I whimpered. I couldn't help it; she felt not like a ghost but like a corpse. A dead body.

Corpse house.

They had laid bodies out here, probably many of them. Decades and decades worth. And this particular body had been one of the revolting little house's temporary occupants.

"Nova?" she said again.

"H-how do you know m-my name?"

"He told me. He told me your name and said you would play with me. I'm lonely here all by myself. It gets so lonely, you know?"

"I'll bet," I whispered.

Poor kid. It's not her fault Lucifer is using her to mess with my head.

I had to master my fear. Surely Gage would be done playing soon and we could leave this place. Until then, I had to hold out no matter what happened.

"W-what's your name?" I said, my voice barely audible.

"Isabella." Now she sounded even sadder.

"How old are you, Isabella?"

"Fourteen. How old are you?"

She had died at the age of fourteen? God, that was sad. I wondered what had killed her.

"I'm twenty-two," I said, trying not to give away my sadness and fear.

"Do you like to play games?"

I swallowed, trying not to gag at her smell. "Sure. Yeah, I like to play games."

"Oh, goody." She clapped her ghostly, rotting hands together.

The poor chick didn't seem to know she was dead. How could that be? Couldn't she smell herself? Maybe she was used to it after all this time, or maybe her nose didn't work anymore.

Just how long had she been here anyway? Probably since the day she'd died, but I had no idea when that had been. Maybe I could find out from her.

"So, um, Isabella, do you know what year it is?"

"Don't you know?"

153

"I forgot. I've been really forgetful lately." Boy, wasn't that the truth.

"It's eighteen sixty-four, silly."

"Oh, right. Eighteen sixty-four. How could I forget that?"

She giggled. She seemed kind of silly and childish for fourteen, but maybe she was wrong in the head. Or maybe kids were different back then; I had no idea. History wasn't my strong suit.

"What kind of games do you like to play?" I said.

Part of me gaped in utter amazement that I could sit here and talk to a ghost or revenant or whatever she was, all casual like she was just another person. Another part of me still wanted to run and hide. But I couldn't leave the building, so running wasn't an option.

"You have a guitar," she said.

"Yeah. It belongs to my boyfriend."

Her skirts rustled again. "What's that?"

"A boyfriend?" I searched for a more old-fashioned way to describe Gage. "Um, he's like my suitor, I guess you'd say."

"Oh, you have a suitor! Is he handsome?" she said in a dreamy voice.

"Extremely."

"Can you play his guitar? I love music."

Was Lucifer keeping this innocent girl in hell? Why? I couldn't understand how she'd come to be trapped here or what a girl her age could have possibly done to deserve this fate. But then Declan hadn't deserved his fate either.

"Yeah, I can play a little," I said after an awkward pause.

"Would you play something for me?"

＊＊＊

Gage:

The heat hammered at me, drawing sweat out of me in rivers. The rotten-egg smell no longer made me want to gag, though. I think my nose had given up and was now playing dead.

I improvised a long intro to the first song, as a kind of warm-up. The noise, the howls, continued on as if nobody could hear a note I played. And maybe they couldn't. Maybe Old Nick had lied about that part. There wasn't much I could do about it now, so I told myself it didn't matter.

All I had to do was play. The rest of it was up to Fate, or God, or someone. Not me, though.

Sometimes when you start a session, you're not really feeling it. You're just going through the motions, almost like a musical robot, playing note after note with no emotional involvement, no love. And

154

then it sort of creeps into you, the music does. It steals inside you and strokes you from the inside, softens you, makes you come alive in some way you weren't before.

When that happens, whatever it is that stands between you and the music, it just dissolves away into nothing. That's when you kinda forget who you are, what you're supposed to be doing and how you're supposed to be doing it. There's no *supposed to* anymore. There's just the notes, the rhythm.

Music is more than words, more than thoughts. It's thoughts and feelings given sonic form, so they get inside you and change you before you even know you've been touched.

The songs flowed out of me, one after the other, like they were connected, part of each other and part of me and I was part of them and there wasn't anything between me and the notes. No boundary, no thought, nothing but feeling and sound.

My voice soared, and caught, and rasped, and I didn't care. I didn't care how it sounded, I just let it flow out of me. In the notes was my love for Nova. All of it. Every moment of yearning or laughter or tenderness or passion, it all flowed out through me and the guitar.

The last note faded into silence. I opened eyes I hadn't realized I'd closed.

Silence.

The hell noise had stopped. The howling, screaming, groaning awfulness had paused at some point during my play and I hadn't even known it. The creatures, the demons, all stared at me, their glowing eyes fixed on me with expressions I couldn't read.

How do you interpret the facial expressions of demons?

The human figures—they stared at me too. All of them, at least the ones I could see. They faced me, and they were still, not writhing anymore.

I looked at Lucifer. His pale brows were crimped together, his eyes strangely vulnerable. The shark-like coldness was gone.

"You have given them a gift," he said.

I slung my arm over the narrow part of the guitar body. "They're quiet."

"Yes." He nodded soberly.

"Are you going to honor your side of the deal?"

"I told you," he said, frowning. "I always keep my word."

"So Nova and I can go back to our world and you'll leave us alone?"

He held my gaze, his eyes back to their usual expressionless state. Was he going to refuse me? Was this all just another elaborate joke with a totally un-amusing punchline?

The sour, acid taste of bile—I was beginning to be all too familiar with it—rose in my throat. If he denied me, if he took Nova away again, I didn't know what I'd do. How do you fight the devil?

Just as I thought he was going to say no, he nodded.

"Yes, Gage, I will honor our agreement. You and Nova are free to go."

I peered at him. "And you won't harass us anymore?"

He cocked his head. "Won't you miss me?"

"Not at all."

"Ah, you wound me," he said, pressing his hand to his chest.

"I doubt that. Are you going to harass us?"

"No. I will not harass you, nor will I send anyone else to harass you."

I held the guitar out to him. "Then I'd like to rejoin Nova, please."

Chapter 25

Returns

Nova:

Isabella leaned close to me in the blackness of the Tool House. I couldn't see her, couldn't see anything. But I could feel her cold presence. I could smell her.

Her breath stank the worst, like a disgusting blend of ancient crypt and open sewer. It gave me shudders, but I didn't want her to notice that. I started breathing through my mouth to shut out the stench.

"You play beautifully," Isabella said. "I used to play the piano."

"Did you?" Now I sounded like I had a bad cold.

"Yes, but there aren't any pianos around here," she said wistfully.

"No, I suppose not."

We sat together in silence for a few minutes, lost in our own thoughts. I wondered what kind of thoughts a ghost or revenant has. Was she remembering her real life?

I heard some soft notes playing somewhere nearby. It sounded like a guitar. I'd set Gage's instrument down next to me as I took a break.

"Isabella, are you playing the guitar now?" I said.

"No. It isn't me. It's your suitor."

My hands tightened into fists. Was she right? Was it Gage? How could we hear him if he was in hell with Lucifer?

But then he began to sing, and I knew it was really him. I recognized his voice, and the words. They were all about me.

> *The mask*
> *It covers me*
> *No-one can see me*
> *I'm invisible*
> *But you see*
> *You see me*
>
> *The stage*
> *It defines me*
> *It tells me who I am*
> *I'm nothing inside*
> *You know me*
>
> *They look at me*
> *And they see the mask*
> *They see who they want to see*

Smile and pretense
But you see
You see me

They say they love me
They love the mask
They love a fantasy
But you love
You love me

God. The beauty of the notes and his voice, the beauty of the words, all made my breath catch and tears spring up in my eyes. But he shouldn't feel as if he wasn't good enough for me. That was wrong. He was more than good enough.

He started a second song, one I hadn't heard at all until now.

Hollow
I was hollow when I met you
And you filled me up
All the empty spaces inside me
Filled with you
Filled with you

Filled
I'm filled with you
Hot
I'm hot with you
Open
I'm open with you
Hold me together, baby

Cold
I was cold when I met you
And you warmed me
All the frozen pieces of me
Hot with you
Hot with you

Alone
I was alone when I met you
And you took me in
All the walled off heart of me
Open to you

Open to you

Broken
I was broken when I met you
And you made me whole
All the fractured shards of me
Joined by you
Joined by you

Filled
I'm filled with you
Hot
I'm hot with you
Open
I'm open to you
Joined
I'm joined by you

Filled
I'm filled with you
Hot
I'm hot with you
Open
I'm open with you
Hold me together, baby

Tears ran down my face now. He'd written that for me. About me.

He sang a third song, and I barely heard it. I was too busy sniffling over the first two. I'd even forgotten to be afraid of my ghostly companion. All I could think of was Gage.

The music stopped. Isabella gasped, her skirts rustling again. "He's coming."

"Who? Who's coming?" God, were there more phantoms hanging around? Maybe worse ones than Isabella?

"Him," she said, with emphasis. "I have to go."

"Isabella?" I said into the darkness, but I got no answer.

Light flared in the tiny room, so brightly it hurt my eyes. I threw my hand up to shield myself from it. If it was something dangerous, what would I do? I couldn't leave the building without getting lost.

Heavy feet thudded across the floorboards toward me. I cringed backward, afraid to uncover my eyes. Isabella had scared the crap out of me at first, and now I wanted her back. I liked her. She was just a lonely kid; this newcomer—I didn't know who or what it was and I didn't want to know.

Warm, living hands grasped my elbows. A familiar scent teased my nose.

"Nova," Gage said.

My eyes flew open. I dropped the guitar and threw myself at him. His arms closed around me as I clung to his tight, narrow waist.

"Are you all right?" he murmured. "What happened? You're shaking."

"There was a ghost," I said. "She scared me."

"It's okay now. I'm here. There aren't any ghosts anymore."

I pried my eyes open. The light seemed to come from behind him. I didn't want to let him go, so I buried my face against his chest and breathed in the clean, healthy male smell of him. His heart beat fast and hard under my ear and his shirt felt damp with sweat.

"You came back," I said. "Does that mean it worked?"

"Yes." His whole body gave a shudder. "Yeah, it worked. Lucifer says we're free to go."

"Do you believe him?"

"Nova, I always keep my promises," Lucifer said.

I jerked out of Gage's embrace. Behind him stood the devil, looking as pale and handsome as ever. The light came from a candle lantern he held in one hand. In the other, he had a gigantic black guitar.

"So you're really letting us go home?" I said.

"Yes, I am. But you might want to hurry before I change my mind."

Gage and I looked at each other. He looked as alarmed as I felt.

"Let's go," he said.

"Wait. Just a minute." I fixed Lucifer with a glare. "What about Isabella?"

"What about her?"

"Is she in hell?"

He smiled blandly. "She most certainly is."

"What? Why?"

"She murdered her entire family, Nova. Poisoned them at dinner. Unfortunately for her, the poison killed her as well. I think she forgot how many dishes she'd put it in."

I shivered. "She seemed so nice."

"Many of them do."

"What about Declan? Did he do something awful too?"

"Declan is what you might call insurance. I won't be letting him go, so don't get any rescue ideas."

I bent my head at the thought of Declan living on, completely alone, isolated in this strange non-place. "He deserves better."

"If you want to go home, you might consider leaving immediately," Lucifer said. "Because my patience is wearing out."

"Let's go, baby," Gage said, tugging at me. "There's nothing you can do for Declan."

It wasn't right, but at the moment what could I do? Lucifer didn't want to give him up. Maybe someday we could find a way to rescue him, though.

"Okay," I said, feeling another stab of guilt at abandoning my friend. "Let's go home."

***

Driving up to the house Gage had bought felt like something in a dream. Surreal, almost other-worldly. The long, country-style driveway had no lights and we were out in the middle of farmland, so it didn't seem all that different from the world I'd just left. Aside from the fact I hadn't ridden in a car in what felt like forever, the world seemed as silent and empty of human occupation as ever.

But then we pulled to a stop in front of the house. There was another car in the driveway, an old blue minivan. Inside the house, lights burned. The place looked alive, welcoming, happy. I looked over at Gage and smiled.

He grinned at me. "You're back. You're here with me."

"I can hardly believe it."

"Let's go inside. It looks like Brad and Marie and the others are still here."

"What are they doing here?" I said, puzzled.

"They helped me get you back," he said. "Come on. They'll be really jazzed to have you back."

We got out of the car. The shutting doors sounded incredibly loud in the still night air. I could smell the fir trees and cedars that surrounded the house.

Gage took me by the hand as we walked to the house. I wished the others weren't here, because I wanted to get him alone. But they deserved my thanks for helping rescue me.

"There's one thing," Gage said as we reached the front door.

"What's that?"

"Call your parents. They think I murdered you."

I stopped dead in my tracks and stared at him. "What?"

"You disappeared and I couldn't explain where you'd gone. The cops came out and searched the house."

"Oh, my God." My eyes widened. "I'm so sorry."

He shrugged. "It's all right. I can't blame them for worrying about you, but I couldn't tell them what really happened."

"No kidding. I'll call them right away."

It felt like real life was smacking me in the face.

I stood on the wide front porch and used Gage's phone to make the call to my mom. Gage stood at my elbow.

"You can go inside if you want to," I said as the phone started ringing on the other end.

"No way. I'm staying with you."

"Are you sure?" I said, wrinkling my forehead.

"Absolutely. I'm not going anywhere without you."

I think he was afraid to let me out of his sight.

The phone started ringing. I tensed, thinking of what I would say to my parents. How could I explain a situation like this?

"Gage?" my mom said on the other end of the line. "Has there been any news?"

"Mom, it's me," I said.

There was a long pause. My heart beat loudly in my ear. My breath rasped in and out of my throat.

"Nova?" she said, her voice beginning to tremble. "Oh, my God, are you okay? Where are you?"

"I'm at the house. Where are you?"

"Dad and I are still at the hotel. We—your dad thought—where have you been? No-one would tell us where you went."

"That's because they didn't know. I—uh—I just needed some space, so I took off for a while." It was the only lie I could think of on such short notice.

Another long pause. "Space? You took off without your truck?"

I should have given my cover story more thought. "Yeah. You know, I really didn't think it through."

"Well, how did you get wherever it is that you went?" She sounded like she was starting to get mad.

"I—uh—I hitchhiked."

"You *what?* Nova, you know better than that. What in God's name were you thinking? You scared everyone half to death. Your dad practically accused Gage of murdering you. He called the cops and everything."

"I know. I'm sorry." I glanced at Gage and he winced. "I should have told someone where I was going. I didn't think."

"Don't you ever do that to us again."

"Of course not." I started to pace back and forth along the length of the front porch.

"I can hardly believe this," she said indignantly. "Just wait until your dad gets home."

I laughed. I know, totally inappropriate. But I couldn't help it; she sounded like she thought I was still eight years old.

"This isn't funny, Nova."

"Yeah, it is. I'm sorry I scared you, but I'm not a kid anymore. If I want to take off, I have that right. And I'm not happy with Dad at all. He had no business accusing Gage of hurting me."

My mother sighed. "You have no idea what it's like to lose your daughter."

"No, I don't. Mom, what happened—I wasn't—it was just something I had to do. I can't explain it any better than that, so don't ask me. I'm not going to talk about it anymore." I had to shut her down before she tried to get the whole story out of me.

"Your dad is going to have questions."

"I'm sure he will, but I won't be answering them. I can't. So just let it go."

"You're scaring me, Nova."

"I know. But that can't be helped. I have to go now, Mom. I'll see you and dad tomorrow, okay?"

I handed Gage his phone and he pulled me into a tight embrace. He felt warm and solid against me, like home. I put my arms around him and kissed him right where his shirt buttons were open and showing his warm skin. My lips hit the spot between his collarbones.

"She's mad at you," he said, playing with my hair.

"Oh, yeah. She thinks I just wandered off."

"I'm sorry I got you in trouble with your parents."

I smiled up at him. "You're a terrible influence. She'll probably ground me for a year."

"Let's go inside and let the others know you're okay."

The house seemed palatial compared to my little otherworld apartment. I'd been so proud of that place, at least until I'd figured out something was very wrong with it. The whole apartment could probably have fit into the foyer of this house Gage had bought. Okay, maybe not the foyer, but definitely the foyer plus the front porch. Or the kitchen.

Yes, our kitchen was bigger than my entire apartment had been.

I thought of Declan helping me bake Valentine's cookies and suddenly felt sick to my stomach. How many other people were trapped in that place?

Someone needed to help them.

We walked into the family room hand in hand. The monumental gray stone fireplace surround was just as I'd seen it in my dream, and a fire burned on the hearth. A small crowd of people filled the room—

Marie, Brad, Max, and two people I didn't know, a blond man and a blond woman with extremely curly hair.

Marie jumped to her feet from her place on the couch. "You did it, Gage!"

"Yeah," he said, grinning hugely. "I got her back."

Everyone crowded around us, all talking at once, patting me on the back, hugging Gage. He seemed so much more relaxed with Marie, Brad, and Max, as if he considered them true friends. Once, during the time we'd been snowed in at the cabin, he'd told me he didn't have any real friends, and here he was surrounded by them. It made me happy to see that.

From now on, Gage was going to live a healthy, normal life. Even if I did have to share him with Hollywood once in a while.

Chapter 26

Tzadqiel

Gage:

I stood in the family room gazing out at the back yard. A single light glowed out there, sending odd shadows across the lawn and up into the hedge that surrounded it and gave the house privacy. The darkness of night made me uneasy in a way it never had before—not for myself but for my girl. Lucifer had promised to leave us alone, but that didn't mean I wasn't worried.

It was one o'clock in the morning, and no-one showed any sign of wanting to go home. I couldn't blame them. They'd stood by me through a frightening challenge and risked their own safety to help me. But I did want to get some alone time with Nova.

She handed me a mug of coffee and smiled up at me as she slid her arm around my waist. My arm wrapped around her shoulders, holding her securely to my side. If I had my way, I wouldn't let go of her for at least a week.

"You look tired," she said.

"A little."

Something moved in the back yard. I tensed, thrusting my head forward as I stared at the shadows. There it was again—movement. As I focused on it, the shape resolved into a tall, dark figure lurking in our yard and staring into the house. Watching us.

"Gage?" Nova sounded worried. "What is it?"

"Hold this for a minute." I thrust the coffee back into her hand. "I'll be back in a few."

I strode toward the French doors that let onto the back area. I'd put a stop to this bullshit right here and now, or I'd die trying. The others turned to stare at me as I yanked the doors open and stormed outside. Damn Lucifer anyway.

Redundant, I know. But you get the idea. How dare he continue fucking with us after he'd given us his word? What was it going to take to get him to leave us alone?

I caught a whiff of spicy-sweet smoke and knew it was Suit Guy. Didn't he have anyone else to spy on?

"I know you're out here," I called.

He came strolling out of the shadows around the hedge, dressed in the same black suit, his cigarette giving off its usual fragrant clouds of smoke. "You saw me."

His voice was deep and mellow. Not exactly what I'd expected.

"Yeah, I saw you. Now fuck off. Your boss promised me he wasn't going to send anyone after us anymore."

Suit Guy's gaze focused intently on my face. His eyes were some dark color I couldn't make out in the low light. "My boss? You think I work for Lucifer?"

I blinked. "Don't you?"

He grinned, his teeth flashing white. "No. Not at all."

"Then who are you and why are you creeping around here? You're scaring my girlfriend."

His grin disappeared. "I'm sorry for that. I never meant to frighten her."

"Who do you work for if not Lucifer?" I said, taking a menacing step toward him. I was ready to pound him into the mud, just on principle.

He held up his hands. "You don't want to fight me."

"Who the fuck are you?" I got right in his face. "Who sent you?"

"Gage," he said gently. "I work for the opposite team."

"What?" Was he trying to claim he was an angel? "No. No way I'm buying that."

His shoulders lifted under the ebony jacket. "It doesn't matter whether you do or not. The fact is I was sent to watch and give what help I could."

"Nova almost got lost on the other side. Couldn't you have done a little more?"

"We're not supposed to interfere. I had very limited powers where you were concerned, but I did what I could."

I snorted and shook my head. "Sure."

"You got the guitar, didn't you?"

"That was you, huh? Figures. I saw you watching me on the street that day." And I'd been sure he was the devil himself, or at least some demon lieutenant.

"The guitar is a powerful tool. Take care of it."

"I thought it was Jeremy who sent it," I said, remembering how the homeless dude who'd given it to me had looked just like my dead best friend for an instant.

"He helped me out a little." Suit Guy stared at me with disarming sincerity. "He wanted to make sure you know he doesn't blame you for what happened to him."

I shrugged that off. What did an angel know, anyway?

"I should have done more to help him."

"Perhaps. But it's too late for that now, and Jeremy forgives you. Besides, the drugs he took were ultimately his responsibility. You know that, don't you?"

He didn't sugarcoat things, which I guessed was good. At least he was honest. But I did not want to have this conversation.

"Sure," I said. "Look, it's late and I'm tired, so maybe we can talk about this some other time." Like never.

"All right. I'll let you go, then. But I'll be around, if you ever need me." He gave me a sketchy salute and turned on his heel.

"How would I get hold of you? If I wanted to, that is."

"My name is Tzadqiel. You just have to say it out loud and I'll hear."

I frowned. "So I just yell out Tzadqiel and you poof in?"

"Pretty much." He cocked his head, still watching me. "I know you don't believe me about Jeremy, but it's the truth. He forgives you. Now you need to forgive yourself."

***

Nova:

The family room was too big, too open. Sound seemed to echo off the high ceiling and hit my eardrums in a way that rattled my nerves. The enormous windows stared at me with glassy black eyes, making me think of all the creatures who might be on the other side, looking in at me.

I glanced around, noting the stunning floor-to-ceiling feature wall of stacked gray stone and the woodburning fireplace, complete with primitive yet chic barn wood mantel. It looked exactly as I'd seen it in that dream of mine. The gorgeous cream-colored sofas and red-orange club chairs, too.

Was that why my apartment had so much red in it? Had Lucifer been trying to remind me of the house I'd so briefly shared with Gage? I couldn't see the purpose of it, though, unless he simply hoped to drive me crazy.

Then again, that seemed like exactly the kind of thing he would do.

The air still carried a hint of woodsmoke, and a cinnamon-apple perfume that made my mouth water.

There were too many people in the room, though. They made me jumpy. Brad, Marie, Max, and a young woman I thought was probably his girlfriend Caroline. Plus the new guy. They all smiled at me and patted me on the shoulder as if they knew me, and I wanted to run and hide.

What was wrong with me? I should be overjoyed to be home, but at the moment the apartment I'd left behind felt more like home than this place.

The posters I'd picked out, the rug I'd chosen, my two fluffy throw blankets, the playlists on my mp3...I'd lost all that. None of the stuff in this room really belonged to me.

Except none of the stuff in the apartment had really belonged to me either. It was all just an illusion created by Lucifer to trick me into thinking that half-world was the real thing.

Gage had walked out into the back yard, leaving me alone with all these people I hardly knew. They were more his friends than mine now. I stared out at the windows, but the darkness outside made them so reflective I couldn't really see what he was doing.

Marie touched me on my forearm. "Are you okay, honey?" she said, her dark eyes warm with concern.

"Yeah." I ran my fingers through my hair. "Yeah, I'm fine."

"You look kinda overwhelmed."

I gave her a stiff nod, along with an even stiffer smile. "I guess I am."

"That's understandable. Do you want to talk about what happened?"

She meant well, and eventually I would want to talk. But at the moment, it felt too raw, too new.

"I—I can't. Not yet." Declan's face rose into my mind's eye, his face wistful as he gazed down at his own gravestone. "I left someone behind, Marie."

Her gaze sharpened. "Who?"

"His name is Declan. He's trapped there, just like I was. We got to be friends and I had to leave him behind. I feel awful about it. He'll come looking for me and I won't be there. I couldn't even say good-bye."

"Maybe we can get him out somehow." She patted my arm. "We'll see what we can do, although I hesitate to open the gate of flames again. That wasn't a ritual I look forward to repeating."

I gave her a relieved smile. At least there was a possibility of getting Declan out.

"Yeah," I said, "that gate was pretty scary from our end, too."

My gaze moved back to the window. I could just make out Gage's tall bulk, standing in a broad shaft of light coming from the family room. He gestured at something. I frowned. Was he talking to someone?

"What is it?" Marie said.

"I think Gage is talking to someone outside." I pointed.

She turned to look. "I see him too. Who is he?"

"I don't know. Wait." I grabbed onto her. "That's the guy who was following us. The one who smokes those weird cigarettes."

She drew herself upright. Her full height was about the same as mine, so it wasn't especially impressive. But her manner changed, her energy grew stronger and more focused, until she actually seemed pretty formidable.

"I'll take care of this," she said.

I trailed behind her as she marched over to the French doors leading onto the back patio. Just as she opened them, Gage turned toward us. I could no longer see the black suit guy. Had he vanished?

Gage loped toward me, his movements relaxed and open. He sent me a big grin and I let out all my breath in relief. Whatever had gone down out here, it couldn't be too bad.

Gage grabbed me up in a bear hug and spun me around. I clung to his waist, giggling in giddy relief. Black suit guy wasn't here to threaten us. That was all that mattered to me at the moment.

"Did you chase him off?" I said.

He set me on my feet. "No. I didn't have to. Nova, he's an angel."

"What?" I tipped my head back to stare up at him. "Really?"

"That's what he said. His name is Tzadqiel."

"Well, why didn't he give us any help?" I cast a glowering look around the darkened back yard, hoping to catch this Tzadqiel dude and give him what for. He seemed to be long gone, though.

"He left. Poofed off, or whatever it is they do." Gage laughed softly. "An angel. I never would have guessed that."

"Why didn't he help us?" I said.

"He sort of did, according to him. He said they're not allowed to interfere much. But he sent the guitar, which helped me with the music, and that's what saved you."

"From what I hear," Marie said, "angels are like that. They won't do anything directly if they can get you to do it for yourself. They'd rather stick to hints and nudges."

"I guess that's better than nothing," Gage said.

His arms were still around me. I rested my forehead against his chest. All those days in that apartment, when I'd felt something missing—this was it. This was the piece I'd lost.

"We're free," Gage said against the crown of my head. "Lucifer told me he wouldn't try anything else against us."

"I'm not sure I trust him."

"Neither do I, but I think in this case he's telling the truth."

"Nova, you want some apple pie?" Marie said.

I turned my head and smiled at her. "Is that the awesome thing I smelled inside?"

"Yep," she said.

"Yeah, let's go in." Gage squeezed me tight. "I need to let my mom know you're all right. She was worried sick."

"I'll bet," I said dryly.

Knowing Nancy, she'd been more worried about her own skin than mine.

We re-entered the family room to find Nancy already there, along with my parents. Gage's mom wore pale-blue satin pajamas and low-heeled white mules with little white bows on them. Wasn't she just precious? My parents were both in jeans and sweatshirts, and my dad was giving the whole company the glower of the century.

"Hey, Mom and Dad," I said, waving without enthusiasm.

"I had to make sure you're really okay," my dad said, advancing on us.

"Of course she's really okay." Nancy minced along behind him, hands on her hips. "What are you implying, Ray?"

"I'm not implying anything, Nancy. I don't trust your son."

"Jesus, Dad." I shook my head. "This isn't the time. Can't we just get along?"

"No. He did something to you. I know he did. Don't lie to me about this."

I could have let go of Gage at that point, the better to confront my dad. But I didn't. I kept my arm around his waist, kept him close to me.

"Look," I said. "I'm only going to say this once. Gage was not at fault. He didn't do anything. I went away, and now I'm back. This whole thing has been totally stressful and if you keep bugging me about it I'm going to lose my shit. So let's drop it."

My dad glared at me, his jaw moving back and forth. My mom put a restraining hand on his arm and spoke softly to him, so softly I couldn't understand what she said.

"He helped me come home," I said. "Gage came and got me. If it wasn't for him, I wouldn't be here."

Okay, that probably wasn't the smartest thing to say, as it hinted at the terrible *something* that had happened to me. My dad's jaw dropped. Then he resumed his glare with even more heat.

"You need to tell me just exactly where you've been, young lady."

I flushed. All these people were here, openly listening, and he still treated me like a little kid.

"No, I don't, Dad. I'm not going to explain myself because if I did you wouldn't believe me. Are you going to trust me and respect my choices or not?"

He looked at me as if I'd transformed into someone else. A mythical beast, maybe—like a harpy or a some other female monster. My mom leaned up to whisper in his ear again.

I could see the resignation come over him. His shoulders dropped, along with the corners of his eyes and mouth. Now he looked like I really had died. He bowed his head for an instant.

Was this going to be the thing that irrevocably broke our relationship? I hoped not. I loved my parents and I wanted them in my life. I simply needed their respect for my adult decisions.

Finally he lifted his head. He looked right at me and said "okay."

"Okay?" I said, lifting my brows.

"Okay. I'll take your word for it."

I pursed my lips. "Thank you."

Nancy gave my dad a triumphant glance. "See? I told you."

God, if only we could muzzle her.

"Mom, don't," Gage said.

"Why not? He practically accused you of murder." She minced farther into the room, not swaying drunkenly at all. At least she'd chosen to stay sober on the night my parents showed up.

"Yeah, and we've got it settled. Let's not stir up anymore dirt," Gage said. "Now, Nova needs some apple pie."

"I'll get it." Marie bustled into the kitchen, probably relieved to get out of the line of fire.

"Now we can pack up and go home," Nancy said. "Right, Gage?"

He gave the biggest sigh I'd ever heard from him. "No, Mom. I told you. I'm staying here with Nova."

"What?" Her eyes went so round it looked comical. "You're not. No, you're not."

"Yes, I am. I can manage my career from Oregon."

Her mouth turned down in an arc. "Gage. You'll destroy your career."

"I have enough money to last me the rest of my life. I'll be fine."

Our occult friends were still listening to the family drama, but I thought Caroline was looking a little ragged around the edges. I knew the feeling.

"Nothing will be the same," Nancy said.

"That's the point, Mom. We're free. The Deal is over." He looked down at me and grinned. "We're free."

Epilogue

Two Years Later:

Nova:

Red and white roses, accented with black ribbon, seemed to adorn every surface of the family room. They trailed in garlands over the white pergola on the back patio and spilled out of exuberant arrangements in various urns and vases around the two areas. The heady scent of roses filled the warm summer air.

I stood at the French doors, my father at my side, and gazed out at the temporary arbor at the far end of the back yard, where Gage waited for me. He looked more beautiful than ever in a black tuxedo. Max stood beside him as best man.

A guitarist played a beautiful arrangement of the wedding march as attendants opened the doors for me to walk outside. Marie and Caroline walked behind me as matron-of-honor and bridesmaid, both wearing elegant black dresses. Yep, these were dresses they really could use after the wedding.

I wore a knee-length strapless gown with a full tulle skirt. It was frilly and romantic, probably the girliest thing I'd ever owned. With my hair in an elaborate, curled and braided updo including white roses, and high-heeled white satin shoes on my feet, I felt like a very different, almost unknown version of myself.

My dad and I began the slow walk up the aisle. Gage turned to look at me in my wedding dress, seeing it for the first time. His eyes lit up. He gave me a lazy smile. My heart started pounding nervously.

Everyone seated in the chairs on either side of the aisle was staring at me. There weren't many guests, but it was still more attention than I was used to getting. My family was there, of course, and Gage's mom— who'd chosen to stay sober for a change. We had some of my high school friends and a few of Gage's closest Hollywood associates, plus Adam Freiberg and Brad.

Declan was also in attendance. We'd managed to pull him from Lucifer's half-world into ours, but he was still adjusting to the realities of modern life.

No paparazzi. We'd kept plans for the wedding super-secret in order to have privacy. In the two years of our engagement, no-one outside of our two families had known the truth about our relationship. Everyone else thought we were merely boyfriend and girlfriend, not that we planned to get married.

Gage and I had gone to great lengths to keep our lives private, and it helped to have magically adept friends. Their spells allowed us to have some breathing room. He was focused more on his music, while still seeking roles that interested him. I was studying art full-time.

He seemed so much happier now that he wasn't so tied to L.A. and the high-profile lifestyle he'd lived before meeting me. As for me, I was happier than I'd ever been. My life had taken such a strange turn when I'd met him. I didn't have to pretend anymore, and neither did he. We were both pursuing the goals that meant the most to us, instead of those imposed on us by others.

We'd agreed to have a long engagement because I was so young when we met and because we got engaged so soon after meeting. And we'd learned so much about each other in the past couple of years; I knew we'd made the right decision.

My gaze met Gage's. My dad handed me off to him. The minister was talking, but I hardly noticed a thing he said. All I could take in was the man I was marrying.

He stared at me, apparently just as transfixed as I was. His blue eyes were sober now, full of the seriousness of the commitment we were making to each other. His hands felt strong and warm around mine.

We repeated our vows staring into each other's eyes. When the minister told Gage he could kiss the bride, Gage drew me hard against his body and captured his mouth with mine as if no-one were watching. I wrapped my arms around his neck and opened my mouth to him. He tasted like mint and he felt so warm, so erotically wet that I found myself moaning against his lips.

Dimly, I heard the sound of clapping behind us.

"I love you," he murmured against my ear.

"I love you, too."

"You're mine now, Mrs. Dalton." He grinned down at me.

"Forever," I said. We were going to make it. We'd beaten the devil. We could handle anything now.

The End

To sign up for Tori's mailing list: Get news of Tori's new releases before anyone else! http://www.toriminard.com/mailing-list/

Tori Minard has published sixteen romance and erotic romance novels and three novellas, in addition to a handful of short stories, both under her own name and as Tessa Tremaine. Her series include The Amaki, Legends Of A Dark Empire, Avery's Crossing, Fortunata: The Jhidris Conspiracy, and Tales Of The Demon Kin.

Tori wrote her first story in elementary school, with a lamentable lack of punctuation. In high school, she spent more time writing fiction than doing homework. Her early stories featured demonic dogs, dolls possessed by evil spirits—no, she'd never heard of Chucky—and politically incorrect post-apocalyptic romance.

She discovered science fiction in the sixth grade, with her dad's recommendation of Edgar Rice Burroughs' *At the Earth's Core,* the first book in his Pellucidar series. Prior to that, her reading had included ghost stories, animal stories and adventure tales. Around the same time, she was discovering the joys of erotica by sneaking her mom's books and reading all the naughty bits. Her mom claims to have skipped those parts.

After a long detour for such grown-up pursuits as working boring full-time jobs (State of Alaska, U.S. Postal Service), getting married and having a child, she returned to her first love—storytelling. She was born and raised in Alaska, and now lives in the Pacific Northwest with her husband, son, and micro-dog

Discover other titles by Tori Minard

Tales Of The Demon Kin:
Novellas:
Malefica
Fury Enchained
The Devil You Know
Taken By Storm

Novels:
Lucifer's Castle
Mastered By Love
Taken By Desire

Short Stories:
Stainless Steel Vampire, story number one in the Skye Donovan series
Love Potion Number Ninety, Skye Donovan story number two
If I Should Die; a Legends Of The Dark Empire story
Price of a Rose, a sexy fairy tale (novelette)
Lemon Drop, a sweet erotic toy possessed by a sex spirit

Amaki Novels:
The Heart Moon
Dragon Moon
Blood Moon

Avery's Crossing Novels:
Rush
Bad Company; Gage and Nova Trilogy Book 1
Bedeviled; Gage and Nova Trilogy Book 2

Fortunata Novels:
Dirty Magic

Legends Of A Dark Empire Novels:
Temple Of The Heart
Darkness Awakened
Darkness Forbidden
Darkness Beloved
Darkness Embraced

Connect with Tori online
To learn more about Tori, visit her blog at http://www.toriminard.com
Twitter: http://twitter.com/#!/ToriMinard
Facebook: http://www.facebook.com/toriminard.paranormalromance
Pinterest: http://www.pinterest.com/toriminard/